Rune Tooby is a smartass rebel and closeted gay biker with The Born Soldiers motorcycle gang. Rune life centered on casual sex and less-than-legal employment, until a pickup truck full of homophobic white supremacists rammed into his bike, destroying his hearing and shattering his life. Learning to live deaf and silent overwhelmed Rune's, sending him to humbly beg help from the last people he trusts completely: the rich and powerful Dominants of the Manse, who trained Rune in the arts of BDSM.

Oliver Hughes, cocky day trader and sexual Dominant, lives a life of indulgent luxury. Despite this, he feels adrift and unneeded since his beloved submissive, Jackson Whitney, became absorbed into life as a family man and cardiologist, leaving him little time for his Master. When a meeting between Rune and Oliver is carefully arranged by the men of Manse, it starts a wild ride, sweeping up everyone who gets too close to the explosive pair. Rune and Oliver find themselves on a path filled with frustrating miscommunications, rage-filled vengeance, and painfully unearthed secrets. (MMM)

Also recommended...

You may also enjoy these other ForbiddenFiction works:

Bare by Lynn Kelling

Ev Myers was looking for trouble when he signed up to do nude art modeling, but he wasn't expecting this much trouble. All he'd wanted to do was rebel against the moral limits of his strict religious family and the PR requirements of his father's senate seat. He saw how much bigger his world could be when Professor Adam Buchanan opened Ev to new passions and new experiences but when Ev's family learned how far he had gone, they decided to resort to kidnapping and brainwashing to save their son from sin and scandal—even if it kills him. (M/M)

Driven by Nicholas Kinsley

Mitchell Morgan is a quiet young man with dangerous secrets. One of those secrets is a psychic power over metal that makes him far more than just the handsome, blue-eyed owner of Advanced Auto Repairs. The other traps him in a world of organized crime and intense violence.

Trevor Lewis is a graphic designer with a passion for drawing, drumming, and his incredibly hot auto mechanic. He meets Mitchell over a broken tail light, and despite—or perhaps because of—Trevor's awkwardness, Mitchell is charmed. Trevor's curly hair and brilliant smile bring light into Mitchell's complicated world. Mitchell would do anything to save Trevor from the dangers of his criminal life—but first Trevor has to save Mitchell from his own darkness.

Hush

A Prequel to Bare

Lynn Kelling

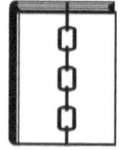

ForbiddenFiction
www.forbiddenfiction.com

an imprint of

Enspire Publishing
www.enspirepublishing.com

HUSH

A ForbiddenFiction book

Enspire Publishing
Hayward, California

© Lynn Kelling, 2018

CREDITS
Editor: Rylan Hunter and D.M. Atkins
Cover Designer: Siolnatine
Cover Art Credits:
Production Editor: Kaye O'Malley
Proofreading: Siol na Tine from a photo by Y Photo Studio @ Shutterstock
Font: Wellrock Slab, by Manfred Klein

SKU: LK1-1.000332-01 FFP
ISBN: 978-1-62234-347-8

Published in the United States of America

DISCLAIMER

This book is a work of fiction which contains explicit erotic content; it is intended for mature readers. Do not read this if it's not legal for you.

All the characters, locations and events herein are fictional. While elements of existing locations or historical characters or events may be used fictitiously, any icit erotic content; it is intended for mature readers. Do not read this if it's not legal forresemblance to actual people, places or events is coincidental.

This story is not intended to be used as an instruction manual. It may contain descriptions of erotic acts that are immoral, illegal, or unsafe. Do not take the events in this story as proof of the plausibility or safety of any particular practice.

Such content should not be read as a depiction of the desires, opinions, or fetishes of the author or the staff of ForbiddenFiction.com.

Dedication

For the seekers
of simple kindness,
understanding,
and support
in the face of life's greatest trials.

Contents

Chapter 1
Wreckage

He should have been dead. Rune Tooby remembered all of it—the whole-body clench and rush of cold terror before the crash. The light blue Ford truck had cut him off and slammed on its brakes. Rune flew through the air over the front of his bike, landing with impact on the jagged rocks beside the steep road. The glare of headlights had swung over, piercing the inky night. His skin tore away in large patches, but that wasn't even the bad part. He lay there frozen, unmoving, knowing something was wrong in a bad, piss-your-pants kind of way.

That dread only faded with time rather than being a one-and-done deal.

His clearest memory? The sounds before the crash.

He'd braked hard, wheels screaming as the road chewed rubber, the roar of the wind dull in comparison. The thud of his bike against the back of the pickup had been jarring in mental ways as well as physical.

All of it was chaos, noise, and violence, followed by only eerie stillness and pain.

And silence.

Lots of it.

He'd flown through the air and landed in Hell.

Before the crash, he'd had his own place. It was small but pretty sweet. Total privacy. Manageable rent. A landlord who rarely came around as long as the checks were sent on time. No one had been in his business. He sold product without The Born Soldiers—the motorcycle gang he'd been a member of since he was eighteen—getting mixed up in it. Sometimes the transactions were more of a trade than an exchange of money. He'd been able to afford it.

Now? Not so much.

The phone rested in his hand. His old contacts were all still there. His regulars and less-than-regulars.

He'd had a type.

Gay curious, closeted, tough on the outside while secretly slutty, totally submissive bottoms on the inside.

Some had wives. Others showed up with girlfriends, told them to wait in the car while they handled the deal. The girlfriends never knew what was really going on.

Staring at his phone's screen, Rune tapped the name of the last guy who'd pulled that trick. Denis Coleman. The dude wore Nautica and American Eagle. He wore seven hundred dollar white sneakers. All of that shit. Had an effortless, just-rolled-out-of-bed beauty that took a solid hour and a half to painstakingly create. Dark blue eyes, chocolate brown hair, solid chest. Rune smiled at the memory of Denis scanning the cluttered room, nervous as a ten-year-old working up the nerve to shoplift a candy bar for the very first time. A peek through the blinds provided Rune with a view of the blonde waiting in the jeep two stories down, playing on her phone.

"Lookin' for the discount?" Rune had asked, playing dumb, all wide-eyed and relaxed. "No big deal if you can't handle it, long as you've got the full amount."

Denis looked everywhere—the windows, the doors, the empty pizza boxes, the retro phone on the coffee table Rune had picked out of the trash in front of some McMansion in Berwyn. He stared at the black and gray ink wrapping both of Rune's arms, starting at his wrists, crawling up his shoulders and hugging his neck. Denis glanced down at Rune's crotch and bit his lip like he was hungry.

Fuck yeah, he was hungry.

Rune had fought back a cocky grin at the time. He played the game a little longer, just for fun.

"How much did you bring?"

"Fifty," Denis grunted.

Not enough. Rune was ecstatic, flying on a natural high. He watched that trust-fund-baby bite his lip, his mouth watering for a taste, and it made Rune start to get hard, so he palmed himself, grabbing a good handful. Denis's gaze went right there, staring at Rune's inked fingers squeezing his thick bulge.

"If you wanna make up the difference, gonna have to work harder than last time."

"Mm-hmm." Denis nodded, jaw clenched, turning slightly to face Rune more directly, like he was a half-second away from getting on his knees. "Whatever."

No more eye contact. There was only one thing on Denis's mind. Did he even want the pills, Rune wondered? Or were they just an excuse?

Rune took his time walking over, and it seemed to drive Denis crazy. Denis actually inched closer to hurry it along. Rune stopped when he was invading Denis's personal space. Denis wouldn't look up. His gaze was trained downward, on Rune's body. Rune had been barefoot, wearing a pair of jeans and a black sleeveless tank with The Born Soldiers' logo sprawled across it like a cheap whore.

Rune grabbed him roughly by the back of the neck and yanked him in for a kiss, but it was Denis who tried to slip Rune his tongue and moaned when Rune allowed it.

Pulling away before Denis seemed ready, Rune growled, "Get on your fucking knees."

Panting, Denis fell. His hands scrambled at Rune's fly, yanking it open, pulling him out, rolling on the rubber. There had been another moan when he'd swallowed Rune down to the root, his dark blue eyes closing with peaceful bliss as his lips stretched around the thick column. Holding Denis's head with both hands, Rune had begun fucking his mouth, not letting Denis tongue him leisurely like last time, slamming into the back of his throat, making him struggle to bear it.

The pace, the whimpers, the hunger and submission drove Rune on hard. It had been perfect.

But Denis had stopped him, pulled away, wiped his mouth with the back of his arm.

"Wait. Just… wait."

"What d'ya fuckin' mean, wait?"

Denis kept his gaze down, locked on Rune's wet, hard dick.

"You just remember you had more cash or what?" Rune demanded, getting angry as Denis got to his feet.

"Just wait," Denis had babbled. His hands went to his own fly and he turned around, got on the couch on his knees and pushed his pants and underwear down to mid-thigh.

And Rune had laughed, bright and loud, as Denis bent himself over, sticking out his ass.

"Well, okay then," he'd smiled, grabbing hold of his rigid cock and aiming for a new target.

It took a good five minutes to stretch Denis enough to take two fingers on an easy slide, but Denis had been beating off the whole time, breathing like a runner on their final sprint. When Rune started to make him take cock instead, Denis shot over his fingers, his cry breaking off, his body convulsing with orgasm as Rune held him by his narrow hips and drew his ass back onto the dick impaling it.

He'd breathed easier for the rest, making soft cooing sounds like it was the best thing he'd ever felt. Rune came, filling the condom and they just stayed like that for a minute or two. Denis kept clenching on the dick like he wanted to make sure it was still stuffing his hole.

"Keep the money," Rune had told him. "We're square."

"No, I'm good for it."

Rune pulled out, watching his dick slide free, staring at the wet, loosened ring of muscle that was Denis's sphincter. He stayed there, bent over the back of the couch, breathing hard, as if waiting for round two. As the silence drew out, he got the hint, pulled up his pants, dug out the fifty and dropped it on the cushion. After palming his purchase, he ran out of there without another word or backward glance.

That had been over a year ago, and Rune hadn't gotten laid since.

He looked around the old storage room they'd cleared out for him when he'd gotten evicted. That had been seven months ago. It had a small cot and some boxes full of his stuff. There were a few bright lamps scattered around the space, because seeing clearly had become sickeningly important. There was a small whiteboard and a marker. The side of his hand always seemed smudged with black ink from the marker rather than his tattoos. Luckily it blended in.

It was just so fucking quiet.

He'd loved heavy metal music, kept it cranked to a low roar until his neighbors banged on ceilings or floors. The smooth tenor of his voice had been his charm, his in. It connected him with the guys in his crew. He'd always been chatty. Outgoing. Over-confident.

Now, he never said a single fucking word. His pride wouldn't allow it. Way back when, he'd said fuck you to speech therapy. Hated that he couldn't tell what was coming out of his mouth. Lost all of his plentiful confidence. Did an about-face and began keeping to himself, all the time. Stopped using his voice which only made it worse to try starting again. He could see it on their faces, from the first, how they shied away from trying to communicate with him. Maybe he sounded off. He didn't know and was too afraid to ask. One thing he knew for sure was how uncomfortable he made them, for being so different than he'd been.

Most people that Rune encountered those days acted just like Denis in one respect—they never looked him in the eye. Their gaze slid off like he wasn't really there, or like they were afraid he'd try to communicate with them and then they'd need to figure out how to do it in return. There was no desire, no hunger. No one wanted him to do anything except go away and stop making things awkward.

He didn't sell anything anymore. His accounts had long been drained from the medical bills. Sometimes he did odd jobs for pocket money, but he had no steady gig. He didn't have a place to live, or a bike, or a purpose.

There were no more calls from horny or hard-up guys like Denis. He still had an account on Grindr, but it would have been a joke if he tried to hook up with anyone. He pictured it—some hot, hard-bodied guy showing up at the club, a grizzled senior member like Axe pointing the poor bastard to the storage room, and Rune standing there with his board scribbled with "Hi, I'm Rune," like the biggest shmuck in the world.

It never would have gotten that far, even if he was desperate. For all that Rune mocked his customers for staying in the closet, he'd never set a foot outside either. None of his friends knew he was gay. None of the crew. None of his family. Not even his therapist, or the people he found through Meetup.com to practice American Sign Language, ASL for short.

The crash should have killed him. He'd fractured small bones in the base of his skull, which had caused ossicular chain discontinuity, which meant he was completely, one hundred percent deaf. There was a slim chance surgery might improve his hearing, but he couldn't afford it and was too scared of disappointment to try.

The road rash along his arms, legs and back had healed. He'd been slowly, steadily covering the scars with new tattoos. But he'd always be broken.

It had been about six months since the accident. His road rash had disappeared after a few weeks, but it took a lot longer for him to adjust to the other injuries and the many practical and financial consequences. He'd felt instantly distant from everyone and had no idea how to claw his way back to normalcy. What the long months had taught him was that now, no one wanted him. No one needed him. He was only trouble. A hardship. A weight his friends shouldn't have had to carry.

Part of him needed to do something about the accident and the people who'd caused it, but it was hard to care enough to take the first steps at getting some revenge when he was barely getting through the days. Soon though, he told himself. Once things started to click again, he was going to act. The promise of that helped keep him going.

He hated the fucking quiet. It boiled his blood, brought out his rage. Made him want to smash things or scream or throw himself off the side of another cliff.

He opened his mouth, took the deepest breath he could, filling his lungs to bursting, and yelled as loud as he could, with all of his strength, until his throat ached.

Nothing.

Silence.

The lamp by the door began to blink—on, off, on, off.

It was the crude, light-based doorbell system the guys used for him. Because he was staying in the storage closet, the light switch was on the outside of the door rather than the inside. They flicked the switch a few times to let him know they were there. He sighed, rubbed his hands over his unshaven face, the bristles abrading his palms.

The door opened slowly. Max stuck his head in. He had a full, wild gray beard, a cap on his head and black, hard eyes.

His hands made shapes which meant: *Are you okay?*

But it was still silent.

The gap between the constant noise in Rune's head and the rest of the world was a vast chasm. His options to explain what was wrong were so fucking limited. He could use the board, scribble a few words. He could make shapes with his hands, which only three people in his life understood. He could type words on his phone and have the phone read them aloud. He could pull his head out of his ass and say something he could never hear, in softened, rounded words.

And he was so tired of trying, so he just sat there, staring at Max, waiting to see how much might come over in the angry glare alone.

Max deflated a little, came in and shut the door behind him.

Rune decided to try a sign after all. He pointed his index finger up at the underside of his jaw and folded the other fingers in, his thumb stuck out. He mimed taking the shot, his head blowing back.

Max drew up a chair from the dusty corner of the small room and sat heavily in it, leaning forward. With his hands, he said: *Go out. See something.*

Max was learning how to sign. He was the only one who'd made the effort, but he was an old dog trying to tackle a new trick. His signs were simple, but they were better than nothing, especially since Max's poor vision made using phones to talk nearly impossible, and the sad fact was that Rune was kind of shitty at lip-reading—especially with mumblers like Max— getting much less than the typical seventy percent of words that most lip-readers did.

Rune flopped back onto the bed.

Max smacked the side of Rune's leg to get his attention, knowing if Rune wasn't looking, he wouldn't know if Max was trying to say something.

Rune understood Max's frustration. It didn't have to be this hard. Rune could speak, he just wouldn't.

Once again, Rune made a gun of his hand and pointed it up at the underside of his head.

Max hit him again, hard enough to hurt.

Rune bit down on his tongue and closed his eyes.

Sometimes he didn't bother signing his desperation. Sometimes he just pointed the one hundred percent real gun he owned and always carried at the underside of his chin instead, finger on the trigger, safety off, chamber loaded, waiting to see if he'd do it.

He'd been hiding in that closet for almost a year, with the dusty boxes and other forgotten, unneeded things.

His hand was taken up, folded into another, pulled away from where it had been pointed. Max gave it a squeeze with his callused, leathery palm. Rune glanced up at him, saw him mouth something that might have been an apology. It didn't really matter. The feel of that hand in his meant a lot more, showing him that maybe he wasn't really as alone as he felt.

Max nodded toward the door, stubborn as a mule. He did it again and again, yanking at Rune's arm.

Rune stopped fighting and let himself be pulled. There was nothing out there that scared him more than what waited inside anyway.

Chapter 2
Doctor's Orders

Jackson Whitney's wife, Josefina, had always compared him to a dog with a bone—once he had it, he wouldn't let it go or leave it alone. They'd met toward the end of his four years training in medical school, before the three years he spent training in internal medicine and the three years following that in specialized training to become a cardiologist. She'd been by his side through a lot, but now that he had his own private practice and was out there doing what he'd trained so long to do, not much had changed.

He still tackled things the same way. He latched on to an idea and wouldn't let it go. No argument persuaded him. He didn't bark or bite, but he protected his interests as ferociously as needed and he didn't relax until everything he'd set out to do was done.

In practical terms, this made him a workaholic. He knew it was a bad habit to keep things to himself as much as he did, but he didn't know any other way to be.

All day, each day at his practice, everything rested on his shoulders. The tough calls and the search for solutions that could save a life never ended and no one else could make them. The pressure was immense. His employees and his patients depended on him just as much as Josefina and their two kids, Jada, who was five, and Kayla, who was three.

Sitting in his Lexus, the engine started but the car parked beside the professionally manicured landscaping outside his office, Jackson blew out a breath and tried to let go of the tension built up in his body. His neck was stiff, his back in knots, his stomach unsettled. The two antacids he'd taken earlier hadn't done much.

The dim glow off the dashboard soothed him, a welcome contrast to the harsh fluorescents from the patient rooms he'd been in and out of since eight that morning.

The past year had showed him his plate was only going to get fuller as time went on. Jada was in school now and enrolled in cheerleading as well as gymnastics. Josefina—Jo for short—struggled to manage the home, the nanny, and the kids without much help from him, especially with her father in ill health as dementia set in. She leaned on Jackson as much as she could, and he did what he was able to for her. She did likewise, but he knew there was a lot he had to shoulder on his own.

Or, well, almost on his own.

He called Oliver Hughes before making any conscious decision to do it. Instinct took over.

Oliver answered, laughing. It was a deep, throaty, sensual sound. "Had a feeling. Guess it was right."

Jackson imagined him in his penthouse apartment, standing by the windows overlooking the city, sipping some scotch, wearing a perfectly tailored suit with the silk tie loosened just a little at the neck, the top two buttons of his shirt undone. His brown hair would be swept back, his hazel eyes fiery and searching, full of energy that never lessened in its intensity or dulled its edge.

The mental image soothed like nothing else could.

Blowing out another breath, letting Oliver hear how bone-tired he was, Jackson said, "Can't go home yet. I'm just sitting here... stuck."

"Jo expecting you?"

"No."

"Then don't go. Where's here?"

"Parking lot at the office."

"Good. I'm close then."

"You are," Jackson smiled, something unknotting in his chest. It was strange to depend so much on a man over ten years his junior—and a white, unabashedly privileged one at that. Many people would have judged Jackson harshly for it, but luckily no one else's opinions mattered, other than Oliver's, his own, and Jo's. They all understood the arrangement, had been equally involved in setting the ground-rules, and had been satisfied with the results for quite a while. "I'd like to stop by, if you're free."

"Excuse me," Oliver said with passion and dominance, "you'd better fucking stop by. That's an order. I forbid you to go home."

Jackson's smile grew. The thrill of Oliver's low voice tickling his ear spiraled down through Jackson's body, twisting behind his balls, stiffening his cock. He palmed it through his pants, squeezing. "Mmm. Yes, sir."

Oliver was the cleverest, most intelligent, cunning human being Jackson had ever met. He was wicked hunger incarnate. He feared nothing. Never met a challenge he couldn't best with one arm tied behind his back. Everything he encountered only made him stronger and more determined to master it all.

Right away, Oliver knew exactly what Jackson needed to hear. Jackson didn't know how he did it, but he always came through.

"Do you need me to call her for you?"

"Please."

Jackson always struggled most with justifying his most selfish needs.

"What else is bothering you? Is it something you can say over the phone?"

"I don't know." He didn't want to get into it, but it was Oliver on the phone and Jackson felt able to just let it go and get the words out. He didn't have kids running around his feet, or staff lingering nearby, or worries about his father-in-law to cloud his mind. It was a lot less complicated in Oliver's world. "One of my patients is dying. They're just a year older than I am. There's nothing I can do."

Oliver jumped right in, without a hint of tiptoeing around the touchy subject. "You're not God. You do your best, always. You're a fucking excellent doctor and you're doing everything you need to for them. Does Jo know?"

"I can't tell her right now. She'd just worry," Jackson admitted.

"You can't manage other people's emotions for them. First chance you get her alone, just tell her. Total honesty. Promise me."

"Yeah. Yeah, okay."

Oliver effortlessly hacked all the bullshit away. Jackson let Oliver's confidence and assurances wash over him like cooling waters. Some of the tension was already gone, diverted from his shoulders to his cock. He used to feel a monstrous amount of guilt about how much he'd given himself over to Oliver, pieces that should have belonged solely to his wife, or so he'd thought. Oliver had worked him through it. Time had shown him the power of trust and true love as they'd opened their relationship, allowing him the ability to devote himself to acting as Oliver's submissive while Josefina took a boyfriend to help sate her own needs. If anything, it had strengthened their marriage. Now, the only thing that scared him was how badly he needed Oliver when the urge struck.

"Is there anything else?" Oliver asked, knowing him too well.

"No."

"You fucking liar. Put the call on speaker."

He pushed the button to transfer the call to the car's speakers.

"Okay. It's done," Jackson told him.

"How hard are you?"

Jackson squeezed himself. "Enough."

"Control it. Right now."

Jackson took deeper breaths, tried to wrest his thoughts away from the filthy, tempting promise in Oliver's suave voice. They'd practiced this, but it was still a challenge.

"Can anyone see you?"

10

"No. The others left as soon as we closed up." It was one of the reasons why he'd waited a few minutes before making the call to Oliver, which he hadn't realized until just that moment.

"Good. Open your pants. Pull your cock out. Then check the center console."

Jackson glanced around, just to be sure, but the parking lot was empty. As he unbuttoned his pants and slipped his heavy, stiffened dick out from beneath his boxers, he thought of the set of car keys he'd given Oliver, months ago. When Oliver demanded access, he got it.

Jackson lifted the top on the center console. Inside was a small, sleek metal case and a tube of lubricant. He palmed both and felt his breathing quicken, his energy becoming jittery with anticipation, his worries vanished.

"Is this what I think it is?" he asked.

"Who takes care of you?"

"You do."

Jackson took care of many people, Josefina most of all, but, as much as he'd always love her, there were some ways she couldn't fit all of his varied needs. And there was only one person who took care of him the way Oliver implied, no matter what or how or why. Jo wasn't into BDSM, but Jackson didn't need her to be. He loved her with his whole heart and always would. She was the mother to his children. She made their home. She was the perfect wife. But tension built up in Jackson in ways she had never known how to vent. It would have changed him, damaged what they had together, if not for Oliver. She gave Oliver Jackson's darkness. She trusted him with it with her whole heart.

"Do you want it?"

"Fuckin' hate this thing," he groaned, slipping it from the case, feeling the thin metal with the ring on the end, cool against his palm. "Yes. Yes, I want it. Something's wrong with me."

"No, you're perfect just the way you are," Oliver told him, and Jackson could hear the smile in his voice. "It's going to hurt."

"Yeah, no shit it's gonna hurt," Jackson murmured, spreading plenty of lube on the metal, especially the flared end with the pointed, dull tip.

"Do you want it?"

"Yes, sir," he answered, without doubt, giving into his fear and letting go of everything else. Oliver was in control.

"I want to hear you. Understood?"

"Yes, sir," Jackson said a little stiffly, his nerves getting the better of him, his heart pounding.

"Are you softer?"

"A little."

"Good. Insert it. All the way. Don't stop until it's completely seated."

"Fuck," Jackson breathed. He took a few deep breaths, then lined up the pointed end of the urethral plug with the slit in his cockhead. "Oh fuck."

He let the weight of the metal pull it down. Gravity drew it down and the lube slicked the way. It was slow torture and he did try to hold in his cries at first, but as the flared end spread his opening, and he did nothing to stop it from continuing its way down into his cock, Jackson let go of that too. His cries started short, low, abrupt. They were little bursts as he began to tremble. He steadied the end of the plug with his thumb, barely adding pressure, and his shout rattled the car's windows.

"How deep?"

Jackson glanced down at his lap, sweating now. "Ha-halfway."

"Good. Keep it going. Don't let it stop. You can't stop it. Only I can stop it, and I want it inside you."

"Yes, sir."

"Do you feel that? How much that hurts? Focus on it. There is nothing else besides the pain. Let it take over."

Jackson added more pressure with his thumb and the pain spiked along with his yell. Then it softened again, and he gasped, shuddering, knowing Oliver could hear all of it. Soon, the plug was stuffed completely inside his cock, with only the ring protruding.

"It's in."

"Good. Just sit there. Don't move. Just feel the pain. Enjoy it. Sink down into it."

Jackson moaned, his eyes rolling. He was getting harder again.

"Wrap your hand around your tip, then squeeze."

Eagerly, Jackson obeyed, even though he knew how much it would ache to increase the pressure from outside as well as within. He tried to swallow his scream.

"No, you will let me fucking hear you!"

Jackson let his lips part and it erupted from him in a stream of curses, his thighs quivering, his stomach cramping. The pain was a red hot spike driven into his most sensitive part.

"Stroke yourself until I give you permission to stop. Use plenty of lube."

Jackson squirted lube into his right hand, then began to tug, his dick slipping in and out of his fist, the squelching loud and obscene.

"Faster," Oliver barked.

Jackson jacked himself. A guttural moan burst from him. Pain swirled with pleasure and knowing he couldn't and wouldn't come made it all so much better. His panting climbed in pitch. Soon, he was begging.

"Please. Please... Fuck. Fuck!"

"Stop."

Jackson shuddered, his dick so hard and throbbing he let it go with shaking hands, unable to think past it.

"I forbid you to touch yourself until I give you permission to do so. I forbid you to close your pants. I'll meet you in the garage. Drive safe."

"Love you too."

Oliver laughed, then ended the call.

Chapter 3
Help

"Mr. Hughes, please hold for Mr. Davenport."

"Absolutely," Oliver murmured, trying to keep from waking sleeping beauty.

A couple of minutes later, a seductive voice purred in his ear, "Olly. Been a while. How are you?"

"Well, I was already good, but I'm even better, now," Oliver grinned, tracing the edge of the doorway with the pad of his thumb. With Master David Davenport came good things, without fail. He was the closest thing to a gay man's fairy godfather, and Oliver couldn't wait to see what surprise the call might bring.

He'd been too invigorated to sit after showering. Jackson was sprawled—naked and unconscious—across the king-sized bed. The strong cut of his jaw caught the dim light, his lips soft in slumber. They'd gone at it in a few different ways for hours and the scent of sex filled the air. Night twinkled through the vast array of windows as a purple haze wrapped over the city.

Only three people ever called Oliver this late. One was dreaming away in the bed. The other was many time-zones away, traveling on a quest for obscure painting inspiration. The last was David Davenport, billionaire CEO of Davenport Industries, owner and operator of Manse, the best gay club in the state, and sly, suave fucker that he was.

"I'm sensing an emergency, given the hour. But what flavor? Business? Pleasure?"

"Need."

"Mmm. Yours?"

"In a way, yes."

"Intriguing. I live to serve, Master. Name your desire."

"How are things with Jackson?"

A diversion? Interesting. He wondered what on earth could cause such a conversational shift. It drew him in even more.

"Fine. Fantastic."

"Have you told him?"

Oliver sighed. The words dried up. His gaze slid like poured, viscous liquid over the dark curves of Jackson's body caught in moonlight. He could still feel the delicate touch of Jackson's lips feathering kisses up the center of his back, over the edge of his ear. A promise of fleeting paradise.

"I'm taking the silence as a no," David observed.

"Hasn't been the right time."

"Have you told Adam?"

Adam as in Adam Buchanan, Oliver's best friend and closest confidant. They'd trained at Manse together, and been each other's most stable support system since childhood.

Oliver smiled. Said nothing at first.

"Olly..." David sighed with disappointment.

"He's away. Traveling."

"You could call."

"It's not his problem."

"He loves you."

"What do you want, David?" Oliver asked, cutting the interrogation short, no matter the breadth of his respect and patience.

"I want you to talk to Jackson about what we spoke of on your last visit. As soon as you can."

"Why?"

"Because you're needed. There is no one else. Not for this."

"Look, if you need me to take a night to break in a new sub—"

"Don't presume. This is serious."

Oliver shouldn't have unloaded on David in the first place, even knowing a secret was safer with him than with any other soul on the planet, Adam and the Pope included. But it was too late to take it back now.

"I need you, Olly. Your background matches up. You're smart. Damn smart. You don't play games, and you're familiar with extremes. You're an expert at control, almost to a fault."

"And you really think you know what I'm looking for here?" Oliver snapped, unable to dull the edge of his anger.

"I do," David answered, his tone gentle. Oliver marveled that a man with the world in his hand could pull off such a thing. "I'm telling you that *you* are needed, Oliver. You. But maybe you're not up for the challenge."

Oliver bristled, turning his back on the gorgeous, married cardiologist slumbering peacefully in the penthouse suite, so exhausted from fucking and hardcore play that even an accidentally slammed bathroom door hadn't stirred him.

Walking swiftly down the hall to his kitchen, Oliver kept his voice lowered. "Like hell, I'm not."

On the other end of the line, David laughed, knowing he had Oliver already.

"I need you here. Tomorrow night. Eight o'clock. I'll be an optimist and have papers drawn up."

Papers?

Craving greater sobriety like air, Oliver poured some ice-cold spring water into a glass and took a deep drink.

Breathing harder and hating that David could likely hear it, Oliver said, "That's a little presumptive, don't you think? One scene, a few nights, that's one thing. I don't sign papers unless I want to sign them, no matter what the situation is. I've made my commitments already. They come first."

"Spread too thin, then, Olly?"

He swallowed a growl, remembering the conversation they'd had months ago after a very long night at Manse, surrounded by freshly fucked submissives who'd done nothing to quell Oliver's private horror at his recent revelation.

Call it an existential crisis. Call it a child of wealth's inability to stop wanting more, to never having enough. But the void inside would only be filled with truth and purpose.

Adam had his calling. Jackson did too—a wife, children, and his practice.

Oliver was a patch on the crack in Jackson's perfect world, not a partner. And as far as Adam went—a friendship didn't make a life.

No matter how soundly Jackson slept in that bed, within the hour he expected Oliver to wake him so he'd be home before the children woke and noticed his absence. And once again, Oliver would be alone.

Quitting his job as a successful journalist to look for a new calling hadn't helped.

Increasing the frequency of his affairs with Jackson had no effect.

His missing best friend had no way to enlighten.

Maybe it was time to trust David.

"Maybe you're too young for this," David pondered.

"Like hell," Oliver shot back.

"Then you'll come?"

"Tell me about him."

"No. You need to meet him to understand."

"Suspicious, David. Very suspicious."

"Maybe. Tomorrow, then?"

"Yes. Tomorrow."

With his favorite drink in his favorite cup held between his palms, Jackson gave Oliver a searching stare. The Eagles mug filled with green tea and a little lavender honey let off soft plumes of fragrant steam. Oliver had delivered it to him as an ominous sort of peace offering. Jackson wore only a pair of briefs, his clothes still slung over the back of the chair by the door. Oliver had requested Jackson put on the briefs in order to help him maintain concentration.

"I can't believe he called you. He hasn't called you in years. Not since that incident during training."

Oliver didn't respond, too busy gathering the right words to explain. He smoothed wrinkles in the down comforter, hating the press of time against his struggle to open up to someone he was supposed to keep no secrets from, and did.

"Why is David Davenport calling you in the middle of the night?" Jackson asked, sounding stunned.

"Says he needs me," Oliver told him with a slight grin that died quickly under the weight of his dread.

"For what?"

"I don't know, actually. But I'll be heading over later tonight."

Jackson shifted closer, laying a warm hand on Oliver's leg. "What's wrong, Olly?"

Oliver blew out a breath. He laid his hand on Jackson's, touching his wedding ring and the deep indent it made on Jackson's finger after many years of wear. And Jackson followed Oliver's gaze, watched him slide the pad of his fingertip over the gleaming gold.

Keeping things locked in, safe and secure, was his mode of operation. Jackson knew it, and related to it. So did Adam. It's why their relationships worked. But as natural as it was for Oliver to help others with their issues, he only came up against roadblocks when he tried to do the same for himself by opening up.

"Do you have any issues with me going to see what this is about tonight?"

Jackson met his gaze, reflecting only affection and acceptance. He had the wisdom of age and experience on his side—something of which Oliver was always aware. In a way, it kept them a little off balance, but it would never have been enough to drive them apart.

"Please tell me if you do," Oliver added.

"Taking another sub?"

Oliver bit down on the inside of his cheek, refusing to let his gaze waver, even though he could see the doubt in Jackson's eyes.

"You're my priority. You know that."

"I'm kind of amazed you're even considering it, though," Jackson laughed, showing some of his hurt. "You don't do commitment, Olly."

It felt like a jab to his weak spot, and he knew his reaction showed.

"Oh my god," Jackson breathed, sitting back a little.

"I can't help who I am," Oliver replied, angrier than he'd have liked. "And that's the biggest fucking problem of all."

"What even is this, though?" Jackson's face screwed up with confusion. "The reason why we work is because of Jo. You know that. And it's not like we've ever been exclusive, here. You go through men like no one I've ever seen! You've had every chance. I'm not trying to hold you back."

"I know you're not. I'm the problem. Not you."

"Just fucking say it, okay? That's what you do anyway. You just say it. So please." Jackson gestured widely with his hands and the mug, giving Oliver the floor.

"No one needs me, Jackson. You're married to *her*. Chalk it up to ego. Go ahead. It's definitely part of it. I'm looking for an anchor, and David said the magic word. I don't know what this is. Could be a clusterfuck and a mistake. But maybe not. I trust him."

"Oliver," Jackson sighed with heartache, setting the mug on the nightstand and moving in to clasp a hand to the side of Oliver's face. "I need you."

Oliver's eyes burned. He glared through the blur into the darkness of Jackson's eyes and all of his intimidating confidence. "Don't."

"*I need you.* I'll always need you."

Oliver grabbed hold of Jackson's arm, trying to wrench him away. They were an even match, though. Always had been. This time, Jackson won out and dragged Oliver in against his will, wrapping him clumsily but urgently in his arms and breathing hot against Oliver's neck, one hand palming the back of his head.

"You stupid shit," Jackson hissed.

Oliver fought, pushing back. Jackson tightened his hold and let him, radiating calm. Panting, Oliver let the fight consume him, because it felt cleaner. Better.

"Just stop," Jackson's smoky voice growled. "I promised you always. I fucking meant it."

Slowly, Oliver lost, and he sank into the defeat, letting go of pride, struggling for breath. The steely strength of Jackson's hard body wrapped around him was everything. It kept Oliver from breaking, got him back in control. There was shame, but plenty of love, too.

"Go. See David. I trust you. I'm not going anywhere. Ya hear?"

Oliver greedily breathed in the scent of Jackson's beautiful brown skin, rolling them both, getting on top. He found Jackson's mouth, moaned as he bit, then licked, sank in for a deeper taste. And Jackson gave over, taking them right back to where they belonged.

The past had an ugly way of catching up with you. Things that didn't fit anymore, discarded and left behind, sometimes showed back up anyway, cocky and smug.

Rune knew he looked angry. He wanted a drink or five. Though he'd never used his own product, he would have then if given the chance. The only thing keeping him there, when he wanted more than anything to get on a bike and drive out onto the nearest congested freeway going ninety miles an hour, weaving and dodging as a glorious *fuck you* at fate, was his desperation.

He'd trained as a submissive as soon as it had been legal for him to do so, starting right on his eighteenth birthday. For years, it had been great. It felt dangerous, sexy, like he was right on the edge, dancing on the line. No one who knew him knew he did it, but the secret had been a great one. It got him off, made him feel like a god when he was really just a punk throwaway kid without any smarts, talent, or money.

But too soon, his personality started to get in the way. He got sick of taking orders from men who got off on his helplessness. It became less about glorifying in giving in, and more about fighting the anger at the people keeping him down.

There had never been love in it, or much emotion at all. He'd never signed a contract, or found a match that worked for more than a few nights. Doms got sick of his attitude. They didn't like how Rune would spit in their face or cuss them out, laughing. He didn't break, though they tried, since he liked pain as much as pleasure, but his ego never let him surrender completely.

As a last-ditch effort, they gave him to a Dom named Elet. A big, black motherfucker with a cock the size of a tree trunk and a wit to match Rune's cheek. Funniest part was how Rune fought back as hard as he ever had, and Elet had no issue with it. Verbal sparring, shot for shot, punctuated sex that made Rune feel like he was being split in half. He'd been chained and bound ten different ways to keep him from lashing out, and it had been incredible. The best he'd ever had, by far.

It was the last time he went to Manse, his training grounds. After that night, he joined The Born Soldiers, hooked up with a supplier, and started the next chapter of his life without looking back.

Shea nudged Rune's arm, passing him the phone. A few questions were listed on the screen. When Rune didn't move or blink, Shea touched his back gently, caressing. No one else could see the touch. The room was dark. He sensed David and Elet arguing a few steps away, in another world beyond Rune's reach.

The frustration ate him alive. He hated the silence so much, his blood boiled with the desire to scream at all of them, to light a match and burn David's mansion to a pile of ashes, to walk out into traffic with a bright smile and arms wide.

But it was way too late for that. He was surrounded. They all knew. David wouldn't let him out of the room, which was lined on all sides, at all exits, with armed private security trained in kung fu and who the fuck else knew what. Elet likewise had his sites on Rune, and knew him on the inside better than anyone should have. Shea, David's collared submissive and long-time partner, was the sweetheart of the bunch, killing with kindness in a way that only made Rune angrier—at himself mostly. Then there was Max, who'd insisted on driving Rune to Manse. He didn't trust Rune behind the wheel, or the handlebars, because he knew how psychotically suicidal Rune had gotten. David had told Max something about taking control and keeping Rune there, but Rune had caught the look Max had given him, saying without speaking that he wasn't going anywhere for a while. He was probably out in the parking lot right now, smoking, listening to shitty classic rock and casually taking in the view of rolling hills dotted with horny queers in all directions.

Rune closed his eyes, rubbed his hands over his face. Shea's hand rested against the middle of Rune's back. Rune wanted to throw it off, but couldn't. Something inside stopped him.

He'd become a joke. Karma's example for all of them to laugh at, showing up on David's doorstep as a last-ditch effort to get it together somehow.

He'd sent an email the night before. It had been long and he'd had to re-write it several times to sift out that fury. It described his accident. That fucker who'd cut him off, slammed on the brakes and ripped Rune's life away from him. It also described the aftermath and his resignation to existing in misery for the rest of his life, short as he hoped it to be.

Within the hour, he'd gotten a reply. An offer of transport to the estate on David's dime, or a personal visit. Or funding to get psychiatric treatment as needed.

Rune had answered that he wasn't a charity case, thanks very much. He just didn't know what to do, or how to shatter the invisible walls he'd been living behind for months.

And now there he was, in David's compound, under guard, with the lot of them trying frantically to communicate with someone who couldn't hear a single fucking word they said and had little patience for acknowleding how helpless he'd become.

Shea's nose brushed Rune's cheek. His forehead rested gently against Rune's temple. A shiver raced up Rune's spine and he felt himself leaning into the touch despite everything, yearning for the contact like a man dying of thirst offered a sip of cool, clean water. The scent of Shea's light cologne, the soft touch of his skin, the welcoming nature of his energy—it all loosened some of the knots wound around Rune's state of mind.

There was movement in front of him. Glancing up, he saw Elet drawing up a chair, then sitting heavily in it, facing him.

His hands started to move and Rune was too stunned to look away.

The explanation poured out in a flurry of fingers, shapes drawn in the air between them. Rune's eyes tracked everything, scanning his recent studies of sign language to grasp as much of what Elet conveyed as he possibly could.

The gist of it seemed to be that David and Elet felt Rune needed someone taking care of him. Elet wanted to do it, but was in a relationship with his sub Thierry which didn't allow for other long-term commitments to specific subs. So they'd found someone else. Someone with previous signing experience who had been invited to meet Rune that evening, and would be arriving soon.

How? Rune asked. *How do you know how to sign?*

My grandmother was deaf, Elet explained. *She helped raise me, and recently passed away.*

Shea nudged Rune again, gesturing with the phone. He shook his sandy hair back out of his ocean-blue eyes, which were framed with faint little lines. He seemed so young but he'd been around the block longer than Rune.

Rune relented, taking the phone and reading.

The question glowed up at him:

What are you looking for in a Dom?

Rune began to type:

More than sex. A lot more.

He tapped the button to let the phone read the words aloud.

Then he added:

Someone who can communicate with me without the phone.

Shea's fingers brushed Rune's hair at the nape of his neck, tempting him to close his eyes again just to concentrate on the pleasant tickles it stirred. Rune didn't know why he'd always fallen so hard for other submissives, other than the thrill it gave him to feel someone give in to temptation, and want to be with him in a way that was more powerful than logic or excuses.

It was comfort and an imbued sense of power he got from being with men like Shea, or Denis.

But that's not what he craved. It wasn't what he needed. The anger was too big, the fear too real.

He wanted someone like Elet, who scared him half to death, knowing exactly what the man was capable of doing to him, and gladly so. He wanted someone who'd take all of his shit without batting an eye, turn it around, and use it to keep him in place, where he'd be safe, seen, and understood. He needed to get the rage out. He needed someone willing to kick his ass. That wasn't Shea.

Shea had taken the phone. He passed it back.

A new question read:

Someone who'll stay?

Rune nodded, keeping his head bowed to hide the panic he felt might have showed in his eyes.

Rune signed, *Who is he?*

Elet replied, *David and I trained him. He's fearless and a pain in the ass, like you.*

The smile spreading across Rune's face shocked him. He bowed his head to hide it, too late.

Elet warned, *You won't be smiling once he gets his hands on you.*

Rune just smiled and waved them forward, willing them to bring it on. He was ready.

Chapter 4
Hell of an Introduction

"David, you've lost your mind," Elet hissed, his back turned and lips moving near his companion's ear, but not bothering to lower his volume much. "We're looking to help this child, not scar him further. It's a bad match. We should call it off."

"First, he's not a child," David argued. "Second, helping is what I'm doing. For how many decades have we been friends, El? Have I ever given you reason to doubt me yet? Oliver can do this. He's changed since you've last seen him."

Oliver hesitated just outside the doorway to the room tucked away on the far left of the ground floor of Manse. The party that Saturday night was in full swing, but this section was mysteriously cleared of guests. Oliver had been directed to the room by one of David's staff, but he intended to feel out the situation first before revealing his presence and giving up all control of the situation to one of the rare people with the ability to intimidate him.

"Are we speaking of the same Oliver?" Elet asked in monotone. "He's never been loyal to a submissive other than Jackson, and even that is questionable. His contract is with a happily married man, with stipulations that he can dip his wick in any hole that appeals to him. All he's looking for is the night's biggest thrill. What on earth makes you think he's the right companion for this poor boy?"

"Please, El. He's twenty-four years old," David sighed. "Neither of them are boys. They act their age."

Oliver could see them standing off to one side, dressed to impress in tailored silk shirts and pants, voices barely hushed as they conversed. David was fair-skinned, though sun-tanned, his dark brown hair immaculately styled, the top two buttons on his shirt undone to reveal a glimpse of his golden chest. Elet's inky complexion, shaved head, and towering height set him apart, though the strength and power in him had always both intrigued Oliver and got his guard up. They were both glancing toward something Oliver couldn't see. He wondered who they were talking about, and where this person was. Oliver didn't appreciate Elet's dismissiveness towards him, especially given the fact that they hadn't had a conversation or been in the same room in years. Once, years ago, they'd bonded a little after discussing some similarities in their upbringing and history, but the connection quickly faded once their personalities began to clash. Since then, it was David, alone, Oliver confided in. Maybe Elet's complaints applied to the naïve person Oliver had been during training, but it didn't anymore. Plus, knowing what he liked didn't make Oliver any less trustworthy, it made him smart. But David's insistence on Oliver's suitability for whatever mysterious task he had in mind also put him on edge, wary of going along with someone else's schemes, their motives unknown.

"No matter his age, Oliver will do more harm than good," Elet insisted.

"You sound pretty sure of that," Oliver commented, finally rounding the doorframe with a smile, his posture relaxed as he strolled into the room.

Elet looked him up and down with a hint of a sneer. "I stand by my convictions."

"Don't we all?" Oliver countered.

"Oliver, thank you for coming," David said, extending a hand and crossing the distance between them as Oliver tried to get a read of the room. Something strange was going on. David held a small white board and marker in his left hand. There were two additional people in the room, previously hidden from view.

They were seated on a couch. One of them Oliver knew well. It was Shea, David's devoted partner. The person next to Shea was utterly unknown to Oliver. He had black, tousled hair, dark eyes, many tattoos peeking out from his collar and the ends of his sleeves, and a slouched posture as he leaned forward, elbows on his knees, his gaze trained on the gadget in Shea's hands.

Right away, part of him knew why David had called. The mystery guest was absolutely Oliver's type. The curling pout of his full lips seemed designed by God for cock-sucking. The dark air of angst and rebellion surrounding him begged for taming, binding, and a good, hard, scream-until-the-windows-rattle fucking. Though dressed in a formless maroon hoodie and frayed, worn jeans with motorcycle boots, Oliver could tell he had a nice body, though the particular size of his bulge and shape of his ass was temporarily hidden from view. Oliver made a mental note to get a better look the first chance he got.

Best of all, the cozy way the dark-haired stranger sat with Shea and the air of deference exuding from him marked him loud and clear as a submissive.

He did seem young, though Oliver was young too.

His imagination ran away with itself, guessing at the taste of his prey's tongue, imagining how he'd look in bondage, dreaming of the way he'd quiver and hump a cock as it rode his tight, rosy, wet pucker, stretching it wide open.

Distracted with fantasies, Oliver shook hands with David, who gave him a sly hint of a grin. "I thought you'd like him," David said softly, following Oliver's gaze.

Something was still off, and he couldn't figure it out. Why were they all there? Why so official? Oliver had rarely been allowed to get this close to Shea without guards breathing down his neck. The guards were still there, by the various entrances to the room, but they hung back. The two who lingered near the doorway he'd come through kept watching him without watching him. If David wanted to set him up for some entertainment, he needn't have involved Elet and Shea as well, or even been present himself. The memory of David's insistence that Oliver was needed rang in his mind, the magic word keeping him interested despite any and all alarms.

Shea typed furiously into the phone, with the mystery guest reading as he did, the screen held out so he could. Now and then, he'd nod or shake his head, as if in response to the typed words. Neither of them said a word.

Strange.

David and Elet exchanged a wordless glance, communicating something. A decision was made of which Oliver, Shea, and the mystery sub were not privy.

Elet stepped forward, quickly crossing to the sub beside Shea. His bent finger beckoned, drawing the boy to his feet. Oliver grinned to see how much rebellious fire blazed in those dark eyes at the summoning, the boy's tense posture screaming out a desire to fight back.

Clasping a hand to the back of the boy's neck, Elet moved him towards Oliver. Hands folding together behind his back, the boy bowed his head, though seemed to peek up at Oliver through thick eyelashes, his chest swelling with heavy breaths.

Elet's low voice shivered the air as he said, "The real question is, Master Oliver... do you want him? He's not Jackson. He won't make things easy for you."

"Really?" Oliver replied. He brushed the back of his finger along the boy's clenched jaw, seeing how he gritted his teeth and froze up at the contact. Taking hold of the boy's jaw, brushing the pad of his thumb over his plump bottom lip, Oliver tipped the sub's head up for a better look. Eyes obediently down, the boy growled softly but allowed it, his body frozen and wound tight.

"He's been trained?" Oliver asked.

"Of course."

The sub was even more stunning up close, making Oliver want to strip away the clothes and explore everything hidden beneath.

"Though he hasn't submitted to anyone for quite a while."

"I can tell."

Oliver dragged a knuckle down the front of the boy's chest, feeling the firmness of the muscle there, tracing each quickened breath as the sub seemed to resent the touching and treatment. To test the theory, Oliver let his hand lower even more, and began to carefully, lightly map the bulge in the jeans.

Instinctively, the boy snapped into movement. His arm came around too fast to see. He grabbed hold of Oliver's wrist with an iron grip and yanked it away. His dark eyes flashed up, a sneer on his face. It was almost too good to be true.

Licking his bottom lip, Oliver waited a moment, the others circling around them in his peripheral vision. Elet had backed off a couple of steps but hadn't gone far. David was there too, in grabbing range.

Oliver moved, pivoting, pulling the sub's arm up behind his back, getting hold of his other arm as well, pinning them both together and wrenching them high enough to hurt, straining his shoulders. The sub grunted with strain, still fighting to get loose, but not budging an inch. Keeping hold with his left hand, Oliver circled his right hand around the sub's slim body, taking a handful of his flesh at the junction of his legs through the slouching jeans. He rolled the sac in his palm, stroked along the length of thick cock, feeling it twitch in his grasp.

"Mmm. Promising," Oliver grinned.

He focused his rubbing around the head of the sub's swelling erection, feeling the way it made his fight grow, small grunts and growls barely audible from him. Like a caged animal, he squirmed to be fingered and made vulnerable in a room full of intimidating men who watched the whole thing happening. Oliver caught David's eye as the boy shivered in his arms...

Then broke free and threw a sharp elbow back into Oliver's stomach.

Elet's laughter rang loudly through the room as Oliver's breath woofed out of him. He recovered quickly. The sub had spun, cocking an arm back to throw a closed-fisted punch. Oliver slammed into him, throwing himself forward and catching the sub by the fist and the throat, slamming him back into the nearest wall.

An unmistakable flicker of lust heated the sub's dark eyes, his lips softening but no sound coming out. Oliver tightened his grip on the sub's throat and let go of his fist. Eyes narrowing, the sub reached to hold Oliver's arm, prying at it. His lips softened, working soundlessly as his breathing was restricted.

Wasting no more time, Oliver yanked open the sub's fly and plunged his hand inside, pushing into the boxers and taking hold of his dick. It was hard, wet. Oliver swiped a finger over the tip, holding the sub's gaze to show he was had. Then let go of his cock, freeing the hand to pull the sub's jeans and underwear down to show the others. Eyes closing completely, the tattooed young man let his head fall back against the wall as Oliver traced the exposed erection with his fingers.

He loosened his grip on the sub's throat and asked, "What's your name, slave?"

There was no reply. Eyes still closed, the boy shifted his grip on Oliver's arm, thrusting a little into the next stroke of his shaft.

David cleared his throat behind them, but Oliver was too engaged to look.

"I asked you a question," Oliver warned. The sub didn't even blink. So, Oliver shouted, "Hey!"

"Oliver," Elet began, still two steps away.

"I'm not talking to you. I'm talking to him," Oliver snapped.

The sub's eyes cracked open. A smile spread over his lips like sin incarnate, and Oliver felt his lust slam hard into him, telling him to conquer, fuck, and tame.

The sub puckered his lips, blowing Oliver a kiss that distracted him enough that he didn't see it coming when Oliver's leg was swept out from under him and the sub used the leverage of the arm at his throat to spin Oliver around and slam him down against the floor.

Smiling even wider as Oliver groaned and fought for air, the sub climbed onto Oliver's hips, pinned Oliver's arms above his head, and winked.

He fucking winked.

Elet walked around them in a circle until he was standing behind Oliver's head.

"Oliver, this is Rune," Elet explained. Oliver tipped his head back to look at him, standing there, and frowned as he saw Elet's hands signing along with his words. "He seems pleased to make your acquaintance."

Oliver glanced between Elet, David, Shea, the nearest armed guard and the gorgeous creature sitting on his hips, absolutely undaunted by the fact that his erection was still exposed to them all.

"What the fuck is going on?" Oliver demanded, his voice a little strained with exasperation.

Rune let go and shaped words in the air as Elet did. Oliver had no clue what it meant.

"If I may translate," Elet said, barely unable to contain his laughter, "Rune says, I'm deaf, you moron."

"Oh," Oliver said with blaring sarcasm, "well that's just fucking fantastic."

Rune bit his lip, seeming quite pleased with himself. He undulated atop Oliver, thrusting against him, rolling his hips and leaning down close to get more contact. His lips barely brushed against Oliver's, sending a jolt of need right to Oliver's straining cock. Then he pecked a kiss to the tip of Oliver's nose, staring him dead in the eyes without an ounce of fear or intimidation.

David spoke up, "Of course, if that's a deal-breaker for you..."

Oblivious, Rune shifted to lay even more fully atop Oliver, and thrust directly against his aching, completely erect cock, prompting a counter-thrust from Oliver, who reached to cup Rune's bare ass and hold him there, wanting more than anything to feel Rune's butt cheeks in the firm grip of his hands.

Rune was too quick, of course, and rolled off before Oliver could do it, then sprung to his feet and tucked himself back inside his pants, fastening them up again.

Oliver sank back down to the floor, sprawled there.

"You know... fuck all of you. The whole bunch. Especially you," he said, flipping them all off, then pointing at Rune.

"So you're not interested then?" David clarified.

Adjusting himself without any discretion, Oliver groaned. Then flung his arms wide in defeat, closing his eyes. They all moved to stand around him, looking down with self-satisfied smirks that he didn't like at all.

"You know, David, you can be a real asshole sometimes," Oliver said. At that, David moved closer to Rune—who looked pretty damn pleased with himself—wrapped an arm around his shoulders and kissed his cheek. Jealousy was a monster clawing at Oliver's chest, throwing daggers at David, who just smiled down at Oliver. "Just get the fucking papers, okay?"

Elet cleared his throat. "Olly, like this..." he shaped the signs slowly as he spoke. "Get... the fucking... papers... okay?"

"Oh, okay. You?" He pointed at Elet and stuck up his middle finger. "Fuck you most of all."

"Do you need to see it again?" Elet asked.

Oliver growled, swallowed the curse, then matched Elet's signs exactly. Rune looked surprised, glancing at David, Elet and Shea in turn with a brutal mix of hope, fear, and humility.

Groaning one last time, Oliver closed his eyes and lamented, "God, I'm so screwed."

Chapter 5
Gutter Rat

Rune appreciated that Elet was interpreting most of the conversation for him, but he was having trouble concentrating on mentally translating the endless stream of complex signing. He interrupted once to ask him to slow down, but there seemed to be too much to say for it to slow down enough for Rune's boner-induced delirium.

He, David, Elet, Shea and Oliver were in an office. The ever-present security guards waited at the door, facing out. Paper lay on the desk. David and Oliver were hashing it out but Rune just kept staring.

Oliver was actually younger than him, just by a year or two, though he looked older. He looked straight out of a high-end men's fashion ad with a five-o'clock shadow on his chiseled jaw, chocolate brown, perfectly styled hair sculpted into place, a mid-length, black woolen coat that fell open to reveal a crisp white button-down shirt with three buttons open at the neck, untucked over tight black pants, polished boots and a silver wallet chain hanging at his hip. It was just the right ball-busting mix of elegant, sexy and badass, keeping Rune hard and unable to stop staring. Because it wasn't just the clothes. The way Oliver held himself, the intimidation techniques that seemed so second nature, Rune was convinced Oliver wasn't even doing it consciously. Standing beside David, who had the power and ability to buy and sell them all like cattle, trained in the finest schools and board rooms, Oliver held his own, standing straighter, squaring his shoulders, clenching his jaw and charging the air. There was something dangerous about him. David hid his danger well, under many layers. Elet didn't try as hard, but being David's best friend had rubbed off over the years, marking him as elite.

Oliver though... his body was hard. Rune had felt it, so he had some first-hand knowledge to work with. His amber and green eyes, his expression, his body language—they blared warnings loud and clear that he wasn't someone to fuck with, which Rune thought was kind of ironic, given the situation.

Especially because Rune knew he was a gutter rat. His looks and charm had gotten him in the door at Manse, way back when, but his attitude and willingness to break the law and do things like make a living as a dealer had gotten him the boot. Now what was he? Hopeless, mostly. And broke, in many forms and senses. He was a penniless, damaged asshole begging for scraps from the richest of the rich.

Maybe they all got off on his ballsiness, basically kicking Oliver's ass when he'd been trying to intimidate and impress.

He was like a party trick. The entertainment. Hired for a few laughs, then sent out on his ass when it wasn't fun anymore.

Rune knew from what Elet was translating that they were filling Oliver in on the backstory Rune had typed out in his email, sharing some of the necessary info. They were treating this like it was legit, and Rune still wasn't able to believe it for a minute.

He gave up trying, slouching back in the leather couch, picking at his nails, legs spread to reveal a hard-on he had no reason to hide in present company.

Elet smacked Rune's leg, scowling down at him for the attention lapse.

So Rune flipped him off.

And Elet hit him again. Then David yelled something and Rune rolled his eyes.

When Elet stepped back and David crouched down in front of where Rune sat, then Elet and Oliver cleared the room entirely, Rune felt some dread. A heavy pit sank into his stomach and the need to run rose back, clawing at his will.

Inches away, touching Rune's knee, David let his lips shape his words carefully.

What's wrong?

Rune bit his tongue, feeling like a bug under a microscope—something gross, caught, and twitching.

David nodded to one of the guards, who pulled the door shut, closing the two of them in.

Even Rune could tell the stillness had intensified.

Rune sighed, pulled out his phone and typed.

He doesn't want me. He just feels sorry for me.

He let David take the phone to read it without raising his gaze. But then David grabbed hold of Rune's chin and forced eye contact. It was kind of incredible how confident David was. It was all right there in his eyes. Not a doubt in the world. Must have been nice.

David relented long enough to type a message:

Oliver doesn't fuck around. Not with something this serious. Doesn't have it in him. Doesn't lie. Doesn't waste the energy. One of the smartest people I know. He wouldn't be here, learning as much as he can about you, if he wasn't interested. You proved yourself. This is just technicalities. You'll be okay, Rune. I promise. You can trust him.

Rune took the phone back, reading, then couldn't raise his gaze again but just sat there, huddled over the device, clutching it like it was his last lifeline. David pulled him in, kissed the side of his head, and Rune nodded. Finally, he looked up and David gave him an encouraging sort of smile. Rune slung an arm behind David's neck and hugged him, pouring his gratitude into the contact. Fingers tangled in Rune's dark hair, David clutched the back of his head and kissed his hair again, then patted his back and let go, nodding toward the door.

Rune nodded. David gave the word and the others returned.

While David filled Oliver in, Elet gave Rune a disappointed look, so Rune signed an apology. Holding his closed hand in the A handshape with his thumb held next to his index finger, his palm facing his body, he circled the center of his chest to show he was feeling sorrow.

In just a few minutes, they were filling out the forms to cement the agreement making Oliver officially Rune's Dominant. All of David's carefully crafted rules applied, protecting both Oliver and Rune. It was all spelled out in black and white, from Rune's safe sign—the shaka sign which resembled the American Sign Language letter for Y, and was widely familiar to even those who didn't know ASL as the sign for "hang loose"—to the miniscule list of what was off limits for both of them.

Oliver inked his signature first. Once Rune did the same and watched it dry, he felt strangely trapped and not as relieved as he'd hoped.

But before he could get himself together, he felt Oliver grip his shoulder and turn him so they faced each other. Using David's white board, Oliver began writing a long message in small, sharp letters.

I learned ASL as a kid. One of my nannies was hard of hearing. My parents thought it would benefit me later, but I've forgotten a lot. I talked to Elet about ASL once, years ago, which is how they knew I can do it. I'm going to study my ass off to get up to speed. In the meantime, I want you to move in with me. I have the space. Over my dead body will you continue living in a storage closet. It's not a discussion, it's an order. You'll have your own room and anything else you need. Just name it.

Rune took the board, wiped it clear and wrote: *How? Are we going to be passing a board back and forth for months? During sex? You've gotta be fucking kidding me.*

Rune raised an eyebrow. His scribbled reply from Oliver read: *Gimme a few days, sweetie, okay?*

S-W-E-E-T-I-E? Rune finger-spelled.

Elet shook his head and rolled his eyes.

When Rune made eye contact with Oliver, he didn't see any condescension or pity, just a warning that he had every intention to continue their sparring session as soon as it was possible, because he wouldn't stop until he won and had Rune exactly where he wanted him—conquered, fucked and pleading.

Oliver gave him the barest hint of a smile—dangerous and intoxicating as it was.

Challenge accepted.

Elet signed without speaking from over Oliver's shoulder: *Watch your ass, sweetie.*

Rune grinned and winked at him.

Then Rune gave Oliver a deferential nod of submission and acceptance.

They proceeded from the room. Oliver gripped Rune hard at the base of the neck and guided him out without giving him the slightest chance to get the upper hand again.

David was right, Rune thought. Oliver was fast learner after all.

"No. No way," the grizzled old guy barked. He wore a leather jacket bearing the logo for something called The Born Soldiers across the back, with various patches and adornments on the lapel and sleeves. Oliver was impressed with his beard and general vibe the biker gave off. He also appreciated that Rune had someone watching out for him. "You ain't leavin' with this guy. No way. You don't know him from Adam!"

"Adam's a great guy though," Oliver chimed in. "Bit of a queen sometimes, but still—"

"What?" The guy gave him a quizzical look. "I ain't talkin' to you." Turning back to Rune, he opened his mouth to yell some more.

"I'm Oliver Hughes, by the way. And you are?" Oliver edged in, extended a hand, forcing an introduction as easily as he always had in his time spent digging up quotes and interviews when he was still writing for the Post. He'd placed himself between the guy and Rune, who watched with amusement. "I can tell you care about Rune, and I can assure you he'll be well taken care of. Much more living space than the broom closet provides. Plenty of attention of whatever sort he's in the mood for."

The biker had been gesturing wildly while he spoke, though Oliver was pretty sure it hadn't been actual sign language. Still, it was pretty informative in its own way. Now, the guy let his arms hang at his sides, squinting up at Oliver like he was a cop coming to drag Rune to jail.

"Tell me your name. Please," Oliver interjected as the guy sucked in air to begin a new tirade.

"Max. Who the fuck are you? He ain't a whore. He ain't for sale. He's got a home. He's got people."

"Mmm, see, I think as a grown-up, Rune gets to choose what he wants. We," Oliver said, gesturing between him and Rune, "have come to an agreement. He's coming with me tonight. We'll be in touch soon. I'm happy to provide my number and address so you can contact me or find him whenever you like."

Max jabbed a thick finger in Oliver's face. "That's rude. You ain't even tryin' to sign. You ain't typin' your words. That's rude."

"Well, I'm learning, but I think Rune gets the gist. Don't you, sweetie?" Oliver smiled to Rune.

"He ain't your sweetie. He ain't nuthin' to you," Max argued.

Rune stepped forward, laying a hand on Max's shoulder, his expression pleasant and good-spirited. He lightly slapped the side of Max's face twice then signed something.

"The fuck is this, kid? He only wants one thing from you! You're better than that! Just come home, okay? We'll figure something else out."

Oliver could tell Max wasn't signing all of his words, and Rune wasn't even paying much attention to those Max did sign. But there was love between them. It was clear.

Rune signed again and Max glared at Oliver.

"Max, what's your number?" Oliver asked, drawing out his phone.

Growling, Max recited it.

Tapping into his phone, Oliver said. "Wonderful. You should get my message any moment now with all of the information you need. You're welcome to come by in the morning, let's say eleven, and check out the place."

Rune went to the beat-up truck parked a few paces away and drew a duffel out of the back, slinging it over his shoulder. Oliver gestured to his black Jaguar, conveniently also parked nearby.

Max flapped his arms and made a desperate type of sound. Rune walked away, his back turned, so Max didn't bother calling out again.

"Okay, Oliver Hughes. You listen to me. Rune has friends. He's got a crew. You harm one hair on his head and we'll come for yours. Get me?"

"Max, he came here tonight for a reason. He knows what he's doing. Trust that, even if you won't trust me. You know where to find us. Have a nice evening."

Chapter 6
Testing the Waters

The drive took a while. Rune spent the whole time online, Googling Oliver's name, learning everything he could. Oliver's biography was listed on a few websites, identifying him as a journalist. Many stories came up with his name in the byline. There was nothing recent though, and no social media accounts came up, which was a little fishy.

Rune checked Grindr, found nothing.

So he kept digging, kept reading. He wanted to protect himself, get some ammunition to work with, but also wanted to fill the time to settle his nerves. Because he was in it now. No getting out. Either he'd just signed his ass over to a psychopath or at the very least, he was in for some super awkward encounters.

Because the silence was maddening. Oliver couldn't sign. Couldn't divert his attention from the road to type. They had few means of communicating, but Rune felt compelled to gather every means of self-defense he possibly could. The wrestling at Manse hadn't been a joke or an act. It was imperative that Oliver understand he couldn't expect Rune to roll over and beg for no reason. Trust and respect was crucial, but it also had to be earned.

Those signed papers meant Oliver could put Rune in chains, strip him down, fuck him dizzy and do any number of things to him. Sure, consent was key, and Rune had his safe sign, but even having David and Elet vouch for the guy didn't really take Rune the whole way towards trusting his safety to the man behind the wheel.

He also still couldn't figure out why someone like Oliver would want him anyway. His motives were in question.

Why take on a project like Rune? Why go to the trouble, when Manse was packed full of hot men who'd kill to suck Oliver's dick and could hear every single command he'd give?

What the hell was Oliver getting out of all the hassle?

They pulled up to a huge old building that looked like it had once been a factory of some kind, and parked in one of a series of private garages along the side. Oliver cut the engine and reached for Rune's bag. Rune smacked his hand away, but Oliver was determined. He didn't let go and just stared Rune down until he gave up.

Blowing out a breath, Rune let Oliver take the bag and got out of the car.

Unable to quite believe where he was or what he was doing, he let Oliver guide him to a bank of elevators. Rune glimpsed enough in the lobby of the place to understand it had been renovated and was no longer functioning as a factory. So there was that, at least.

He felt the instinct take over to go deep into his head and detach. He didn't even see what button Oliver pushed, or bother to check if he was trying to communicate at all.

The doors opened and Oliver stepped out. Rune trailed him to a door, which they went through, and into a space with brick walls, massive windows, steel and aluminum in the exposed ceilings, wood floors, leather furniture, high end finishes and more. For someone who'd been living in a dusty storage room, and otherwise was homeless and unemployed, it was slightly intimidating.

Mouth dry, struggling to swallow, Rune's head spun.

He didn't belong there. Standing in that immaculate place made him feel even more like a piece of shit.

He needed to hook Oliver. Show him the deal had been worthwhile. Rune also wanted to prove himself and establish his place.

Feeling more nervous than since before he'd trained at Manse, Rune tried to fake his way through it. Oliver set the bag down, then turned on some lights in the massive kitchen.

Rune walked over to him, staring at Oliver's slightly exposed chest, trying to breathe normally. He put himself in Oliver's personal space, inhaled the scent of Oliver's skin and lack of cologne, nearly brushed his lips against the tan skin of Oliver's neck and grabbed a fistful of his coat. Closing his eyes, he went for Oliver's mouth.

A hand wrapping his jaw pushed him back.

Eyes springing open, Rune bit down on his back teeth and watched Oliver seem to struggle with what to do.

So Rune reached for Oliver's crotch and palmed his bulge.

That hand got yanked away too.

A single word, mouthed carefully: *Stop.*

Oliver's thumb brushed Rune's lip, his eyes staring right there.

Growling, Rune fought the holds, which only made Oliver's hand slip down to Rune's throat. Oliver walked him back two steps to the brick wall, his expression washed over with sudden calm as he squeezed.

The air ran out, and Rune bucked reflexively. Oliver slipped a knee between Rune's thighs, brought his arm up and around above his head, against the wall. His teeth scraped Rune's lower lip. He licked, light and quick, over Rune's top lip and kissed the end of his nose, then relaxed his hold on Rune throat.

Shaking his head slowly from side to side, Oliver held Rune still.

The moment drew out.

Then Rune fought back, trying to move, to break free. Oliver had to work to contain him, his effort showing in the flushed look of his face, the tendons standing out in his neck, and the strain of his muscles, but he managed to do it, no matter how hard Rune pushed back.

Oliver mouthed again: *Stop.*

Rune relaxed, stopped fighting. Slowly, Oliver let go, stepped back.

Rune charged him, knocking Oliver back into the counter's edge, before sinking to his feet. He began sucking wide, obscene kisses to the hard bulge between Oliver's legs, licking a wide stripe over the fabric.

Oliver's hand locked under Rune's jaw, pulled him up off the ground and to his feet. Rune winced at the pain, grabbing Oliver's arm with both hands.

Oliver tossed him away. Frowning, he grabbed the duffel, then turned to walk towards a hallway through a living area carpeted with a thick, white rug.

Neck throbbing, Rune gathered all his will and ran, knocking into Oliver's back, sending him flying awkwardly into a couch where he landed on his side. The bag dropped from his grasp as he moved to brace his fall. Wasting no time, Rune climbed on, straddling Oliver. He undulated down against him, showing Oliver he was hard, letting him feel it as his erection dragged against Oliver's hip. At the same time, he scraped his teeth against Oliver's neck, then sucked a kiss there.

Oliver threw them both sideways, rolling them onto the carpeted floor with a thud that drove some of the air from Rune's lungs.

Dazed, Rune wasn't able to stop Oliver from getting on top and pinning him more completely in place by his hips and both arms. Panting against Rune's ear, Oliver showed him as he worked to calm down. His breathing slowed. His lips dragged against Rune's jaw, causing Rune's cock to twitch. He bit down on Rune's earlobe, sending an extra jolt of pure pleasure.

Rune felt the sound get past his defenses—a whimper, a plea.

Oliver caught his eye, then kissed him hard, licking back into Rune's mouth, forcing his jaw to open wide. Rune let Oliver use his mouth, tongues twisting, teeth scraping, lips teasing. By the time they broke, Rune was breathing hard, his need huge just to be had, owned, and claimed.

It all came to the surface, and Oliver stayed just far enough away to watch it, studying him, preventing Rune from sinking back into the kiss, or breaking free, or getting off. He was just trapped and seen, wound up and with no release in sight.

He just wanted it over. He wanted to stop thinking. Stop worrying. Stop fighting.

He wanted to know he hadn't made a huge mistake. That he wasn't worthless. That he wasn't just a joke, good for a laugh, then thrown away in the garbage.

He wanted to show the rich man to whom he'd pledged his obedience, who had no way to know what Rune was so fucking scared of, that he could still make it feel good, even if the rest was a total useless mess.

Once again, he heard the scream of tires, felt his skin tearing away, heard his own cry for the last time, saw the doctor's pity and felt his crew's gaze sliding right off of him like he wasn't even there. He felt Oliver, a stranger, his Dom, holding him out of reach, like he didn't want Rune kissing him again, looking at him like he was a puzzle with no answers, and he broke his own biggest rule.

"Please," Rune begged.

Something shifted behind Oliver's eyes, and Rune looked away, biting hard at his lip, turning his head away, knowing that next Oliver would let go and point to the door. Rune was already mentally pulling out his phone, texting Max for a ride, ready to crawl back into his hole and give up for good.

But then Oliver sank down, lying completely atop Rune, circling him with his arms in a gentle embrace, pressing his lips in a kiss to Rune's temple and just breathing, just holding on.

Rune wound his arms behind Oliver's back, a slight tremor shaking him, and gave in.

Oliver carried the tray into Rune's room. It was the largest of two guest rooms, with its own bathroom and walk-in closet. The tray was filled with an array of breakfast foods—everything from vegan to sausage, and coffee, tea and orange juice, just to cover the bases. There was still too much Oliver didn't know about his new submissive.

Rune was still deeply asleep as Oliver walked in. Barely a trickle of sunlight escaped the thick curtains blocking the large windows. Oliver set down the tray beside where Rune curled up on his side in the bed, pillow folded under his head and a peaceful expression on his face. For just a moment, Oliver took advantage of the chance to study Rune while he was totally unguarded. His handsome features were somehow only enhanced by all of the black and grey-ink tattoos. He was stunning with his pale skin, nearly black hair, thick, dark eyelashes, and soft, full lips. Since he was shirtless, Oliver had his first chance to not only check out more of Rune's body, but also his ink and the long swaths of scarred skin along his arm and back.

Rune awoke while Oliver was looking him over. Inhaling sharply and reaching up to rub his eyes, he tried to shake himself awake fast. He pulled himself upright, tugging at the sheet in a glimpse of self-consciousness. His phone lay on the nightstand, charging with one of Oliver's spare cords. Unplugging it, Oliver turned it on and passed it to him. Then Oliver woke up his own phone and passed it to Rune to read from.

Good morning. We need to correct the communication issue. Elet's on his way over to help me catch up. I plan to use the next few days just to study and get you situated. We'll move your things here so you're comfortable and I'd need you to take some time to tell me about yourself. I'll return the favor as best I can. Send me whatever questions you have.

I've sent you a text with my email address and list of things I'm curious about. Things I need to know about your past, your goals, and your preferences. All the basics and broader subjects, like what's important to you in life and what you eat for breakfast. I wasn't sure on that last one, so I got a little of everything.

Regarding last night, I'm keeping hands off until we're better able to understand each other. I won't jeopardize your safety. I need to be absolutely clear on what you're feeling at a given time, and that means learning about each other first. That's why I stopped you. It's temporary. I'm a quick study.

We also need to make some rules for your safety for when we do get into some scenes. I'm still putting them together. First off is no blindfolds and no binding of your arms at any time that would thereby impede your ability to communicate with me, or see me communicating with you.

Sorry for hitting you with all of this so early, but we've got a lot of ground to cover and it's already driving me crazy to have you here and not be able to do anything about it.
The basics about me: I'm stubborn. I don't do bullshit. I get what I want. Right now, all I want is you.

Oh, and I already have a submissive. You'll meet him soon. His name is Jackson. Married. House. Two kids. He's here when he can be. I'm hoping you'll get along. I think you will.

Staring at the small glowing screen, Rune blew out a breath that sounded like it would have been followed by a hearty, 'fuck me,' if he was the speaking sort. He ran his hands back through his hair, tousling it in a hot, absolutely un-self-conscious way that made Oliver want to rip the sheet back, tear off any clothes in the way and have at it, rules and logic be damned.

But he could see the questions piling up in Rune, ready to burst out. And it was killing Oliver to not be able to just have a conversation with eye contact and everything, so he gestured at the tray, took his phone back and pointed to Rune's.

Clearing the screen, Oliver typed instead:

I'm not going anywhere. I'll be out in the living room if you need me, studying. Take your time. Relax.

After reading Oliver's screen, Rune typed a quick response:

No work?

Oliver answered:

Day trader. Work from home.

Rune nodded in understanding, biting at his lip, seemingly caught between deciding to eat, type, go take a leak or get dressed first, waiting on Oliver to go before he could.

When Oliver saw Rune's gaze sweep up and down his body, hand on the tray like he was about to move it aside, Oliver held up a hand and gave him an encouraging look before turning to go.

Chapter 7
Working Hard or Hardly Working

By the time Max showed, Rune was sprawled out at the long, elegant black dining table in the main room, surrounded by the remains of his breakfast, a fresh mug of coffee, a notepad and his phone. With his feet up on the table, he typed away, sipping idly and keeping an eye on the pair of Doms in the sitting area as often as he could.

The list of questions from Oliver was so extensive, Rune wouldn't have believed it possible even if Oliver had stayed up all night writing it, if not for the tip about him being a writer by trade. Or at least, used to be.

He knew it was going to take him all day. Maybe that was the point.

So Rune was glad for the distraction when Max sent a text to let Rune know he was at the door.

Barefoot, dressed in old jeans that fit him like a second skin, tight black V-neck shirt and finger-combed hair, Rune felt underdressed for his company and surroundings. Once Max walked in outfitted in full biker regalia—leather jacket, boots, the whole deal—Rune felt instantly more at ease. They were two pegs that didn't fit, but it became clear, fast, that seeing where Rune was helped set Max at ease.

The conversation was simple, short, and consisted mainly of Max checking out Oliver, the place, Elet, and Rune's general vibe. He handed over another duffel full of more of Rune's things, as requested via text message earlier in the morning.

Rune opted out of trying to translate the verbal back and forth going on, even though Elet attempted to interpret for him, waving them off and going back to his seat to type some more.

Oliver showed Max out with a handshake, which was as good a sign as any.

Grabbing an apple, Rune tossed it in the air, caught it, and brought it and his new bag full of stuff back to his room.

He closed the door behind him, dropped the bag on the bed and parted the zipper.

He was just removing his handgun and checking the chamber when he felt the air shift behind him as Oliver walked in.

With a sigh, he didn't fight it when Oliver stalked over and took the gun out of his hands, wearing a royally pissed off expression and shouting something Rune didn't bother to catch. He sat heavily on the edge of the bed, elbows planted on his knees, one eyebrow raised as Elet came to join the fun.

Diving right in, Rune signed: *It's for protection. I won't wear it in here if you don't want me to.*

When asked if he usually wore it, he nodded enthusiastically.

When asked why, he explained as simply as he could that he'd either been a target or had product worth stealing for years. He didn't sell anymore, but after the accident, he wasn't taking chances.

They asked what he meant by that.

Rune hesitated to explain.

Oliver asked who was targeting him. Or, demanded, rather.

Rune explained: *I don't know. Got a partial license plate and a good look at the white power and Nazi stickers on the back of the truck.*

Oliver and Elet exchanged looks. Rune bore it, though wished he didn't have to explain this part before he finished some of the more basic questions Oliver had first.

You think the accident wasn't an accident? Elet signed.

Rune shook his head.

Why?

I was meeting a guy at a pull-off in the middle of nowhere. A date. Local guy I met on Grindr. He never showed, but I saw the truck parked nearby. I left to go home. I never got there.

Everything got still. It drew out. Then Oliver started to talk to Elet and he wasn't translating anymore. Rune moved to grab the bag, slung it over a shoulder and signed: *I'll go. It's not your problem. I'm sorry.*

Oliver stopped him with a hand to his chest, took the bag from him and pushed him back down onto the bed before setting the bag aside, by the wall.

Have you told anyone else? Your crew? Elet asked.

Rune shook his head.

Why?

I'm not out to them, he explained.

Oliver covered his eyes with a hand, like he was getting a headache.

You think they targeted you through Grindr for being gay? Elet asked.

Who knows? I'm also Jewish, Rune replied, then pointed to the star of David that was on the back of his left arm.

They all stared at each other for a minute.

I'm keeping the gun, Oliver said via Elet's translation. *For now.*
I have a license to carry, Rune added.
Good, Oliver replied.

Rune had never done so much typing in his life. For three weeks, they lived in a weird limbo. It turned out Oliver had an IQ high enough that he skipped three grades and graduated at the top of his class at university. He also had a knack with languages. He spoke four of them—Mandarin, French and was passable in Russian. Most of that was due to his parents, just like with the ASL. Oliver said that'd had a passion for making him as multilingual as they could, starting when he was a toddler, by hiring nannies who didn't speak English or paying for special lessons.

He did nothing from dawn to the middle of the night but learn sign language, either via Elet in person, Elet on Skype, colleagues of David's who were also fluent in sign language on Skype, or via internet tutorials. He was also in the process of hiring a tutor for them both, to meet with them individually to work on expanding their vocabulary and fluency. The man was a sponge. He quickly knew more than Rune, and so included him on the lessons. Rune got the sense from Oliver's behavior and the email conversations they had that it was a compulsion with him. When he found a goal, he threw himself into it until it was conquered, possibly to the detriment of other facets of his life. For instance, though Oliver had mentioned his submissive, Jackson, Rune had yet to meet the guy and could only imagine he was feeling neglected.

Since Rune's personality was more of the slow burn sort, he couldn't relate to Oliver's fervor for knowledge, especially if it was just in the interest of getting laid. They could fuck without conversing, but Oliver was having none of it.

When Rune wasn't in lessons, he was typing out messages to Oliver, which were mostly clarifications of questions from questions about questions. It felt a little like an interrogation, so soon Rune was slacking off, going for walks and playing online games when Oliver thought he was actually working.

Already, Oliver knew a ton of things about Rune—everything from details about Denis, to Rune's consistent status as a troublemaker in grade school, to his intention to cover as much of his body with ink as he could so at least his scars were completely obscured. He knew Rune's parents split up when he was five, that he hadn't graduated high school and started living with friends at sixteen after his mom's drunk boyfriend smashed a bottle over his head and caused a laceration that took twenty-three stitches in his scalp to close. He knew Rune had been a straight-A student before things had taken a nose-dive thanks to circumstances like mom's shitty boyfriend, and that Rune had always gotten in lots of trouble for sticking up for the underdog in school and in his neighborhood.

He knew Rune had been a chatty smart-ass when he was the hearing, talking sort, and now preferred to hang back and observe rather than make the effort to engage people. That was a habit he knew Oliver was trying to save him from, claiming it was a sign of depression, encouraging Rune to find things that energized him again.

Rune knew a lot about Oliver, too. He'd seen photos of Jackson, who was pretty hot and unlike anyone Rune had been with before. Jackson was bi, much older, serious, and worked so hard trying to save people that he kept stressing himself out, which was where Oliver stepped in, releasing pressure so Jackson didn't explode.

He knew Oliver's BFF was a guy named Adam Buchanan that Oliver was weirdly devoted to in a soul mate type of way. Adam was an intense, ginger, blue-eyed artist who'd been born to be a lawyer until fate intervened and plunged him into the tortured painter role instead, driving him to distant countries in search of escape from his problems and inspiration for his muse. Rune was curious to meet the guy and see just how intense Adam really was. Oliver implied that he, personally, was one of the rare people who could deal with the dude on a consistent basis without feeling claustrophobic and attacked. Instead of putting Rune off, it amused him and made him more curious. Especially since Oliver also confessed he and Adam often shared submissives, including Jackson. Before, having sex with one guy had been crazy enough for Rune. Being in a threesome, foursome or fivesome was way beyond his imagination's capabilities.

It was weird to share so much with someone via text alone, making everything feel secret and sacred somehow. Yet, he could see the things they'd talked about reflected in Oliver's expression when they were together or simply looking at each other across the room. It helped lessen the feeling of being trapped on one side of a vast chasm, because he'd found a messenger system to send notes rather than getting over the gulf entirely.

Having Elet there to translate had the opposite effect, like nothing was private and everyone was involved in any conversation that was had. Privacy vanished completely. That was why Rune favored the emails as a way to catch up and stay engaged.

Running snippets of phrases and thoughts through his head, Rune lingered in the shower attached to his room. He'd never been big into grooming before, but the bathroom was like a spa, with high end fixtures, a jetted tub, mood lighting, a two-person shower with a rainfall shower-head and three other shower-heads spraying from various directions. There was also a speaker system built in that Rune was tempted to use just to fuck with Oliver if he was listening in and put on Celine Dion or something at full blast.

He scrubbed his arms, liking the way the bubbles mixed with ink and scars. Rune had two full sleeves and a massive back piece. There were smaller tattoos on his fingers and some trailed up his neck to wrap behind his ears. It had pissed him off when so much of the work he had was torn away, the asphalt working like a cheese grater on his skin.

Scanning the areas of his arms with newly blank patches of scarred skin, he tried to let the shapes spur possibilities for new tattoo ideas.

The steam was filled with masculine aromas which added to the sense of being in a strange, indulgent place. Most of the time he just showered with plain soap and water. Oliver didn't even have soap. He had a bunch of scented body washes and expensive-looking shampoos, conditioners, scrubs and all sorts of weird shit. Half the time Rune spent in the shower was in deciding what to use and how.

He liked it, though. He took two showers a day now—morning and night. Might as well, right?

Stepping out of the cavernous, tiled shower, Rune did a rough pat-dry and barely remembered to wrap the towel around his waist as he went back into his bedroom.

Where Oliver was lounging on the bed.

Rune cocked an eyebrow at him, holding onto the ends of the towel a little more securely but not out of shyness. He just didn't quite know what was up.

At first, Oliver didn't even seem to notice Rune's confusion. He was way too busy ogling every inch of bare skin showing.

Rune waved to get Oliver's attention, then pointed to his eyes.

Oliver smiled slyly and shrugged.

Rune re-secured the end of his towel, then signed: *Tired of studying?*

He wasn't sure the question would be understood, so he was pleasantly surprised to see Oliver tilt his flattened hand back and forth. He also screwed his face up a little as he signed: *Frustrated. I want to talk to you.*

Frustrated? Rune echoed, letting his confusion show in his face.

Oliver thought a minute, then slowly explained in a simplified way that if it was him, he'd be going crazy. Then asked if Rune was okay.

Feeling a little on the spot to be near-naked and having his first real face-to-face conversation with Oliver, Rune knew the bout of shyness showed. Fearing a blush as Oliver kept looking places Rune wasn't used to men looking so blatantly, he resigned himself to his vulnerable state and tried to own it.

I'm okay. It's better here, Rune explained. *Your studying means you care. It helps.*

Oliver asked if Rune was angry.

Unsure how to reply, Rune watched Oliver's eyes for a minute, but they gave away little besides endless hunger for knowledge and satisfaction, as usual. He was engaged, though. He was paying close attention.

Rune shrugged, holding things back, masking his expression.

So Oliver repeated himself.

Maybe, he admitted. *It's not your problem.*

I'm your Dom, Oliver argued, his brow furrowing.

Rune nearly smiled. Oliver was expressive enough without the signs to convey plenty of his intention, just in his body language and the contortions of his face.

The levity didn't seem to please Oliver, who signed one thing: *Revenge?*

Then, Rune did smile, but kept his cards to himself.

Oliver signed a deliberate NO, wearing a stern expression, bringing his index and middle fingers together once with his thumb, the other fingers curls inward.

Rune shrugged and made a circle of his thumb and index finger, his other fingers extended in the sign for okay.

He wanted to change the topic. Luckily, he had the upper hand. He was the one who'd been pushing to get physical. He had the ability to drop the towel and cross the line.

Something held him back. Call it uncharacteristic bashfulness. Call it a reluctance to look a gift horse in the mouth. If Oliver was disappointed in what Rune had to offer sexually, it might mean he'd be back on the street again, out of luck.

Leaning back against the pillows, ankles crossed, fully dressed with his shoes and everything, Oliver leaned on one elbow, holding Rune's body in his sights. He uncrossed his legs, spread them a little as he bent one knee and leaned back. He adjusted himself and Rune looked away.

When Rune looked back, Oliver was the one smiling.

Was he calling Rune's bluff? Seeing if he'd strip and try going for a wrestle again? Oliver seemed awfully cozy on the bed, like he was settled in for a long stay.

Rune wished he hadn't just come from the indulgent shower, fit for Gods. It made it a hell of a lot harder to do something that risked his newfound luck. One wrong move and he'd have to say goodbye to such luxuries.

Then again, if he was going to get kicked out, he wanted to know sooner than later. Get it over with.

So, he held onto the front flap of the towel, and tugged the back flap loose. The towel unwound, exposing Rune's backside, the fallen towel held tightly in front to mask his crotch and tease a little, testing the waters.

Heart pounding, it amazed Rune to see Oliver's confidence and hunger only grow. He seemed to leisurely drink in all of Rune's nervousness and feigned cockiness. An almost bored demeanor encouraged Rune to try getting the upper hand, like it wasn't even possible.

Rune had never been with a guy like that before. He was too used to scared-shitless, closeted, middle-class wimps looking to suck or get fucked. Now, Rune was the prey, and he was being hunted.

Standing there, barely covered, his ass in the wind, at first Rune was shocked when Oliver dropped his gaze and pulled out his phone, like he was uninterested or had a call to take.

But then he tapped the screen a few times and pointed the back of the phone at Rune, holding it there.

Skin prickling with goosebumps, Rune realized he was being filmed. It made him want to seem more confident, when he'd never been more intimidated.

The tension of that moment wasn't anything like it had been at Manse. It wasn't a game. It wasn't about getting laid. It was about proving himself to someone who had demonstrated for going on a month an ability to provide and care for him, long term.

There were stakes. Oliver had barely gotten any work done so he could learn a new language as fast as humanly possible. All for Rune.

The silence crowded in. His vision began to black out at the edges and the pressure behind his ears increased, so he closed his eyes, hoping it would pass. His hands stopped feeling the towel's terry cloth texture, or the room's slight chill, or the drips of water sliding down his back, or anything else.

He knew he cried out in surprise, feeling the exclamation voice from his throat when he felt a touch. He trembled a little, uncontrollably, as a body pressed close to his back. A hand cupped the side of his ass, squeezed, and a warm mouth sucked a kiss to his jaw. Oliver's cologne filled Rune's head. Rune kept his eyes shut as Oliver's other hand caressed Rune's chest, pausing to twist his left nipple.

The hand squeezing his ass relaxed, rubbed over to his crack and traced up to his pucker. A pair of fingertips circled the opening, teasing it for a moment. Before Rune had gotten over the shock, the hand flattened on the center of his chest, braced against him, and a single, dry finger pushed through his rim. It kept sheathing in him and quickly bottomed out. There were several reactions.

Oliver's heated breath exhaled against Rune's neck, and he held it there inside him. Rune, trying to stay silent, knew sounds were slipping free despite his best efforts, and the worst part was he couldn't hear them to know if he should have been embarrassed or not. This caused him to tense up, even as his cock clearly enjoyed the power play, getting hard in record speed.

He didn't throw any elbows or fight it. Oliver pumped his finger gently, testing his new submissive, waiting to see if Rune would submit. But there was no drive to top from the bottom like he'd done before. In that moment, he didn't want to challenge Oliver. He was exhausted from trying to act like everything was okay, that he was handling his isolation fine, and that the chaos of his life wasn't a big deal. So, he gave in.

He shifted his legs slightly more apart.

Oliver peppered light kisses down the side of Rune's neck in response, then pulled out. Gripping Rune by the back of the neck and pushing with a hand to his back, Oliver walked him forward, to the end of the bed, then guided him to bend sharply over at the waist. Rune dropped the towel, bracing his hands on the bed.

For a moment, he couldn't feel Oliver at all.

Then there was heat behind him.

A wet fingertip teased his rim. The touch was unhurried, lingering, like Oliver was watching Rune's reactions, letting him feel vulnerable.

And it worked, if that was what he was going for, because Rune understood he wasn't in control at all. Oliver had him—physically, sexually, practically, psychologically.

Two wet fingertips slowly filled his hole. Just the tips held inside him, and god how Rune wished he knew what noises he was making so he could filter them better. His thighs and stomach muscles quivered.

How long had it been? How many years since he'd been taken by another man?

The math eluded him.

Oliver spread the fingers slightly, testing the stretch of Rune's hole, causing him to tilt his hips even more to receive and struggling not to clench; to just allow it. But the patience and terrifying strength of the move, showing how Oliver was willing to take Rune apart slowly, thoroughly, no matter if he fought or not, unraveled some of Rune's protections.

He sensed Oliver moving, but the fingers stayed, didn't sheath in him, just toyed a little longer with his rim.

Then Oliver's other hand grabbed Rune's left butt cheek and teeth bit down just above where it gripped him. Hard enough to make Rune voice his surprise and pain. Oliver used the hand to spread Rune's hole and took a long lick up Rune's cheek. He did it again, closer to his opening but not quite touching it. Rune panted, trying to be still, his cock dripping.

And Oliver kept going. Kisses, teases with the pointed end of his tongue, wider licks as if to taste him better. The whole time, the fingers moved in and out of him, shallowly. They left him alternately empty, stretched, poked, and tickled. Rune knew Oliver watched him closely, studying every tremble, hearing every whimper. Rune had no way to protect himself, or hide, or pretend it wasn't making him hot. That he didn't want it, offering up his ass to a man much smarter and stronger than him in all the ways that really counted.

Rune reached for his cock, needing relief.

Oliver smacked his hand away, the skin stinging where it was struck.

Oliver gathered up Rune's balls, tugging them back between his spread legs, mouthing over them, and gradually let his fingers stuff Rune's ass, entering him inch by inch, widening in a V the whole time, increasing the ache, fast.

Rune wanted to beg. His pride kept him from speaking, but he allowed more desperation to enter his cries.

Oliver's hand pulled out. He stopped touching, kissing, or licking Rune.

Without any warning, Rune felt intense pressure as he was entered. It wasn't slow, or patient.

Oliver drove into him, pulling Rune's ass back onto his cock, not easing up until he was fully seated.

Throbbing, aching, Rune was stretched wider than he'd been in several years. He wasn't used to it and it fucked with his head as well.

There wasn't time to adjust. Oliver thrust hard into him a few times, knocking Rune forward on the push, tugging him back on the withdrawal as his body fought to bear it, his practically-virgin ass gripped tightly around Oliver's cock. It was humiliating, his face reddening with a rush of blood to heat it, his breathing out of control, his heart pounding. It just made him grateful at least they weren't face to face.

As if reading Rune's thoughts, Oliver slowly pulled out. He smacked Rune's ass with an opened hand, pushed him onto the bed and manhandled him to his back. Grabbing hold of Rune's legs, Oliver pushed them back as far as they'd go, spread wide.

The dark predator in him shone from behind his eyes, in the flash of perfect, white teeth and the glistening sweat on his skin.

Driven to look away, Rune lowered his gaze to Oliver's long, thick, dark cock. It was rock hard, wet. Rune wanted it. God, how he wanted it. Shocked at himself, Rune grabbed his ankles, holding himself open.

Oliver climbed on, drove in, and Rune's mouth worked, his back arching up off the bed as Oliver went deep. His hand dragged up Rune's neck, the fingers folding around his chin to rub his lips, pushing between them to trap his tongue. Rune sucked, frowning at the pain and helplessness.

Oliver pulled on Rune's jaw, forcing his mouth open wide. He bit down on Rune's nipple in a sharp jolt, then tugged on it with his teeth. He let go only to scrape his teeth next against Rune's chest, scratching the skin. He bit down on Rune's shoulder hard enough to leave the mark, maybe breaking the skin. Pain spiraled around pleasure in a dizzy swirl that made him crazy. The whole time, Oliver fucked Rune at a hard, rough pace and it was all Rune could do to hold on and survive.

Chapter 8
High

Oliver was drunk, his head spinning, but not from anything as banal as alcohol.

He couldn't get enough of Rune's sweet purrs, whimpers, and panting breaths. The sound of them was of a prideful young man's walls shattering, exposing things no one had ever witnessed before. Oliver was in new territory. Everything he discovered was his to own and keep. No one else could have it.

Not holding back, he let the animal in him loose, fucking like he was angry, like he was desperate to get so far inside Rune, his legs wouldn't work for days and he'd never get Oliver out again.

He could tell Rune hadn't been fucked in years, and it was glorious. It was like being with a virgin, only better, because Rune knew what it meant to surrender to a man like Oliver.

Not only was he tight as sin, he stayed clenched up with fear and discomfort, making it impossible for Oliver to last as long as he wanted. Oliver felt every flutter of Rune's inner muscles, every inch of his passage, because they'd both gotten tested the week before. They'd agreed to only lose condoms with each other for the foreseeable future, but this was the first time Oliver got to enjoy the glorious sensation of going bareback with a partner.

Oliver kept his hand clamped around Rune's lower jaw, lip and tongue, forbidding him from closing up and hiding anything. Oliver wanted everything. Every cry.

Bracing a hand on the bed, Oliver leaned down over Rune. Oliver looked him dead in the eye and slammed into him one last time as he came, shuddering and unloading into Rune.

The orgasm had Oliver tingling from head to toe, the aftershocks drawing out as he kept fucking Rune more gently, his thrusts wetter now. He maintained eye contact, thinking of Rune's history. He knew Rune had been failed by all of his previous Doms in one way or other. Even Elet. They didn't get him. Couldn't see what he needed. Mistreated him out of their own selfish pride, arrogance, and blindness. They let him think he was the problem, just for knowing what he wanted, what worked, what didn't and not settling for anything less.

Maybe before, Rune's own arrogance had been an issue, but it wasn't anymore. No, instead, now he was too broken, too fragile underneath the standoffish exterior. He thought there wasn't a place for him, and he'd been right. But now things had changed. Now he had Oliver, and Oliver saw him. Clearly.

Rune's eyes were filled with fear—of not being enough, of being a disappointment, of being lost again, of hoping things might get better now that Oliver had signed a contract.

Oliver was so used to the way new subs held back, or tried to put on an act to show off, or the way Jackson sometimes got lost in his own head; he was struck by Rune's bare terror and secret frailty.

Recovering, Oliver drew Rune into a hug, wrapping his body around him in the embrace without pulling out. Rune grasped Oliver's back, holding on gently, breathing heavily. He tucked his chin over Oliver's shoulder and wrapped his legs behind Oliver's back. His hands flattened against Oliver's skin, grasping him. A subtle tremor shook Rune, from deep inside. He kept making soft sounds as he tried to catch his breath.

It was more intimate than any moment Oliver had experienced in ages.

When he did pull back, Rune glanced away, turned his head, jaw clenched. Oliver caressed down Rune's toned chest and abs and grazed the tip of his swollen, red, wet erection. It jumped at the contact, begging for attention. Caressing back up, Oliver trailed fingertips over Rune's arm and the twisted scars along the outside of his left arm. There had been more along his back and Oliver felt suffocated to imagine what Rune had looked like freshly after the accident, bloodied and left on the road to die. It had been a miracle the head injuries hadn't killed him.

Glancing at Rune's face, Oliver saw him cringing. He brought a hand up to cover his eyes.

Oliver set a hand on Rune's chest, feeling his heart hammering away, his breaths broken and hitching.

Oliver drew the hand away from Rune's face with effort, and guided his head with a hand to face forward. Angrily, Rune opened his eyes. They were bloodshot and wet. He held his breath, stopped looking at Oliver, or focusing on anything. Oliver kept caressing him—his jaw, brushing back his wet black hair, stroking his neck, his chest. Rune tensed up, clenched on the cock stuffing him full. He squirmed restlessly at each touch, with his thighs tensed as if he wished Oliver wasn't between them, breathing in fits and starts. It felt like he expected Oliver to punch him at any moment.

Oliver reached for Rune's hand, brought it down and wrapped the fingers around his shaft. Rune still wouldn't make eye contact and his hand threatened to fall away. Oliver reached for the lube and drizzled some over Rune's dick. Covering Rune's hand with his own, Oliver squeezed up to the head and down again, then let go. Rune didn't continue, but he didn't let go.

Oliver rubbed up to Rune's neck, grasped his jaw, traced his lips, pushed between them and wrenched open his mouth again. Right away, Oliver heard a broken whine and saw him squeeze his eyes shut.

"Magnificent," Oliver sighed. "God, if you only knew..."

Some of the old fight kicked in then. Rune bucked, but Oliver was in too deep. A hand pushed at Oliver's chest, but it didn't shift Oliver an inch, so instead he grabbed at the arm keeping his mouth opened. With effort, grunting, struggling, Rune pulled. He didn't bite Oliver, or even try to. Arm flexed, Oliver remained, smiling.

Then Oliver let go, freed his hand from Rune's mouth and reached for Rune's neglected hard-on, petting it gently, stroking through the slick. A shiver worked its way through Rune, and Oliver felt it move through him. The gentle fondling made Rune wild. His teeth gritted, he swallowed his protests, refusing to open his eyes.

For a while, Oliver played just with Rune's cockhead, focusing his attention there. He traced it, squeezed it, scratched over it. Despite the humming and convulsing, arms fallen to the bed at his sides, Rune allowed it.

Oliver thrust into him to remind him of his place, then sank down into a kiss to his mouth, opening him with ease, licking as deep as he could reach to force Rune's jaws open wide, then pulled back into a gentler tease of just his lips. Rune bucked against Oliver's fingers, trying to ride them. Scratching up the underside of Rune's erection, which was hard and ready to shoot, Oliver watched his prey's eyes slip open, just a little. With the sweetest whimper yet, Rune came in a flood, shuddering hard through it as Oliver moved to kiss him again, stroking gently and drinking down Rune's soft sob.

Oliver pulled back only slightly, watching. Rune's control slipped entirely for just a moment, and he let some of the sorrow out, teeth clenched, lips drawn back, eyes closed against tears that escaped anyway.

Hushing to him, Oliver brushed a kiss to his cheek, licked away a tear.

Rune grabbed him by the back of the head and chased a passionate kiss that drew out for minutes.

When they broke, Rune wasn't letting go. His fingers played at the hair on the back of Oliver's head, his gaze stubbornly lowered.

Smiling, Oliver pecked a hard kiss to Rune's cheek and pulled out with a groan.

Rune tried to keep him there, grasping at him, but Oliver slipped free and quickly cleaned off. Oliver had put a few new rules in place to keep them both safe while they went without condoms, like establishing that with everyone else they had sex with, they would always use protection, no matter what, and that they'd keep getting regularly tested together.

Oliver saw the relief as he came back to bed and manhandled Rune, who looked utterly exhausted, over onto his stomach. Spreading him wide by pushing his legs far apart, Oliver climbed up, steadied himself and plunged back into Rune's ass with a heavy groan.

Rune cried out with both pain and gratitude, tipping his hips up to help Oliver sink all the way in. Once there, Oliver wound his arms around Rune to keep their bodies flush. Feeling every breath and heartbeat against his palm, Oliver moaned. Restless, Rune tried to move counter to each of Oliver's rolling thrusts, but Oliver's closeness prohibited much. He bit at Rune's earlobe, chased his mouth from over his shoulder, and saw ecstasy painted over his stunning features.

Wanting more of a deeper kiss, Oliver pulled out, rolled Rune to his back and re-entered him so they were face-to-face.

"You're fucking dangerous," Oliver panted, trying to clearly enunciate his words. He forced himself to focus at least that much, as much as he was getting lost in it all. Clenched and begging wordlessly, Rune's hands were splayed on the bedcovers, his ass pushed down firmly into the next thrust. His gaze never left Oliver's lips. "Don't have a clue how much you could fuck me over, do you?"

He pulled all the way back, then let Rune's ass swallow him hungrily, all on its own, inch by inch. Rune reached up to grab a fistful of Oliver's hair, rubbing himself against him like a cat wherever he could.

"Thought no one could reach you, huh?" Oliver rode him, feeling delirious, wanting it to last for hours. "Thought you were safe. Alone. Tough as fucking nails. Untouchable. And now what? How're you gonna keep me out now?"

His palm skimmed over scar tissue, thinking of that damned gun. Of a roaring bike flying down the road, being chased by a truck full of monsters. Oliver let Rune pull him in to another rough kiss.

And knew he was doomed.

He was a fucking goner.

Rune wouldn't look at him. Oliver tried everything short of prying his eyelids open. Rune was curled up in Oliver's arms, facing him, and kissed him eagerly, often, finding his target by touch alone. He breathed hot against Oliver's chest and played gently with the dark hair on his forearm. But he wouldn't look, even when Oliver tried to sign to him. He'd just frown and come at him for a teasing kiss that Oliver would feel all the way down to his toes.

Eventually, Rune fell asleep like that, with his arm and leg wound around Oliver. Oliver had things to do—work, studies, email, calls—but he refused to move even though he wasn't sleepy at all.

How often he'd wished for a submissive who wasn't always thinking of the next thing, or how to politely leave right after the sex was through. With Jackson of course, there were feelings involved. Commitment. But he always needed to get home to the kids. To Jo.

They came first.

Adam had no trouble finding such a thing. Oliver had been jealous of Adam's ex, Italo, for too long, because Italo never left Adam alone. There was no motive. He just liked being around Adam more than he liked being alone. For Italo, Adam came first. Though there were no great feelings there, they were a comfort to each other. From the outside looking in, it was sweet.

Sweet like Rune, who had nowhere to be. No one expected him. Besides Max, who out there worried about him? Anyone?

Oliver didn't know why Rune had gotten upset. Maybe the dam simply broke. The monumental effort of going it alone. Or maybe, instead, it just hurt that much to be truly weak, sharing with Oliver each one of his broken places and giving Oliver every chance to hurt him more by knowing.

So Oliver ignored the need to take a leak. The fact that he was expecting company. The fear of showing Rune he could be weak, too.

An hour later, the apartment's front door opened, keys jingling.

"Olly?" a familiar voice bellowed. It was late, but Oliver didn't sleep normal hours, or much at all.

Instinct told him to shush, to cringe at the yelling.

Then, he remembered.

Stupid.

With Rune nestled in slumber against his chest, Oliver called out, "In here!" Even though it still horrified him to do it. Instincts and habit were funny.

"Am I interrupting? You're in the guest room, so..."

Jackson rounded the doorway. Stopped short. Clapped a hand over his mouth and winced.

"It's okay," Oliver told him in a normal, loud voice. "He can't hear you."

"Why not?"

Oliver smiled, but it was a bittersweet sort of sentiment. He'd told Jackson the basics of what was going on, but not details.

"He's completely deaf."

"Yeah, right," Jackson laughed, eyeing the sleeping figure on the bed, seeing everything the thin bedsheet didn't hide. Already, Oliver saw heat there, and plenty of interest, as he suspected he might. Rune was a fantasy fuckboy, after all. It was like he'd crawled right out of someone's filthy wet dream.

Oliver snapped his fingers beside Rune's ear as Rune dozed away, totally relaxed.

"Oh shit," Jackson breathed, his smile wilting, replaced with a look like he'd been punched in the gut by his best friend, which was pretty close to the truth. "Oliver…"

"It's recent. The injury. Fucked over his whole life."

"When you said he was desperate, I had no idea…" Jackson floundered, a hand rubbing over the warm brown skin of his bald head. Then a switch flipped and Oliver smiled to see it. "Has he seen specialists? Maybe it's something correctable with surgery. Or—"

"He's not there," Oliver cut in. "Not even close. He's used the financial factor as an excuse, but I think that's all it is. An excuse."

Jackson wandered closer, covering his mouth with a hand, his gaze slipping all over Rune. Oliver felt how Jackson was being pulled in magnetically by Rune's relaxed, bare demeanor, his guard totally down. It was why Jackson and Oliver got along so well. They were drawn to conquer in the same ways.

"I'm intruding," Jackson realized. "The way he's holding you… He wouldn't want me to see this. I should go. Or make some dinner while I wait, maybe. It's been hours since I ate anything."

"Sure. Just don't go. Stay as long as you can," Oliver asked, brushing his fingers through Rune's hair. "It's time you two met."

Jackson grunted in agreement, still unable to look away from Rune.

"How was he?" Jackson asked, lowering his voice, his passion and lust evident in the question.

Oliver chuckled darkly, feeling the silky texture of Rune's dark hair between the pads of his fingers. He got lost in the memory of how Rune had grown shy as soon as Oliver was inside him, and stayed submissive, his fight gone while he was being taken like he needed to be had more than he needed to defend his pride, the fight returning only when Oliver wanted him to masturbate. Giving pleasure had seemed much easier for him than accepting it.

"Tight as a virgin," Oliver told him. "His first time taking cock in quite a few years, from what I'm told. But he was… eager for it. Embarrassed."

Jackson ran his thumb over his bottom lip, glancing between Rune's body and Oliver's eyes, a spark of hope charging him up.

"You want him," Oliver observed. When Jackson stayed quiet, added, "Hmm?"

"Of course I fucking want him. Look at him."

"He's a fighter," Oliver warned. "If it was two on one, he wouldn't make it easy for us. You might leave with a black eye."

Jackson smiled at that, laughing a little. "Bring it."

Chapter 9
Meeting Rune

"How'd he lose his hearing?" Jackson asked, loading the last of his dishes into the dishwasher. He'd made some chicken and sautéed vegetables for his midnight dinner, enjoying every bite in peaceful seclusion. It was something he craved about Oliver's apartment—the chance to sit with his thoughts without a worry about waking anyone or having to turn in because Jo expected him. Oliver was a night owl too. Jackson's odd schedule didn't faze him at all.

Oliver had always urged Jackson to treat the apartment as his own, so he did. He had groceries delivered. Kept a closet full of clothes in the other guest room. His toothbrush and razor had a permanent place by the sink.

They hadn't talked about it so directly, but Jackson never intended to leave him. Jackson was as invested in the relationship as he was his marriage. God help him if he ever had to choose between them. He couldn't have done it.

Luckily, Jo understood.

Oliver sighed, leaned back against the kitchen counter with his arms folded. He'd put on a pair of black tailored pants but was shirtless, barefoot, and—Jackson would have bet the entirety of David Davenport's fortune—commando. Oliver didn't do underwear.

The scruff on his jaw made Jackson smile. It was a sign of Oliver's state of distraction. Generally, Oliver couldn't stand any facial hair and shaved it off twice a day. The slight growth on his jaw was a testament to Rune's powers over him.

"You'll get a kick out of this, I'm sure," Oliver grumbled.

"What?"

"Neo-Nazis ran his motorcycle off the road. Intentionally."

For a second, Jackson prayed it was a joke. Oliver's deadpan expression told him it wasn't. Closing the dishwasher door, Jackson straightened. "Oh hell no."

"Yeah. Rune thinks they set him up. Followed him to a meet-up with a guy who never showed. As he was driving away, the truck trailed him, then caused the accident. Hit his head damn good when he was thrown from the bike. Shattered some bones in his inner ear. Lost plenty of skin."

Jackson pointed a finger, getting angry. "Fuck that shit."

Oliver walked over to the wet bar, poured some bourbon in a glass. Then poured a second and pushed it Jackson's way before downing his entire glassful.

"He carries a gun. Had a friend bring it here the second day, but I took it. Jay, I think he wants to go after those fuckers," Oliver said wearily.

"No shit. I want to go after the fuckers too."

"But you won't, because you're ruled by logic first. Head over heart. Jo, Jada, Kayla—they'd keep you from doing it. He's got nothing holding him back," Oliver said, gesturing down the hall to where the shower was running quietly.

"Except you. And you can be a bastard about serious shit. I know you can."

"Yeah. Might not be enough. Not with this. And if he does something stupid, gets a hole blown in his head, I couldn't fucking take it, man. I couldn't."

Jackson frowned, drank his bourbon, letting it burn down his throat. "Cops?"

"Hearsay. No proof."

Jackson set the glass down. Oliver poured them another round.

Not long after, Rune emerged wearing a beat-up old pair of jeans and a white V-neck t-shirt. Jackson thought he was even sexier with his eyes open, like he was built for fucking. His movements were cat-like, fluid, sensual. His wide-eyed gaze was so alert and intelligent; it gave Jackson chills. His silence added to the effect, transforming him into a creature designed to sneak up and pounce. The tattoos made him seem dangerous, dirty, and kinky. Jackson didn't see anything he didn't like.

"Jackson. Rune," Oliver introduced, spelling the names with his hands too.

"You know sign language?"

"Getting there. One of my old tricks I'm having to relearn."

Rune looked Jackson up and down. Jackson had more than a few years and some height on him, and was broader in the shoulders.

Rune signed something, his eyebrows going up in surprise, which Oliver laughed at before translating. "He said, 'you submit to *him*?'"

"As much as I can," Jackson grinned. Letting Oliver tell Rune for him. "Fuck, I need to learn sign language now too, don't I?"

"I believe in you," Oliver replied, coming over to kiss him. Humming, cranked up on lust, Jackson turned it dirty, licked into Oliver's mouth, liking the taste of the booze on his tongue to spice things up a little. They never did scenes drunk, so it was a novelty to have him tipsy.

When the kiss ended, Jackson's lips tingled. He took his refilled glass and went to sit on the leather couch. He sank down into it, legs spread wide, rolling his head on his shoulders.

Then he looked Rune dead in the eyes and raised his glass, "You've been through some shit, kid. I'm sorry."

Oliver kept translating, Rune's gaze dancing away long enough to catch the meaning before coming back.

He signed something to Oliver, to which Oliver replied with a nod of his head at Jackson. "Go on."

Hands hooked in his pockets, Rune slowly, smoothly made his way over, the sway of his hips mesmerizing. Jackson set the glass aside, guessing where this was going. Rune came right up to where Jackson sat and moved to straddle him, sinking down onto his lap. His hands wound around Jackson's neck, his fingers moving over the nape. Oliver circled around behind the couch and stood behind where Jackson sat.

"Permission to touch, sir?" Jackson asked, with Rune watching his lips so closely, it started to make Jackson hard.

"Yeah. Just watch yourself." In a reflection of the glass of a framed photograph, Jackson saw Oliver's hands moving, translating everything for Rune, who glanced from Jackson's lips to Oliver's signs.

Rune rolled his hips in a thrust against Jackson's crotch. Jackson popped the button on Rune's jeans, tugged at the zipper. Rune reached down and grabbed a handful of Jackson's cock through his pants, drawing a deep chuckle.

"Doesn't fuck around, does he?" Jackson commented.

Slipping both hands inside the back of Rune's jeans, inside his boxers, Jackson squeezed a double handful of Rune's cheeks. They were firm. Tight. Thick for a white guy. Rune's eyes closed halfway, gazing down at him, his face in shadow. He traced up Jackson's length, measuring him.

"You like that?" Jackson whispered. "Gonna stuff it deep inside your sweet virgin ass, soon as I get permission. You know that, right? Take our turns with you, all night long." He caught movement in the reflection again, saw that Oliver continued to sign Jackson's words, even the whispered ones.

"If you talk to him, make sure you're enunciating your words so he can lip-read," Oliver instructed.

"Yes, sir." Jackson asked, "Does he beg?"

"Mmm. In a way," Oliver replied.

"Good."

There was a pause. Jackson saw Oliver's hands moving, speaking in a way Jackson couldn't hear. Rune's gaze followed them as he rocked gently between Jackson's hands and his crotch. He drew his hand away from Jackson's dick, brought it back to circle Jackson's neck instead.

"You're giving him orders," Jackson realized.

"I am."

Rune pushed his ass out much farther, sinking down and beginning to trail light licks and soft kisses up from Jackson's open collar, along the side of his neck.

"Touch his knot. Gently."

"Yes, sir," Jackson said, eager to comply.

The first two fingers of his right hand shifted into Rune's crack, causing him to freeze up for just a second, tensing at the touch. Jackson found his hole. It was puffed up, hot. He traced circles over it and brushed over the center.

"He's swollen. It'll hurt if we do anything else to him tonight," Jackson said.

Oliver grabbed hold of Rune's chin, drew his face up again, forcing eye contact, then speaking through sign. Rune sat back a little, just enough to reply in kind. Then told Jackson, "He's not afraid of pain."

Jackson felt Rune shiver, his head bowed.

"Let him go for a second."

"Yes, sir."

Rune got up on his knees, jaw clenched, face flushing but gaze deliberately set on Oliver and not diverting as he pushed his jeans down as far as they'd go, which was mid-thigh. Jackson saw Rune's cock stretching the fabric of his boxer briefs, his hard-on growing. Then Rune sank down again, pushing out his ass, and reached back to pull the briefs down in back to expose his ass. His gaze came up again to look deep into Jackson's eyes and watch his lips.

"Mmm, that's it, baby. We got you," Jackson hummed. "Scared?"

Rune squinted, his jaw clenched. He shook his head.

Oliver circled the couch again, spread some lube over Jackson's fingers, then went back to where he'd stood before, watching over them both.

"Finger him. It's okay to get rough."

"Yes, sir," Jackson said, trusting his Master.

The tip of his middle finger found Rune's swollen pucker and he could see the effort it was taking to maintain eye contact with Oliver. Jackson spread some lube over Rune's rim, then fed the fingertip through to the first knuckle. Rune shuddered, strained, clenched up.

"Deeper."

Jackson pushed it in to the second knuckle, the inside of Rune's ass just as swollen as the rim, gripping him tighter than Jackson had felt in a long time. He gave Rune a moment, seeing him flush a deeper red, swallowing thickly, then Jackson buried the finger to the hilt and rubbed at Rune with it from inside.

"Nice?"

"Real fuckin' nice."

"Give him another. Give it harder."

"Yes, sir."

Oliver reached for Rune's chin, holding his jaw to force his head to stay upright so they could communicate. Jackson withdrew and forced his wet index finger in as well, going in fast in a complete thrust, having to use extra force to get all the way inside. Rune grunted, trembled, arms tensed, panted for air through his nose.

"Finger fuck him. Test him. Spread him."

"Yes, sir."

Oliver tightened his grip on Rune's jaw and Jackson went for it. Pumping both fingers, he set a quick pace, spreading them apart on the withdrawal, stretching Rune's sore hole. He hooked both fingertips barely inside, spread them as wide as he could, drew a harder grunt, made him start to breathe even more heavily.

"Good. Use both hands. Spread him like that."

Jackson slid his fingers out with a squelch, hooked both index fingers inside Rune, and pulled.

Rune whimpered, frowned, started to writhe.

"Hold him."

Oliver let go and walked around while pulling something out of his pocket. A dental dam. He came up behind Rune and sank to his knees.

"Pull out. Just keep him spread."

Jackson couldn't see what Oliver did, but Rune's cry broke free, his body convulsing in Jackson's arms. Oliver's mouth hovered by Rune's exposed, swollen hole, bobbing slightly. Jackson heard soft suckling sounds, then Oliver sat back and reached out with a hand, his forearm flexing as he pushed for his target. Rune gasped, then yelled, convulsing even harder. Oliver steadied him with a hand to his back and kept at it.

Dropping his head, Rune muffled his next yell against Jackson's shoulder.

"I'm massaging his gland very lightly, but it's having quite the effect, don't you think?"

Rune was restless, unable to stay still, but any amount of writhing didn't deter Oliver or free him from Jackson's prying. It went on and on, as Rune's shouts softened to purrs, his body sweat-slicked and twitching. He panted against Jackson's neck, gripped the back of Jackson's head like he needed the anchor. A long, unending moan that broke apart sounded against Jackson's skin.

"Let go," Oliver told Jackson, who complied.

Oliver took hold of Rune by the hip, moving him, pulling him upright and back so he wasn't leaning on Jackson at all. He guided Rune's hands behind his head, his fingers lacing together there. Standing, Oliver reached between Rune's legs and kept hold of his hipbone.

Rune's eyes widened, jaw clenched on a grunt.

"I've got his gland trapped between my fingers," Oliver said, and Jackson knew the technique, manipulating the sensitive area with a finger up the ass and a thumb pressed hard at the taint. "Pull his briefs down."

"Yes, sir."

Jackson stretched the elastic waist out far to get it around Rune's erection, his cock dark, long and curved. It was soaking wet and leaking more in small pulses. He glanced down at Jackson staring at it, then let out a shuddering breath and averted his gaze again.

"Still shy," Jackson smiled.

"Delicious, isn't it?" Oliver did something that made Rune whimper sharply and strain, his arms and legs tensed. "Jerk him off. Spice it up."

"My pleasure, sir."

Jackson fondled Rune's sac, his balls heavy and drawn up, while watching his eyes. A muscle in Rune's jaw flexed as Jackson pulled, stretching the skin and drawing Rune's balls away from his body, then squeezing gently. With his other hand, he wrapped Rune's erection, stroking lightly through the wetness. He saw Rune's eyes roll back and he swayed a little. Clear, viscous pre-ejaculate kept jetting from his slit. Jackson rubbed his thumb over it, pulling gently at the small opening, digging in the edge of his fingernail. Rune bucked, moaned, eyes closed tightly.

Jackson wrapped the plump-shaped head of Rune's cut cock in a circle made by his thumb and index finger, then squeezed gently, more and more.

Rune let out a wavering cry, head bowed, grabbing his left wrist with his right hand and squeezing.

"Obedient," Jackson observed.

"Yes, he is," Oliver agreed.

Rune bucked again as Jackson kept squeezing harder. Oliver gripped him tighter to try to still him.

Jackson let his circled grip slide back to Rune's root, squelching loudly, then stroked back up just as tightly and wrapped his whole hand around the crown, squeezing even harder.

A rough cry split the air. Oliver's fingering moved Rune in small rocking rolls of his hips. Jackson relaxed his hold, then tightened it up, doing it over and over again.

A constant humming sounded from Rune, his face a picture of anguish.

Jackson started jacking him, hard and fast, and Rune shot, gasping, over the front of Jackson's button-down shirt and his neck. Tugging him through it, desperate to taste his hot come, Jackson watched Rune's exhaustion and surrender take over.

Oliver freed his hand and drew Rune back into a hug. Rune's arms overlapped Oliver's, holding on as he tried to catch his breath, his head leaned back against Oliver's. Jackson caressed Rune's thighs, his pelvis, his chest.

"Hard?" Oliver asked from over Rune's shoulder.

"So fucking hard."

"Me too."

He moved Rune with Jackson's help to lay on the couch. They cleaned off with wipes.

Then Oliver turned his sites on Jackson, the darkness in him taking over.

Jackson welcomed it.

For a moment they stood facing each other. Then he yanked open Jackson's pants, possibly ripping the zipper, pushed him around and over the end of the couch.

"Two fingers. Now."

Jackson didn't waste time with lube and shoved two fingers up his own ass, as far as he could reach. He saw Rune watching, wide-eyed and enraptured.

Oliver was probably rolling on a condom.

Glancing back, he saw Oliver's arm draw back far. The first strike hit him hard, square on his right cheek. It stung and more slaps followed. Perhaps letting out all of his anger at Rune's situation, Oliver spanked Jackson until he was growling, his ass on fire, the skin soon oversensitive.

"Pull 'em out."

Oliver wasted no time, instantly replacing the fingers with his cock, driving into Jackson and pulling him back onto his length. Throbbing, Jackson shifted wider with a groan to accommodate him. Oliver kneaded Jackson's sore cheek, scratched hard over it and slapped it again. Jackson clenched in reaction and Oliver hummed, riding him. He wasn't gentle, taking him roughly, spanking every so often to keep Jackson tight and on edge.

Growing dizzy, from the edge of his vision, he saw Rune move, his hands drawing shapes.

Oliver paused. Then drew Jackson upright without pulling out.

"Arms behind your head. Cross 'em."

Jackson obeyed and Rune crawled down the couch toward him.

"Oh no," Jackson moaned.

Oliver laughed.

Rune rolled a condom onto Jackson, then opened wide and swallowed him halfway down.

Moaning heavily, Jackson fought the urge to bury the rest of his length in Rune's throat. Rune sucked hard, cheeks hollowed, tongue rubbing, those pretty pink lips stretched wide. Oliver resumed riding Jackson more gently now while Rune kept using his mouth.

"Fuck... please..." Jackson shuddered, wanted more than anything to grab Rune's head and fuck his mouth. Instead, he let Oliver take hold of his crossed wrists and his hip, giving him complete, maddening thrusts.

Rune pulled off with a pop and a hungry moan, pushing Jackson's cock up against his pelvis, licking with a flattened tongue up to the head, suckling on the crown, stretching his lips wide around it, then took it back over his tongue again and into his throat.

It got Jackson close, fast, but Rune seemed to realize it, so he backed off, licking more than sucking, playing with him with a hand, rolling Jackson's balls.

Oliver came with a sigh, kissing Jackson's neck.

He pulled out. Tossed the condom.

Rune stood, moved off the couch, then walked around, staring at Jackson like a wild animal.

"Uh-oh."

Oliver snickered.

"Olly..."

"Hands off," Oliver ordered.

Rune walked around behind Jackson, who pivoted to keep facing Rune, not trusting him to leave his sight. Rune backed him up to the ottoman in front of the couch.

The shove to the center of his chest drew a startled yell as Jackson fell back, landing square on the ottoman. Rune moved fast, springing onto Jackson facing his cock and not his head, then guided Jackson's legs back as far as they would go. Oliver joined in, holding Jackson in the pose so he was folded in half by pushing on the backs of his ankles. Straddling Jackson's chest, Rune swallowed him down with a hum. Hand tapered into a point, he pushed the whole thing at Jackson's hole, prying it open.

"Fuck!"

Jackson groaned at the stretch, but thrummed with pleasure from Rune's deep, sucking pulls. He held nothing back, taking as much of Jackson's dick down his throat as he could, which was a little more than half.

"Oh, he's so getting payback for this," Jackson panted, then moaned at the continued burrowing of Rune's hand.

"Don't pretend you don't love it," Oliver grinned.

"This little fucker…"

In moments, Jackson came, panting, shuddering. Three of Rune's fingers rubbed at the inside of Jackson's hole, Rune's tongue giving wide licks to the head of Jackson's cock where come pooled in the condom.

"Okay yeah. I like this kid," Jackson laughed, clenching around Rune's fingers.

They let him straighten out, helped him sit up. Oliver handed him a towel and a glass of water. After catching Rune up on some of the threats Jackson made in the height of passion, he moved to massage Jackson's shoulders.

"Seriously though. You told him he's got it coming, right?" Pointing at Rune, he added, speaking the words as clearly as he could, "Watch your pretty ass."

Rune blew Jackson a kiss, waving him on.

Grinning like the devil, Oliver just said, "Hey. I warned you."

Chapter 10
Taking Off

Rune was on his way out of the apartment. He had a ride set up, and explained as much to Oliver, who stood next to Jackson with a displeased expression. Even Jackson seemed perturbed and he barely knew Rune.

Oliver spoke and signed simultaneously, *You need to rest.*

Rune told him he'd rest later, adding that he'd had a good nap. It was enough.

Jackson said something, which Oliver translated as: *He agrees you should rest. You look tired.*

I need some air, Rune countered.

Where are you going?

The clubhouse, Rune explained, though he would have rather kept that to himself. He liked his privacy. He also wasn't used to being under the protection of a compulsive, determined Dom like Oliver. It got to be a little suffocating.

Plus, Rune wasn't collared. He hadn't given Oliver the reins to his entire life. Yet.

He saw Oliver explaining what 'the clubhouse' was to Jackson and waited. *It's not safe.*

Rune grinned, tempted to laugh. *It's the safest place I know.*

No, this is, Oliver argued, his severely furrowed brow and thinned lips indication enough of his current mood, despite all the sex which Rune would have thought might have loosened him up a little.

Rune thought Oliver would have wanted some more time alone with Jackson anyway, without Rune in their hair.

Why do you care? Something happens to me, just get a new sub.

He could tell Oliver hadn't caught all of that, though he might have gotten the gist. The biggest indication was the storm clouds gathering over his head.

He stalked over to Rune, who had edged closer to the door.

Bracing himself, Rune stayed ready for anything.

But Oliver just pulled him into a kiss with an arm slung around Rune's lower back, then embraced him.

A small voice at the back of Rune's mind whispered that Oliver knew what Rune was trying to pull. That the instinct to take off post-coitus was an ingrained thing with him after so long at being a connoisseur at casual sex and totally foreign to real commitment.

Because Rune didn't like how much Oliver now knew, and didn't know how to handle Oliver's tenderness or concern. There seemed to be no motive behind it of a sexual bent, or as a way to assume more power for power's sake, or as leverage to get high, get off, or be selfish.

It was like Rune had fallen into someone else's life. Some of it was too good to be true, and he'd already had enough disappointment to last a lifetime.

He pushed against Oliver, but Oliver just kissed Rune's temple and caressed his back, his arms tensed to prevent Rune's escape.

The silence rushed in anew, reminding him he was adrift, floating out there. But then the sensory data of Oliver's scent, warmth, strength, touch, kisses and unspoken patience flooded him. It filled all the empty places and overwhelmed. It was more specific, more intense than he remembered a hug could be.

When Rune's struggling tapered off, Oliver eased up, let go.

I won't let anything hurt you, Oliver signed.

Jackson had come over too. He reached out and gripped Rune's shoulder, giving him a steady gaze that didn't waver.

You don't owe me that, Rune argued.

Oliver translated for Jackson, then replied. *Someone does. You're stuck with us.* He punctuated this with a smart-assed shrug that said, 'tough shit' loud and clear.

Rune looked at them both, trying to wrap his head around it all or make sense of anything he felt. It was so noisy in his head, nothing came out clear.

He told them, *Okay. I'm going. I'll be back soon.* He pulled out his phone, gave it a wave to show he was reachable.

For a minute, Rune was convinced Oliver wasn't going to let him go, but he stayed put as Rune unlocked and opened the door. He slipped out and didn't look back.

After a quick trip across town, Oliver took an elevator to the top floor, stepped off and brushed shoulders with a teenager with a magnificent pair of full lips who was getting on the elevator to leave. Without knowing if the kid was legal or not, Oliver resisted the tempting backward glance at their ass — but only barely. The teenager had a medium-brown complexion, black hair and carried a backpack slung over one shoulder. They didn't make eye contact, kept their head bowed, and seemed in quite a hurry to get on the elevator and go.

That was his first clue.

Strolling up to Adam's door, Oliver leaned against the frame, secure in the guess he was about to make.

The door opened to reveal his best friend in the world, wearing only a pair of paint-stained boxer briefs and a harried look.

"You fucked a child, didn't you?" Oliver said with amazement.

"What? No! Why would you ever say that? Get in here and stop looking at me like that," Adam commanded.

Oliver just laughed.

"He was carrying a backpack, dear. My strong moral code forbade me from seeing if his jeans were packed with a thick cock or just a well-reamed butt."

"Your strong moral code and my devotion to studying law are both right up there with the pope's fondness for gambling and sloppy hookers."

Adam shut the door with a loud thud, then stalked past Oliver, making a beeline to his studio.

"So, we had a good trip then? Purged plenty of spunk? Painted lots of beautiful boys? Dislodged that thorny stick from your ass?"

Shooting a steely look back at Oliver, Adam added a few daubs of paint to his palette and set a barely-touched canvas on the large easel standing few paces inside the room.

"Why, you want to check and see if it's still there? Jackson not enough for you these days?"

Oliver smiled, dropping his gaze, folding his arms. There were smears on the glass windows, just in one area. His imagination provided some vibrant imagery featuring the boy by the elevator and a grumpy, hard-up Adam.

"Uh-oh." Adam stopped what he was doing and stared at Oliver.

"I really hope you carded that kid, or else you could be headed upriver for a long, long time."

"What happened with Jackson?"

"Could you answer mine first, you royal pain in the sphincter?"

Adam didn't say anything for a long moment, then pulled his phone out of his back pocket and started to tap at it. Oliver managed to cross the distance between them in a split second and snatch it from him.

"Don't do that."

"What the hell did you do to Jackson?!" Adam railed, blue eyes blazing, fire-engine-red hair flying as he whipped his head around.

"Nothing, peaches. He's fine," Oliver soothed as patronizingly as he possibly could.

"Then what the fuck?" Adam yelled, even more angrily than before.

"Seriously, do you need a valium? A handy? Or maybe you were serious about checking for that stick. I mean, it has been a few years since I've taken that particular ride from my favorite ginger, but—"

"Explain. Now," Adam breathed through clenched teeth.

Oliver could only laugh again. "Wow." He strolled around the space, letting his lack of tension contrast gloriously to Adam's temper. "I never knew you cared that much. He'll be flattered when I tell him."

"Something's wrong with you," Adam realized, soft awe creeping into his tone.

"This shit doesn't work on me, you know. I'm immune. You can't trick anything out of me, or psychoanalyze, or bully, or threaten. Learn some patience, my love. Please. Tell me about your latest masterpiece," he invited, gesturing to the smeared glass, though careful to avoid touching anything resembling a bodily fluid.

Adam rolled his eyes and set his hands on his hips. He let his head fall back on his shoulders and addressed the ceiling.

"He's twenty. Get over it. A one-off."

"He was carrying a backpack," Oliver chuckled. "With pictures of the Teenage Mutant Ninja Turtles all over it."

"No, there wasn't," Adam countered, though he seemed slightly unsure, only amusing Oliver further.

"Did he spread for you, or was he too shy?"

Adam didn't answer right away; he'd gone back to studying the mask Oliver had thrown up to conceal his secrets.

"Stop that. We're having a linear conversation."

Adam snorted and reached for a glass of water, sipping it while giving Oliver the side-eye.

"Yeah, right."

"Should I guess? I mean, I didn't get a proper look… maybe you were giving him a private lesson… and he kept staring at your cock, so you pulled it out, let him crawl over and lick at it for a while…"

After considering him a moment longer, Adam said, "Close. He assisted me in class last term. Came by to return some supplies I lent the department for staging models and basically threw himself at me. Had his pants down and cheeks parted before I knew what was happening. Made these soft begging noises the whole time but wouldn't look at me. He did all the work, too, like he needed cock to live."

"Maybe he did. A rare condition," Oliver offered with a tragic air.

Walking slowly over, Adam didn't stop until he was in Oliver's personal space, nose to nose with him, looking him dead in the eye. Not falling for it for a minute, Oliver angled his head to the side, teased in as if for a kiss; Adam feigned back, then held, watching Oliver's lips, then parting his own as if readying for contact.

Oliver gave the center of Adam's top lip a short lick with the point of his tongue.

"You missed me," Oliver whispered.

"Never," Adam lied.

Oliver let the moment breathe, didn't pull away, wondering if Adam would make a counter-move or not. Then Oliver reached down and palmed Adam's cock through the briefs.

"Mmm, almost," he purred, feeling triumphant as he weighed the thickness pressing against his hand. "Love that I still make you hard, sweet cheeks. Feeling's mutual."

Adam shook him off, cleared his throat and—futilely—adjusted the briefs.

"Tell me what's wrong with you."

"...he asked politely," Oliver teased.

"Are you sick? Dying? Is it cancer? That's why you won't tell me, isn't it? You know I'd lose my fucking mind and want to jump off the building. I—"

"Shhh," Oliver hushed, putting his finger over his own lips, then Adam's. "I'm fine. You're *really* wound tight today, huh?"

"Okay," Adam allowed, the rage dissipated but exposed strange things in its wake. "You may not be dying but you are killing me."

"Okay," Oliver sighed.

"Good. Okay." Adam nodded, perking up a little, standing straighter. "Well?"

"There was an emergency while you were gone."

"Fuck," he breathed, deflating. "I knew it. I—"

"Shhh," Oliver repeated, this time sealing Adam's mouth completely with his whole hand. The best part was how Adam let him do it, which raised Oliver's spirits tremendously.

"I do love you, you know," Oliver told him, letting go.

"Yeah, right. Continue."

"Boss," Oliver saluted. "I got a call from David. Davenport."

Adam was momentarily taken aback, blinking at him. "Okay," he said slowly. "About...?"

"An emergency."

Adam covered his face with his hands and groaned into them. "I really might need to hurt you."

"I may have..."

"...yes?"

"...signed a contract."

Oliver glanced away, then back. Adam gave him a mostly blank stare.

"I don't get it."

"Yeah, I didn't either."

"It took you forever to sign the contract with Jackson. Forever. Teeth were pulled. Arms were twisted. You were a total pain in the ass about it. And... what? David calls you. You run over and sign? For some stranger? Why the hell would you do that? What could possibly—"

"Enough. Enough, okay," Oliver cut in. "Yes, it's very funny. My life is hilarious. But I make my own choices and so do you. I don't need your permission for everything."

"But you... you didn't even tell me or call me or—"

"It happened too quickly, and it was a lot."

"A lot of what?"

Hitting a limit he didn't know he had, Oliver turned and walked away, toward the kitchen.

"Hey! I'm still talking to you! We're not done here!"

"You're a real dick sometimes, you know it?" Oliver muttered under his breath.

His arm was grabbed. He was yanked around and his arm came up to block, but he wasn't fast enough. Adam caught him under the jaw, threw him back into the wall in the hallway. Blue eyes searched him, and he didn't know how to keep Adam out completely. He'd never been able to.

"Holy fuck," Adam gaped. "You're serious. You fell for this guy. You... you don't even trust me with him, do you? Even to tell me about him. We don't... keep secrets from each other, Olly. We never have. Not like this. Not when it's important. Did I... did I do something to make you lose trust in me, or..."

"Stop. Stop it," Oliver said tiredly. He yanked Adam's hand away from his throat.

"Olly..."

"It's complicated. It's not about you. I'm not keeping him from you. I wouldn't be here right now if I was. Jackson left a few hours ago. And I was alone and I knew you were back, so," he sighed.

"What's the matter?" Adam asked, spying something Oliver hadn't wanted him to notice. "Something's wrong."

"It's probably nothing. I'm probably overreacting. I—"

"You have never overreacted in your life. You're the most level-headed, even-tempered person I've ever met."

"I'm just... worried. I... I can see it in his face that he's going to do something stupid... and I don't know how to stop him. I don't even know if I can."

Chapter 11
Cards on the Table

The storage closet was just as Rune had left it, his bed waiting for him and all of the things he hadn't brought to Oliver's were still boxed up gathering dust. He lingered in there for a few minutes, missing the solitude he'd run from.

He'd been taking a lot of walks around the city, just to get some air between sessions with Oliver or the tutor. The day before, he'd seen a light blue truck stopped at an intersection that looked suspiciously like the one that had hit him, but he wasn't able to get a view of the back to check the plates or the stickers. He hadn't been able to stop thinking about it since.

For some reason, in light of possibly seeing the truck again, and those dicks that had gone after him, it felt good to be in his old space. It helped him remember who he was. What he'd been through. Regressing into the waiting isolation that room provided, he let it engulf him.

Shaking off the momentary cowardice, he wandered back into the club's main room. The crew was mostly still asleep, but a few rogues who probably hadn't even gone to bed yet lingered at the bar and the table closest to the only window that looked out over the front parking lot. A few waved or nodded to him as he passed, but they knew better than to try to engage him in conversation.

The Bluetooth speaker rested on the counter behind the bar, probably still broadcasting an online stream of the local police scanner. It was one way they watched out for trouble, and not just for their own sakes, though Rune hadn't been the only member engaged in illegal activities. Sometimes they listened for signs of activity from rival crews, or just random assholes stirring up shit where they shouldn't.

Since his accident, Rune had become especially fixated on the broadcasts. For a while, he'd asked that they write down the codes for any serious activity when they could, so he could review it. Then, luckily, he found out the local police station's scanner information was also broadcast on a Twitter feed.

He pulled his phone out, went to his Twitter app, and searched for the feed so he could review the latest posts.

A touch to his shoulder startled him, but it was only Max.

Rune pulled up his text-to-voice app and typed: *Anything strange since I left?*

Max scratched his beard, then shook his head. *Why?*

With a sigh, Rune debated whether to tell Max more. Now he was the only one who knew about Rune's orientation, but he'd taken the news without any issue. He was the closest friend Rune had. Maybe he could act as an ally too.

With a glance around for eavesdroppers, Rune steeled himself.

It wasn't an accident, he explained, pointing to his ear, then some of the scars on the back of his arm.

"What?!" Max bellowed. Rune didn't hear any of it, but knew it had been loud, just from the way others stopped and looked at them. Cringing inwardly, he tried to seem unfazed as Mark and Jason got up off their stools and came over to see what the fuss was about.

Foregoing the app, Rune set the phone down and signed, *I don't want them to know about this. It's my problem. I can take care of it.* He didn't know if Max got all of that though, and seemed driven by his own shock more than anything.

Max gave him a doubtful look. He pointed at Rune's phone, mimed pressing buttons and Rune got the hint. He opened the voice-to-text app and held it out to record what Max explained to Mark and Jason. Rune read as they all talked, discussing the accident and what Rune had learned. Readying himself for anything, Rune waited for them to catch up to what he and Max already knew.

The conversation got more heated. They all looked pissed. They were jabbing fingers at the lot, at him. He mentally matched the gestures with the words he read, understanding Mark and Jason's frustrations and fury.

Jason pulled out his phone, facing Rune more directly. He typed one word and held it out:

Who?

Rune knew it was up to him to say anything or not. They'd never leave him alone now, though. He didn't know if they'd kick him out for being queer, or just treat him differently, but it wasn't like they didn't already. Still, it wasn't their battle to fight.

Jason knocked Rune's shoulder, his scowl deepening with impatience.

Resigned, Rune typed his answer, telling them:

I only got a partial plate, but I know who they are.

The three had gathered around. Seamus, Goat, and Doc wandered over as well.

They waved him on, wanting him to spill the rest, but he hesitated. The next thing he told them would be like throwing a lit match into a pile of explosives.

He typed:

> *This isn't your problem. It's not a crew problem. They didn't go after me because I'm a member.*

Jason replied:

> *Fuck that. Now it's a crew problem. You almost died! Tell us who they are!*

Mark asked with his own phone:

> *Was it a business issue? Deal turned sour? Someone after your product?*

Rune shook his head.

> *Then what?*

There were six of them making a human wall around him out of leather-clad, angry bikers. The fact that they were communicating via typed words on their phones like kids in class passing notes rather than screaming at each other didn't lessen the potential danger of the situation for Rune. Most of them were armed with both knives and guns. He didn't know any of the crew to be outright homophobes, but sometimes people didn't wear that right out on their sleeves like his attackers.

He needed to lie. Make something up.

But they were all looking at him like they could see right through his reluctance to share. He could blame it on being a Jew, but something in that turned his stomach. Maybe it was better to just lay it all out and cut ties if need be. He had Oliver now. It was a safety net if Rune took another fall.

Of course, that was if they let him out of there in one piece.

He felt cold, nauseous, and like he needed to sit. His head started to pound and his scars itched like they were still healing.

Someone handed him a beer. Someone else set a chair down next to him. Others had joined the group, too many to count. So many eyes stared at him. Farther back in the room, conversations filled the air, out of his reach as the news was passed along.

He drank the beer and sat down, rubbing a hand back over his head.

He thought of texting Oliver quickly before telling them anything else, maybe just to say thanks or apologize. All of that work to learn to sign for nothing.

Letting the phone's app read aloud what he typed, he began to tap away at the keyboard.

> They're a white supremacist group called The White Lions. Local. Their jackets read Pride and Power. They set me up. Followed me to a spot out on Route 13 where I was meeting a guy who never showed. Then they hit me with their truck as I was leaving. They went after me because I'm gay.

He couldn't look up. His hands were trembling enough to make it hard to keep hold of the phone. He shut his eyes, chugged his beer, set it down then added:

> I don't want any trouble here. I'll go. I'm gonna clean up my own mess.

Keeping his eyes shut, he waited for it. Maybe they'd drag him off the chair, or hit him across the head with something. He tensed up, breathing hard, holding his phone hard enough the edges dug into his palm.

Someone gripped his wrist.

After a long moment, Rune opened his eyes.

Max was crouched in front of him, looking as steady and unruffled as ever. Sure, he'd seen Rune at Manse, knew he was living with Oliver, but they'd never discussed whether he was gay. Could he save Rune from the other crew if things got ugly? Would he?

Searching his face, Rune didn't trust his peripheral vision showing the crew arrayed around them, unmoving. Max tightened his grip, as if to lend Rune some of his steadiness.

One of the guys passed Max his phone, who gave it a glance before holding it out for Rune.

It said:

> What do you need us to do?

He passed them his mug for a refill, scanning the room for signs of threat, but they weren't riled or looked like they wanted to fight. Were they really okay with it? He couldn't quite bring himself to believe it.

Max held the phone right in front of Rune's face, demanding an answer.

So Rune gave it to them.

I need names. I need to know where to find them. I need to make sure they're not going after other people.

Revenge? Jason asked, a glimmer in his dark eyes, craving permission to attack.

Rune didn't say yes or no, but he gave Jason a level stare and the men around him pumped their fists, jostling each other, talking more rapidly. A few of them came and clapped him on the back.

Mark asked:

What's the partial?

Rune typed it out, had the phone read it aloud.

We'll find them, Max signed. *We'll stop them.*

Not without me, Rune replied.

A weird shift took place that day. For so long, the clubhouse had been the biggest tangible thing making Rune feel isolated. He hadn't been able to confide in the guys. Hadn't fit in anymore. Hadn't been able to contribute or participate. They hadn't known who he really was, or what was really the matter. Sure, they knew about his injuries, but the rest had been held deliberately back.

Now word was out that he was gay, and they knew what his true motive was. A lot changed for him, right away.

He didn't feel like he had to hide away in his makeshift room. The guys were talking with him via cell or with Max's help in translating. They were interested in learning more, asking questions, sharing things they thought might help him track down the cowards who had done this to him.

The guys were motivated, engaged, and riled up. It was something to rally around. It was a noble cause.

Rune's inability to connect with his friends had been the final straw that had sent him to David, in search of someone like Oliver.

He had *found* Oliver.

They were official. The papers were signed.

Rune didn't give a shit about the papers though. What weighed on him were all of Oliver's efforts to connect, as well as what had happened the night before.

Truthfully, he'd gone into it looking to get laid. To prove he still *could* get laid, and his deafness wasn't a permanent cock block.

But whatever was going on between him and Oliver had little to do with fucking. If all Oliver wanted from him was regular access to his ass or mouth, they didn't really need to talk much for that. Oliver could have learned the basics of sign language in one day.

No, Oliver didn't just want Rune's body. He wanted *him*. His mind, his emotions, his total submission and absolute vulnerability. Physical exertion—pain, pleasure, everything in between—was no big deal for Rune. It was the rest of it that sucked.

He'd never had anyone try so hard to get inside his head. To make him so weak, then suspend him in that state until he truly knew his powerlessness. But he sensed no malice in it. He kind of wished he did. It would have made it easier.

So, things with Oliver were complicated. Not only was there all of Oliver to consider, there was Jackson, too. A fucking actual doctor, who seemed just as kinky and sexually aggressive as Oliver. The perfect pair.

It was beyond tempting, but it was also a lot to deal with. Rune hadn't signed up for all of that. He'd gotten sex. He'd gotten a fancier place to crash than a dusty closet. But he'd gotten a lot more than that too—a guy who actually cared about where he was and why; who probably missed him, and expected his return; who no doubt was plotting things to do or say when Rune returned. Maybe there would be expectations of promises made. Maybe Oliver and Jackson would just want to make Rune as weak as they possibly could again, listening to him break in his endless silence, taking him apart piece by piece to better claim him as their own.

So, Rune hung out at the club all day.

Oliver texted a couple of times, asking when to expect him back.

Rune didn't know what to say. He told Oliver he'd let him know soon.

It wasn't that Rune regretted contacting David, he just hadn't known what he was getting himself into.

Trying to resolve the accident and prevent those bigoted douchebags from hurting others was forefront in his mind, bigger than any personal concerns—Oliver included. But he also didn't want to let Oliver down entirely, not only because the guy scared him a little. Rune just didn't know how to handle all of that at the same time.

Jason held up his phone for Rune to read.

Borrow my spare bike. It's in the side lot, next to the oak.

Rune raised an eyebrow at him, then typed his reply.

You sure?

Jason nodded.

Rune glanced over at Max. He was far enough away, so deep in conversation with Mark and Goat that he hadn't noticed the exchange. Good.

Max didn't want him riding. Neither would Oliver.

Rune didn't give a fuck.

Thanks, man. I owe you. I'll take good care of it.

Jason's hand clapped into his and they shook. Jason slipped him the keys, which Rune pocketed quickly.

A few hours later, some information surfaced.

Mark got the location of The White Lions' clubhouse.

No one goes over there until we've got a solid plan, Mark said and typed.

Rune held up his hand, thumb and index finger making a circle, the other fingers extended.

Max gave him a doubtful squinty-eyed, suspicious look, so Rune smiled over at him, trying his best to look blameless.

A Yankees game came on shortly after. Everyone gathered around. Food was ordered. Beers were lined up.

Rune went to hit the john, then slipped out the back door. He texted Max:

Got a ride back to Oliver. Talk soon.

He jumped on the bike and headed straight for The White Lions' clubhouse.

Chapter 12
Alert

Is Jackson there?

Oliver stared at the text message from Rune again, wondering what to think, whether he should be suspicious, or nervous, or what. It had come five hours after the last time Oliver had heard from him.

Can he be? He's got supplies there, right? Basics?

Panic flooded Oliver's system. Because he knew. It wasn't about kink.
Rune was in trouble.
Oliver's replies had been many:

What kind of supplies? Supplies for you or someone else? Are you on your way here? Are you okay? Where the hell have you been?

No response.
"Should I call Adam? He's good at leveling you out," Jackson offered. "You're going to give yourself an aneurysm."
"I'm fine," Oliver insisted, knowing he sounded like a tea kettle boiling over—shrill, bursting, aflame. He so rarely freaked out, he wasn't great at coping whenever he did.
"My ass are you fine. Sit. Sit down, Olly."
Oliver briefly released the hand he had sealed over his lips. "I'm gonna chain him to the bed. Seriously. We're talking leashes. I'm so…" he laughed, and knew he sounded insane. "I'm so fucking pissed at him."
"You don't even know this kid," Jackson said softly.
"I fucking *know* him!" Oliver roared. Then stopped, held up a hand, breathed deeply and counted to ten. "I'm sorry. I'm wound a smidge tight."
"Ya think? Should I call Jo?"

"I think you should call the asylum, because I've lost my mind. What the hell did I get myself into? What the fuck is this?" Oliver said with soft awe.

Jackson stood there, stoic, elegant, dressed in a designer suit, pretty as a picture. He shook his head, then pulled out his phone, tapping out a message. Oliver turned toward the door, forgetting to breathe, unwilling to look away from the knob.

His phone blipped.

A message from his building's security team read:

On his way up now, sir.

Oliver bent at the waist, blowing his exhale out through his lips.

It was a long two minutes before the door rattled, the knob finally turning.

The door shoved open. Rune shuffled in, his hand pressed to his arm, his bowed head in shadow.

A sheet of crimson stained the pale shirt he wore beneath the leather jacket, and the jeans. His arm was bent at the elbow, his hand gripping the middle of his left forearm.

They locked eyes.

In Rune, there was no apology. No guilt. Just exhaustion.

Rune grunted, raised the arm without letting go of it, kicked the door shut and leaned heavily back against the frame.

"Jackson," Oliver murmured.

"Yep."

Jackson ran over, got an arm around Rune's back and guided him to a nearby stool in the kitchen. As soon as Rune's ass was planted, Jackson pulled Rune's right hand away from where it squeezed. The leather was split, blood dripped on the wooden floorboards.

"Scissors," Jackson barked. It startled Oliver into movement, snapping him out of his trance.

Rune looked up at him quizzically, so Jackson mimed cutting.

Scowling, Rune peeled off the leather coat and dropped it to the floor.

More blood gushed free as he moved. Lots of it. Jackson snapped, "Stop! Stay still!" while holding up his hands, palm out. Rune paid no attention.

He set the arm on the kitchen counter at his favorite spot on the large island and gave Oliver a sunny smile. He fucking waved with the arm that wasn't gushing blood as Jackson applied pressure and said, "Olly, my bag."

Shaking with anger, about to explode, Oliver snatched up the satchel and stomped over to the island. He slammed it down, opened it wide and stayed back to give Jackson room.

"Fuck!" Oliver raged.

Rune made a circle out of his right hand, tipped it up as if to drink from an invisible cup.

"And fuck you too!"

Rune just grinned at him and shrugged, pointed to his useless ear.

God, but Oliver wanted to punch him across his smug fucking face.

"Just get him the drink, Olly," Jackson sighed. Rune focused on Jackson's lips, his expression relaxed and content. Jackson found peroxide and some swabs. "It's not that bad. A few stitches should do it. A clean cut."

Oliver went to the sink, reached for a glass. There was a hollow knocking sound.

He turned, saw Rune rapping his knuckles on the granite. He pointed to the liquor cabinet.

Oliver lost his mind.

He flew around the island, slammed into Rune, his hands locked up around his throat, and squeezed. A wheezing gasp sounded from Rune's pretty lips.

"The fuck is wrong with you?!" Oliver yelled right into Rune's face.

Mouth working, strangled wheezes the only sound in the room, Rune didn't even fight back.

"Stop it. Back off," Jackson scolded gently. "Or I'm kicking you out of your own home. Don't think I won't."

Oliver let go, sank into a crouch, hands raking through his hair, pulling hard at the strands nearly hard enough to tear them from his scalp.

Jackson had started the first stitch before Oliver had gotten it together enough to provide Rune with some bourbon, which he downed greedily and waved for more.

The hooked needle pushed through the sliced-open skin and Oliver stared at the blood pooled on the gleaming stone below Rune's arm.

"I hate this," Oliver said, knowing that Rune kept tracking their lips, reading their words. "I hate that he's deaf. I hate him."

"No, you don't. Quite the opposite, I think."

"Oh, fuck off," Oliver sneered.

"Mmm," Jackson hummed, pulling the thread tight and going for stitch four. Rune didn't flinch or react much, to Oliver's anger or anything else. He tapped the edge of his glass on the counter in a steady rhythm.

Oliver went and grabbed a pad of paper from his desk, brought it back to the kitchen, slapped it down on Rune's thigh. Setting a pen in his right hand, he pointed to the pad, expectantly.

Rune gave him an easy, crooked grin, then began to write in tight, small letters.

I'm fine. I'm great. Stop worrying so much.

Oliver groaned, rubbed hard enough at his eyes to see stars.

I appreciate the help, he wrote next. Then he set down the pen.

"Oh, no you fucking don't." Oliver signed and said: "Explain. Now. Right now."

Rune glanced over at Jackson's work, barely reacting to the punch of the needle through his skin as it looped through for the seventh time.

He picked up the pen.

> *Something I had to do. They were targeting black kids. Driving by. Throwing bottles. Laughing. I got their attention. Had them chase me instead. Led them to a speed trap I heard about. Let the cops take over. No big deal.*

"No big deal. I swear to—" Oliver growled. With oodles of exasperation, he signed and shouted, "Why is your arm sliced? Were you on a bike? How? Whose?"

Rune gently scribbled:

> *Like I said, they chased me. Got too close at one point and I got clipped with a knife. They were drunk as fuck. It was easy to get away once the cops noticed them. Just doing my civic duty.*

"Knives. Awesome. Who is 'they'"? Oliver asked.

You know.

"The pricks who ran you off the road," Oliver said. Rune followed the movements of his lips in a way that stirred Oliver's cock in unwanted ways. "How the fuck did you find them? Why were you following them?"

"Why do you think?" Jackson asked.

"You can't do shit like this," Oliver told Rune.

I think I just did, Rune scrawled in tight script.

"Not anymore. I'll stop you," he said, signed.

Rune just smiled, shrugged.

Oliver barely controlled the urge to yank him from the stool, throw him over the counter's edge and fuck him into submission.

He grabbed Rune by the throat.

"Stop, Olly," Jackson pleaded, knotting off the last stitch, leaning down to inspect the wound, prodding gently at the neat work with gloved fingers.

You're mad, Rune signed, his face's expression mimicking the emotion.

He understood all of the implied commentary, everything spelled out in the cool control reflected in Rune's eyes.

Why did Oliver care so much? Was he mad at Rune's good deed? The pricks who'd gone after kids? Himself for giving a fuck about some punk sub who wasn't so easily controlled and ordered around?

Jackson moved to clean up, packing supplies away, wiping down the skin around the wound with peroxide again to clean away more of the blood. Rune sat patiently, watching Oliver, biting at the edge of his lip, his head cocked at an angle.

Rune jabbed his thumb at his own chest, then in the direction of the apartment's door.

Oliver pushed down on the fury and upset as hard as he could, stepping into Rune's space, twisting a hand in the front of the bloody shirt, then yanking Rune closer without pulling him off the stool. Tilting his head, Rune offered his neck, stayed still, calm.

Breathing hard, Oliver's lips skimmed Rune's ear. He pulled back just far enough for Rune to see his mouth as he whispered, "Fuck you." His lips moved to Rune's neck, latched on. His teeth sank into the skin, leaving a mark but not breaking through. He let go, shifted lower, bit again, felt the heat of Rune's body baking the air.

"Rune, you might need a transfusion. You must have lost a lot of blood, but… you look okay," Jackson observed, touching Rune's face, looking into his eyes.

Oliver buried his nose in Rune's skin, breathing in his coppery smell. Jackson's latex-covered hand gripped the back of Oliver's neck. "He's okay, Olly."

Oliver let go, stepped back.

"Hold him," Oliver said softly.

"Yes, sir."

He waited until Jackson had a good grip, then pushed Rune off the stool, spun him around, bent him over the counter's edge, and freed himself before yanking at Rune's belt, then his fly. He got the jeans down, used some lube from Jackson's kit, then moved closer to Rune's backside.

The first thrust drew a strained growl from Rune. Oliver could tell it hurt.

So he pushed harder.

The door opened on his next withdrawal, Rune's breathing getting harder, his body straining against Jackson's hold on the back of his neck and upper arm.

From behind Oliver, a familiar voice said, "Came as fast as I could."

Something in Oliver loosened. He smiled. "Missed you, dear."

"Busy? Who's this?"

"Pain in my ass."

"Mmm," Adam hummed. "Think you have that backward. So this is payback?"

He strolled over, stepping carefully around the blood drips, and kissed Oliver's cheek. Oliver knew it was rude to not warn Rune of Adam's arrival or translate what they were saying, but his sour mood caused him not to care as much as he might. He did, however, see it more as though they were in a scene. If Rune had been blindfolded or wearing earplugs instead, Oliver still wouldn't have alerted him until he was ready to. Voyeurism was built into their contract.

Moaning happily on the next push, Oliver bottomed out and held still inside Rune, kneaded the side of his ass, felt him clench and quiver. The worry, the wait, the tension, he pushed it all together and used it as fuel. Oliver felt Adam fingering the hair at the nape of his neck, raising goosebumps, and moved to ride Rune harder, shallower, faster. Rune's face was turned to the other side. Adam was totally out of his field of view.

Rune strained again against Jackson, his back arching as he struggled to take the pounding, but Oliver kept up the pace until he climaxed. Moving slower on the come-down, he waited until he was fully spent, then bent himself over Rune's body, wrapping himself around it.

"Let go."

Jackson released Rune. Oliver took total control, wrapped him up. Rune's intact arm wound around to overlap Oliver's, which was crossed over Rune's slim hips. Oliver kept his hips tucked snugly against Rune's pale cheeks. He felt Rune's heartbeat—steady, a little quick.

"He's fucking killing me," Oliver sighed.

"Again, beg to differ, what with the blood and all. The hell happened here? Hey, Jay."

"Sir. Thanks for coming."

Jackson had walked around to the sink and began washing up. Adam leaned back comfortably against the counter right beside where Oliver was still buried to the root in Rune's ass.

Oliver pulled out, stepped to the side, signed to Rune.

Rune stayed where he was, watching. Always watching.

Oliver crooked a finger, drew Adam into Rune's field of view at last, saw him tense and flush. But he didn't move. He obeyed the command.

Oliver pulled Adam into his arms, hooked a hand around Adam's jaw, around his ear, angled his head and went in. Adam opened for it, letting Oliver lick deeply into his mouth, sucking a kiss to his lips, took his time. Oliver poured emotion and intimacy into the kiss, giving Adam the tenderness Rune likely craved for himself.

Warning flashed in Rune's eyes. A bit of hurt. Anger.

Oliver savored the selfish victory as much as the taste of his best friend and broke the kiss. He licked the flavor of Adam from his lip.

He finger-spelled the name.

Lynn Kelling

Rune closed his eyes. Surrendered.

Chapter 13
Tête-à-Tête

The sound of the shower's pattering carried far, echoing down the hall, filling the still air in the living space. Jackson's hands tented in front of his nose, the fingertips touching, and he stared at the dark entrance of that hallway, wondering about a lot.

"Here." Adam held out a glass half filled with amber liquid, keeping one of the pair to himself.

"Thanks."

Jackson anticipated the kiss, tilting his chin up to meet it. Adam's lips were warm, tasted like honey whiskey.

"Mmm. That's more like it," Jackson smiled.

Adam sat beside him with a heavy exhale, drinking, reclining back and spreading his legs. The right one rested comfortably against Jackson. Adam's hand rubbed idly over Jackson's back.

"Missed you."

"But not him?" Jackson smirked behind the rim of his drink.

Adam grunted, laughed. His short nails scratched over Jackson's spine, sending shivers down his arms, up the back of his neck. He closed his eyes, enjoying it.

"What the sweet fuck was all of that?" Adam asked quietly. "Gimme the short version."

"Olly's trying to save him. Rune's trying to save the world. I don't know if either of them are going to succeed before they kill themselves trying."

"Hell of a short version." Adam held out his glass. Jackson clinked his against it and they both drank. Emptying the glass, Jackson set it down. "Come on," Adam beckoned. "You know you want to."

Jackson laughed softly, twisted to lay down with his head in Adam's lap, his legs draped over the end of the couch. Adam began caressing Jackson's head and neck, his talented painter's fingers mapping shapes, sculpting visions on his skin. Humming in pleasure, Jackson tried to let go of some of the stress. It was surprisingly easy to do.

"Missed you too."

"How are you? I mean, really? You look like you're carrying a lot. He knows that, right?"

"Oh yeah, he knows. I'm fine," Jackson assured him. "It's mainly work. Trying to balance it all. So much goddamned responsibility."

"Why do you think I went with a career in painting?" Adam shook his head, sipped the last of his whiskey and set his glass down too. His right hand slowly unbuttoned Jackson's shirt, slipped beneath it to lightly sketch fantasies over his chest. His left brushed the frown lines away on Jackson's brow. "I saw what law did to people. When you take on that much, it takes over if you're not careful. But I know you are. What's the worst of it?"

Jackson sighed, frowned again, but happy to let Adam try to coax it away. "A couple of young patients. Men with families. The prognosis isn't good, and they're trying, but you can see them waiting for it to all slip away. The fear of losing people they love."

"Must be hard to see it coming like that," Adam admitted, his blue eyes focused on something beyond the room. "And Olly's been there for you?"

"Of course. But when Olly first took on Rune, we took a break for a few weeks. He needed to relearn ASL. Wanted to ease Rune into it all, because he was in rough shape, mentally. So I took Jo and the kids down to the Dominican Republic."

"No shit?"

"It was *nice*," Jackson smiled, remembering. "A colleague—podiatrist—rents out his villa right on the beach. Turquoise waters. Quiet. White sand. Pool. Kids played on the beach. Kayla was hunting for seashells every day. Jada was making an entire sand kingdom and I was right down there with her, digging out roads between castles."

"Wish I'd been there. Sounds like heaven."

"It was. But I was ready to come back. I missed him too much."

"What's your take on Rune?"

"Mmm. He's incredible. Afraid of nothing, you know? But he's sweet as hell with Olly. Obedient. Most of the time," he laughed. "He's a fighter, though. Gets off on it. And Olly gets off on trying to tame him."

"You don't?"

"Well..." he chuckled. Adam squeezed Jackson's pectoral muscle, pinched his nipple, sending a jolt straight to his cock. Pulling one leg up, he adjusted his pants to make room for his swelling erection. Adam pinched again, twisted, and Jackson's chest pushed into the contact, his neck elongated, his head thrown back even farther. "Yeah. I do," he said, a little out of breath.

"What was that tonight? The blood? The wound?"

"Rune chased off some white supremacist pricks. Caught the edge of a knife for his efforts. Saved some black kids downtown."

"Damn."

"I know."

"But... why? Was he just in the neighborhood?"

"No. He hunted them down. He thinks they're the same guys who ran him off the road, destroyed his hearing."

"So it's not just a one-time thing, is it?"

"I don't think so."

"Which is why Olly's losing his mind."

"Yep."

"And you? What's your take?"

"I think... he inspires me. Gives me hope."

Footsteps approached, Oliver rounded the end of the hall, came right for them. He was wearing a towel around his waist and nothing else. His bare chest was covered in soft brown hair, his nipples dark. His wet, tousled hair hung in his eyes. He was an irresistible sight.

He wrapped a hand around Jackson's jaw, caressed the pad of his thumb over Jackson's lower lip.

"I'm putting him to bed, making sure he falls asleep. You'll stay? Please?"

"Of course."

Oliver's gaze rose to catch Adam's.

"You too?"

Adam nodded.

"Take good care of him."

Adam's hand pulled out of Jackson's shirt, rubbed down to his crotch and rolled the hardened flesh there. Jackson moaned and spread, wanton and desperate. Oliver leaned down and licked into Jackson's mouth, sucked on his lips.

"Tonight, you're his. Okay?"

"Yes, sir." Jackson's breath caught as Adam squeezed his cockhead. "Thank you."

Leaving Oliver behind, they went to the master bedroom. Adam closed the door, turned on all of the lights, and opened the wardrobe tucked in the corner of the room, throwing the doors wide and surveying the contents.

"Strip," Adam commanded without turning, then glanced back and caught Jackson's eye, seeing his expression. "What?"

"You're gonna take your time, right?"

"Of course," Adam scoffed.

"Good," Jackson smiled.

"What do you think this is? My first time?"

"No, sir."

It had been half a year at least since the last time Adam had been there during a scene, and Jackson couldn't even remember the last time they'd been alone. But he knew Adam's focus was intense, sharper sometimes than Oliver's. Adam was even more a voyeur. Where Oliver wanted to feel a man break and submit, Adam wanted mostly to see it, capture the moment for study and scrutiny. Oliver got swept up in the emotion and passion, but Adam never did. There never seemed to be a distraction great enough to break him from his goal of taking his submissives apart, piece by piece.

Jackson had peeled off the mostly unbuttoned shirt. Bare-chested, he opened his pants, stepped out of his shoes, pulled off his socks. He shucked off his pants, pushed down his boxers. His gaze stayed lowered, respectfully, though he sensed Adam studying him already—looking hard at Jackson's body as he decided what he'd like to do to it. There was a cold detachment in it that Jackson craved. Adam's clinical curiosity felt a perfect match to Jackson's mental, emotional chaos. More than anything, he wanted someone to take over, sort his mess, clear the clutter, make him feel, make him yell and give over, completely.

Adam's shirt fell to the floor. His boots clunked against the wooden floorboards, one after the other, as he toed them off. His bare feet padded over, around Jackson.

A blindfold was pulled over his eyes, tied tightly behind his head.

"I want silence. No speaking, other than to say your safeword. No yelling. Nod if you understand."

Jackson nodded.

"Have your preferences changed?"

Jackson thought back to the last scene with him submitting to both Oliver and Adam. It had gone on for hours and he'd needed two days off from work afterward to recuperate. It had produced several indescribably kinky paintings. One of which hung in David Davenport's dungeon. Another hung over the bed in the room in which they stood.

He shook his head.

"Perfect. Hands behind your back."

Jackson brought his hands to his lower back, fists clenched. Something soft and firm wrapped his wrists, yanking them close together. A band wrapped his throat, just loose enough to allow him to breathe freely. Then tension pulled the band tighter, the same tension pulling at his bound wrists. When he flexed his arms to force his arms higher up his back, the pressure on his collar released, and he knew a chain must connect them.

Maybe he should have hated the chains, given cultural history and what they implied. It was another war he fought with himself. The struggle to overcome the world's systemic, overwhelming racism but to also find men he trusted so much that he could be made powerless before them and get lost in decadent sensation, forgetting his troubles and relinquishing all responsibilities for a few precious hours. It was the greatest high to need to do nothing but give in, endure pleasure, foregoing identity, labels and expectation. There was more peace in it than anything else he'd found.

Already his breathing eased. He forgot the look that was on Mr. Thornton's face when Jackson delivered the test results promising little hope and a shortened life. He forgot the blood splashed on granite and the way Rune hadn't flinched with each stitch through his sliced skin, like he'd been in so much agony for so long that something like being sewn back together was nothing. He forgot the eager way Jo had asked if he'd be heading to Oliver's that night, and the relief in her voice when he'd told her he was.

"Widen your stance. Don't move."

He shifted his feet farther apart, past the width of his shoulders. He tensed up, bracing for anything.

His erection was taken in hand. Fluid was swiped over and around the head, then worked into his slit. He swallowed a moan, felt his skin prickle and tighten from the top of his head to the bottom of his feet.

"Remember. Silence."

Something cool, hard, thin and blunt touched his cockhead, found the small opening of his urethra, parting it gently. After an involuntary flinch, he got control of himself and practiced deep breathing exercises, inhaling through his nose, holding the breath, then blowing it out through his mouth.

The pain was a spike and full, expansive ache that radiated into his gut, down through his thighs, as whatever Adam held was fed through the small hole in his dick and gradually, slowly impaled it. Right away, it pushed Jackson into a vulnerable mindset, forced him to surrender in the best of ways, and had him savoring a private thrill at the prospect of what Adam might do before they were done.

It seemed to take forever, which Jackson loved. He wanted it drawn out. He needed every feeling to be magnified and strengthened. Soon, Jackson was trembling uncontrollably. He let his bound arms hang down, which strained the muscles in his neck and choked off his breaths whenever he felt a shout might break free. The sharp, maddening discomfort in his cock contrasted blissfully with the gentle fondling caresses Adam gave Jackson's balls. Coping took all of Jackson's strength. There was no room for anything else.

The instrument was different than the sounding rods Oliver usually used on him, or any of the plugs he'd recently worn, but Jackson didn't dare guess why or how. His heart pounded as he fantasized about the possibilities.

Once it felt like twelve inches of metal was buried in his dick, the movement stopped. By then, Jackson was covered in sweat and his breathing was ragged. The need to lay down, to steady himself somehow, was overpowering. Because he had nothing to lean on. He could only try to stay balanced on his feet and not sway in any direction. The spike in his penis was his only other anchor.

Adam had stopped touching him. The sensation of being stared at, his privacy obliterated, his vulnerability studied, kept the prickling sensation going over his skin and the heat blooming in his face. It also kept him hard.

Then a hand cupped under his balls again, fingers playing with the sensitive skin. The weight of his sac was tested, the shape of his testicles mapped with careful, firm, rolling strokes. His breaths were shaky, uneven.

"You enjoy the way that feels? The pain? The humiliation?"

Jackson felt a wash of cool air over him as a vent kicked on, and nearly swayed. He tensed, catching himself. He nodded.

"Would you like me to photograph it?"

He nodded again, then whimpered softly as Adam stopped fondling him and walked away. His cock twitched, rising more, and he shuddered with need, his eyes rolling up, his head falling back on his shoulders.

He heard Adam over by the wardrobe. Heard a soft whirr and some clicks, then footsteps again. Down low, from directly in front of him, then off to the side, he heard the snap of a camera's shutter.

"I'm going to open you as wide as I can. Take a look inside. Take more photos. It's going to hurt, and if you whimper again, you'll be punished. Nod if you understand."

Jackson shivered, shifted his feet ever so slightly, then nodded. His cock jumped, begging.

More footsteps. A low clunk and a clatter. Footsteps again.

Hands moved him, turned him, guided him forward. A hand held his hip steady. Another hand pushed at his back, bending him slowly over at a ninety-degree angle. He shifted forward again and his knees touched something soft.

"Up. Slowly."

He brought his bent leg up, resting the knee on the soft surface of what he supposed was the bed. Then he brought up his other leg and crawled forward as much as the hand on his hip allowed, which wasn't much. The hand pushed at his back, bending him forward even more, until his shoulders rested on the bed, his head turned to one side, his ass in the air, and the metal stick shifted inside him with all of the movement. His cock throbbed with pressure, pain and the stiffness of arousal.

His sac was gathered in a hand, pulled on and fed through something hard. Pressure closed on the root of his sac, squeezing. He felt something touching him, extended side-to-side across the backs of his thighs, right under his ass. He shifted experimentally, and when he did, it pulled hard on his sac, stretching it even farther from his body.

He pictured the toy—a wide band called The Humbler, meant to keep a submissive bent sharply over. Any struggle or attempts to straighten would yank on their balls, trapped in a hole in the center of the band, its curved ends formed to hug the tops of the thighs.

Sinking into his helplessness, Jackson felt his heart racing, the cool air on his skin drawing more goosebumps. The ache in his balls was no match for the one in his cock.

A wet finger plunged swiftly, eagerly, through his sphincter, going in deep and twisting to rub him. The surprise drew a muffled grunt.

"You're tighter than I remember. Must be all of that time off you had. We'll have to work on that."

The finger kept rubbing at him from the inside. It twisted around again and quickly found his gland, pressing at it.

He couldn't stop the louder grunt, or the flinch that yanked at his sac hard enough to round the grunt into a lower tone, filled with ache.

The finger withdrew.

Unexplained, sudden fire erupted inside Jackson's cock, shooting down the core of it and deep into his gut, and he screamed as it bloomed into a full-bodied pain that cramped him up and strangled the air from his lungs.

The burning sensation stopped abruptly, and he gasped, then panted. A hand tenderly rubbed the back of his neck.

"The sound is wired. If you can't be silent, I turn it on. Longer for louder cries. Nod if you understand."

Jackson fought for control, until he was only breathing hard through his nose, and nodded.

Two wet fingers pushed back through his rim, spread apart. He pushed back onto them, wanting more, wanting Adam to fuck him, unsure if that was something he'd get that night or not.

"Good?"

He nodded.

Adam gave him a third finger and Jackson convulsed with pleasure to be so full, rocking against them ever so subtly.

"No, be still. You get what I give you. No more."

The three slippery fingers rode him with deep strokes, all the way in, all the way out to rub in a circle over his rim, then delved back in once more. It felt so nice, his head spun. The urge to beg, to moan, was maddening.

He'd forgotten how patient Adam could be.

Adam fingered him for what felt like hours, until Jackson's rim was so engorged with blood and oversensitive, he felt his heartbeat there, all of his focus on each touch, and how good it was. He stayed open, welcoming each push, hearing each loud squelch as Adam added more and more lube, until it dripped down Jackson's thighs and was smeared all over his cheeks.

Finally, Adam asked, "Would you like more?"

Jackson keened.

Adam pulled out, flipped a switch.

Jackson stiffened from head to toe, biting back the scream, thrumming, convulsing, then panting hard as the surge stopped.

"I said, would you like more?"

He nodded, the room spinning around him, his body aching in places he didn't know he had.

He barely remembered his name let alone anything else. The world had ceased to exist.

And he only wanted more.

Chapter 14
Surrendered

He sighed with pure bliss as something cool pushed between his cheeks and entered him. The end felt narrow as a finger, but widened instantly, like a cone. He remembered what Adam had said, knew it was likely something clear, something designed to test his endurance.

A hand gripped his hip, steadying him as the pressure spiked. It had barely begun entering him and he already felt stretched to his limit, couldn't take any more. Adam rubbed Jackson's stretched rim where it hugged the toy, smearing lube around, holding the toy in place. He kept the pressure constant, and oh-so-gradually, it moved deeper into him. Jackson panted, fists clenched, picturing what he must look like—ass up, hole spread around a clear monstrous toy, the pink of his sphincter as Adam stared, looking deeply into him.

Jackson fucked air, getting off on the vision, so Adam pushed harder to fill him. That drove Jackson forward, the Humbler stretching his balls, so Adam's hand on his hip drew him back onto the toy.

"Good. Show me you want it. Open wide for me. If you obey, I promise to fuck you. I might even take the rod out of your cock while I do it. Watch you squirt. Watch you lick it all up."

A wave of heat moved through him and the toy inched deeper, just enough that a ridge passed through his outer ring of muscle, locking the toy in place as it narrowed dramatically after. He wanted to thrust against something and get off, get relief, but was terrified to move. His cock jumped and he convulsed a little. Adam caressed Jackson's trapped balls. The heat of him lingering there behind Jackson moved, shifted. Hands came to rest on the backs of Jackson's thighs. A wet, soft muscle petted his sac. Adam hummed, sucked a kiss to the spot, then licked some more. He took most of Jackson's balls into his mouth and sucked on them.

Jackson almost couldn't process the pleasure of that, and moaned.

He cursed through gritted teeth. Adam pulled off. Jackson braced for the surge, growled as it barraged him, bearing down on the toy in his ass.

It stopped.

Everything grew still again. Silent. Adam wasn't touching him, but was there… somewhere.

He heard the whir of a camera's lens, the click of the shutter. The sounds were right behind him, as if Adam aimed the focus right at Jackson's spread ass, which he probably did.

"Don't pretend you don't get off on it," Adam said softly. "I didn't think you'd take the whole thing like this. I tried it on a sub a few months ago, and he cried, used his safeword, and made me promise never to use it again. But you took it like a champ." The camera clicked, its eye seeing into him. "I'll have to show Olly, of course."

He tried to track Adam by sound, but it was difficult. The longer he stayed perched there, stuffed in two ways, bound and pulled, the more desperate he became.

"I have missed you," Adam said softly. "Been searching for someone like you. Haven't found him yet."

The wet, soft touch came back, but this time Adam licked Jackson's stretched, stuffed hole. The tip of his tongue traced the rim, and Jackson yanked his wrists down to cut off his air, fearing a guttural moan. It worked, and he pushed back into the touch, craving it. Adam's tongue moved restlessly, teasing, tasting, claiming. He reached between Jackson's spread legs, wrapping the hand around Jackson's stuffed cock. He stroked the shaft, fingered the head and the place where the end of the rod stuck out.

The most wanton whore, Jackson offered up his ass, prayed a silent thanks for each stroke, being still, being quiet, feeling strung tighter than he'd ever been.

"Deep breath, gorgeous. Hold it."

There was massive pressure at his rim and he refused to exhale or let out sound as the yell bubbled up. The toy's ridge passed, and the rest was an easy slide as it passed from him.

Without it, he felt gaping.

Adam massaged Jackson's rim, and Jackson panted through it, grinding his forehead into the bed, the urge to plead immense.

"Speak. What do you want?"

"Please fuck me, Sir," he begged, shamelessly, fervently. "Please. Please."

Adam plunged into him, hard, deep.

"Fuck," Jackson breathed. "Thank you. Fuck…"

Adam's grip on Jackson's hips was brutal, keeping him perfectly still as he was pounded from behind. Adam was going rough enough to bruise him in other places too. It drove the breath from Jackson's lungs as he moaned and bore it. Adam fucked him like he was angry, like he was trying to drive Jackson right through the bed.

Adam came, sighing, slowing.

He released the chain connecting Jackson's wrists to his collar.

He pulled out, removed the Humbler, massaged Jackson's sac.

All Jackson could do was moan and savor it.

Adam pushed him onto his side, pushed at Jackson's hip to expose his sore cock.

Something lightly covered him there then. He felt Adam suck at the ridge of Jackson's cockhead, tonguing the edge, tracing his slit. The light touch of plastic peeled away. A soaking wet hand began to jack him off, each pull a loud squelch. Jackson rode it, welcoming the painful pressure of the sound stuffing him, shamelessly humping Adam's fist. Jackson felt exhausted and unable to move in any other way except that steady rolling of his hips.

His movements got sharper, more desperate, and he began to whimper.

"Easy. Slow down. Enjoy it."

He forced himself to control the movements, to go slower, but the need to come was intense, inescapable. He convulsed, tugged at his cuffs for comfort, breathed with his head turned to the side.

"Better. Beautiful."

He stayed curled up like that for an eternity, almost in the fetal position, arms bound, collared, stuffed with metal, gently fucking Adam's soaking wet fist like it was the sweetest pussy in the world. He couldn't orgasm with the rod in him, but he kept getting close, and would whimper softly, fighting through it, and keep rolling his hips.

When Adam pushed the blindfold back, then reached for the end of the rod, Jackson begged, his voice breaking, "Please don't. Please. Not yet."

"I'm not leaving you, Jackson. I swear it. Be still. Obey me."

"Yes, sir."

Breathing hard, Jackson lay there as Adam slowly eased the rod free, watching as his pale hand coaxed it gradually out of Jackson's thick, dark, glistening cock. The end slipped free and Jackson moaned.

Adam set the rod aside and reached for Jackson again, touching so lightly. He gently rubbed the sore slit, and Jackson flinched, but bore it. When Jackson began to rock against the touch, Adam shifted to wrap his cock instead, tugging it. He fell back into the easy rhythm, panting, jittery with anticipation.

"Squirt for me, Jay. You close?"

Delirious, he couldn't respond, but just chased the edge, rocking into the fist as if nothing else in the world mattered. In that moment, it didn't. He was peaceful. Consumed.

He shot his load, gasping. It splattered over the bed covers, kept pumping from him with the coaxing of Adam's fist. Jackson got one glimpse of the cold fire in Adam's blue eyes, fervently trying to capture each sight, taking it. Claiming it. Then Jackson closed his eyes and gave over again, in perfect submission.

He stopped moving, spent.

Adam's fist kept tugging, stroking Jackson's oversensitive cock. It was unbearable. He loved it.

The discomfort climbed and he began to writhe.

"No, be still. Obey me. Ride it. Ride the pain. Stay very still."

Curled there, he began to cry out as Adam kept stroking, the squelch, squelch, squelch obscene, but he obeyed. He endured, shaking, his voice breaking.

It went on and on, past pain, into a deeper delirium. Ten minutes became twenty and still Adam pet him, coaxed him, throbbing, swelling, aching.

The sensations overwhelmed, but he pushed down on his discomfort, down right between his legs, letting it fill his cock, then pushing the pain into Adam's restless hand.

"That's it," Adam urged. "Don't stop."

He released the chain on the cuffs, rolled a condom on Jackson, rolled him over to his over side, sunk down and swallowed him to the root, cupping his ass with both hands. Moaning, Adam sucked him. Making soft desperate pleas, Jackson held Adam's head and rode his mouth. Adam's fingers pushed into him, found his gland, pressed at it from inside and out, milking him.

"Oh fuck... Oh fuck... Adam, please... Please..."

When he came again, everything faded to black.

He woke with a redhead in his arms, sleeping naked, warm, and comfortable. Jackson smiled, wondered about Oliver, about Rune, and drifted peacefully back to sleep.

The story—the whole thing—lay on the nightstand, in alternating script styles. Oliver's tight, slanted hand appeared in shorter bursts, mostly questions, between Rune's sprawling, softer, wild penmanship.

It had been the easiest, quickest way. They'd laid in bed, Rune on his stomach, up on his elbows as he wrote away on the tablet of paper. Oliver lay half atop him, unable to stop touching him or kissing his flushed skin, damp from the shower, smelling of woodsy soap, watching each word form as the pen skated across the paper.

The lack of eye contact helped speed the process. Oliver had noticed how Rune clammed up and receded into himself when faced with explaining via sign or in a confrontational way. So he hadn't seen Oliver's reactions to each secret about how he'd come out as gay to The Born Soldiers, or how they'd agreed to help him, or why he'd snuck out the back to scope out the other crew by himself, dumb as it had been. He'd only felt Oliver's kisses and touches, which opened Rune in more than one way.

Halfway down the third page, the word 'careful' trailed off in a long swooping line that slashed the white from end to end. That was when Oliver had entered him. On the line below this, the words were unsteady, barely legible. He'd closed Rune's hand up around the pen, set it back on the line and showed him what was expected. After that, there were shaky phrases, dashed words. The lines fell away in all directions, often, as Rune had struggled to keep control of it.

When Oliver had gotten enough out of him, he'd set the pad aside, flipped it over to keep it sacred, and pulled Rune against him.

That had been nine hours ago.

He'd awoken to Rune weaving his fingers through Oliver's, pulling their linked hands against the warmth of Rune's bare chest. Through that hand, and where his chest was flush to Rune's back, Oliver felt Rune's ribs expand with each breath, and the steady flutter of his heartbeat.

He'd brushed a drowsy kiss to the back of Rune's ear.

He didn't know how to explain in words scribbled over paper, or shaped in the air by fingers, how terrified he was. How he needed Rune to be careful. That he couldn't take chances like he used to.

He knew some of these urgencies were expressed through the bright glare his eyes and the tense set of his jaw. Couldn't help it. But it was in the way their shared body heat only drew Rune closer, in the tuck of his chin over Rune's shoulder, in the clasp of his palm to Oliver's neck and the weave of his fingers through Oliver's hair, playing with the strands, that Oliver really pleaded with him.

There was no reconciling it—the stupid, deaf kid that drove off on a motorcycle, dodging and weaving through traffic with a truck full of drunken, knife-wielding bigots on his tail, getting near enough to slash through his coat and open up his arm, and the shy, sweet lover who cuddled so close and didn't dare let go once all night long.

It was killing him.

Rune's quest was noble, understandable, rash, and dangerous. For someone with nothing to lose, it made sense. But Oliver was too proud to tell him he no longer existed free of ties. Because if Rune couldn't feel it on his own, there was really nothing to say.

The smell of him, the soft feel of his body tucked so close as if trying to get every possible point of contact, began intoxicating Oliver. He bit gently at the side of Rune's neck, the inked skin. Rune undulated in his hold, sighing. Oliver's cock had been swelling steadily and fit snugly between Rune's cheeks, riding the crease. He rolled his hips, grinding back against it, then let go of Oliver's hand, reached behind himself, between them. Taking hold of Oliver's cock, Rune aligned it with his hole and pressed back to take it in. Oliver moaned, thrust and felt the head pop through. Rune let go, his arm coming up to hook behind Oliver's head, fingers carding roughly through his hair. Grabbing a handful, he pulled Oliver in, purred a soft plea as Oliver pressed kisses behind his ear.

"Fuck," Oliver lamented, frowning. There was pain in his chest. A tightness that wouldn't let go. His palm flattened over Rune's heart, savoring each beat. He kept imagining the beautiful body in his arms sprawled on concrete, broken, or kneeling before the barrel of a loaded gun, or crushed under tires. He kept feeling it get away from him, over and over again. As the fear swelled, his hand shook, just a little.

There was someone in the doorway, but he didn't glance over. Didn't care. Rune was all that mattered.

Rune tensed in his hold, clenching up on Oliver's cock, growing perfectly still.

The figure moved, vanished, but came back a moment later.

A shock of red in Oliver's peripheral vision told him enough. The soft whirr of a camera lens focusing told him more.

Rune was wide-eyed, gaze locked on the intruder like a cat stalking prey. His body was strung tight in the curled pose. The hand in Oliver's hair held him tighter, protectively. Oliver groaned, moving within him, riding the tightness, burying his face against the side of Rune's neck to mask some of his bare emotion. His hand held over Rune's heart, shielding it.

The camera clicked again and again.

Rune was about to launch himself from the bed and attack with claws and teeth, so Oliver held him tighter, kissed along his jaw. His sleep-roughened voice asked uselessly, "Stay. Stay with me." His voice broke. "Please."

Adam moved around the bed without a sound. The soft click the only marker of his passage until he swore in a whisper, "God damn, Olly."

Still, Rune tracked Adam, never looking away, barely blinking.

Exhaling into Rune's dark hair, Oliver kept a steady rhythm, trembling slightly on each push.

Adam moved closer, facing them. The nearer he came, the more Rune dropped his arm, bracing it on the bed, like he was about to launch off of it, the warning clear in the hard set of his eyes, the flash of gritted teeth.

Adam dropped the camera, turned it around to reveal the screen on the back, held it out to show.

Finally, Rune's gaze shifted, from Adam to his art.

Rune blinked, softened. The lowest moan slipped past his lips as Oliver tugged back, pushed to fill him once more. He reclaimed Oliver's hand, wove their fingers together, pulled them against him. The tension eased and he was knocked forward on the next thrust.

Adam opened his right hand, facing Rune, the fingers spread, and moved it across his face in a swooping motion, as if clearing away cobwebs.

Beautiful.

Rune stared, smiled, just barely. Laughed soundlessly. Closed his eyes.

Adam sat on the bed, caressed Oliver's arm, then the center of Rune's chest, then gently brushed the dark hair back from Rune's face.

Oliver came, quivering, gasping. Adam's fingers combed back through his hair. Rune hummed contentedly. When Oliver pulled out, Rune shifted onto his back so he could see both of them, his gaze following their lips.

"The hell did you learn to sign?" Oliver rasped without letting Rune go, even a little.

"My phone. Just now."

Oliver breathed out a chuckle, shook his head and kissed Rune hard, moaning into his mouth. The fear hadn't let him go, though. For a moment, it wrapped even tighter, painfully.

"You okay?" Adam asked, the question concerned, tender as he gestured to Oliver and held up his hand with his index finger and thumb making a circle, the other fingers extended. He smoothed the hair at the nape of Oliver's neck.

"I can't lose you," Oliver whispered, speaking the words urgently to Rune. "I can't."

"He knows," Adam assured him. "Trust me, Olly. He knows."

Tearing his gaze away, just barely, Oliver finally saw the camera's screen. Rune's gaze seared into the lens, daring the viewer to come closer, to even think to try. He held Oliver so protectively, powerfully. Though he was being actively violated, he was in total control. Confidence shone from him. Meanwhile, Oliver clung on with desperation, pouring emotion into the tattooed warrior in his arms, who soaked it in, greedily and didn't intend to share.

Oliver couldn't look any longer, but trailed kisses over the side of Rune's jaw.

Rune released Oliver's hand, just for a moment. His right hand rose, flattened, to his lips, the fingertips barely touching. He brought it forward and down slightly, in Adam's direction.

Thank you.

Adam replied by moving his hand in a circle before him, as if tracing an invisible ball, or doing an old-fashioned bow while moving only his arm.

You're welcome.

Chapter 15
On Edge

Jackson had hugged Rune goodbye. Rune was still fucked up over it.

He hadn't signed or said anything, just came over, dragged him in, and smacked a kiss to his head before letting go and leaving.

Who were they to each other? Rune couldn't say. He only knew he missed Jackson once he was gone, even though they hadn't even spent much time together.

But Jackson's presence calmed Oliver. So did Adam's. Rune saw it, plain as day. Oliver's gaze snapped to theirs constantly, checking in, keeping tabs, maintaining balance. They migrated together like magnets pulled by an unseen force.

Rune was starting to feel the pull, too. He fought it as hard as he could. He didn't want to be owned, kept, or monitored. Freedom had always been his biggest driver. There was no use to having ties. Traditional employment killed the spirit. Families came laden with drama. Costly possessions added weight, forbidding ease of movement. Getting off, getting high, having fun, feeling alive—those were worth living for.

Or at least that's what he would have said before the accident.

Now, when he needed to feel Oliver against him in the dark, when the doubts crept in, chewing at him, he didn't know how to face it. He couldn't resist the urge to seek out the comfort he craved, but the shame of caving to the itch was just as big as the reward.

It had hurt just as much to see Oliver's shock at the blood and injury when Rune had arrived the night before as it had to feel the knife slashing at him. Truthfully, Oliver's upset was worse because it hadn't come with the rush of flying down the road through the dark, adrenaline pushing Rune to go faster, and faster. There had only been the stillness and the inability to explain.

He'd welcomed it when Oliver bent him over and reamed him out, giving it hard and angry. He'd even been eager for the humiliation of realizing

Adam was there, watching, and the piercing jealousy of the kiss he'd shared with Oliver. All of it was deserved. None of it was enough.

Adam kept staring at him.

Rune would have thought he'd had quite an eyeful already, after witnessing the lovemaking between him and Oliver, and photographing it, then sitting beside where Rune lay after. Adam's fingertips had skimmed over Rune's arms, back, neck, chest, fingers, scrutinizing each tattoo and scar. Rune had laid there, submitting to it, while Oliver showered and changed. Adam had taken hold of one arm at a time, turning it this way and that, spreading Rune's fingers. He'd tipped Rune's chin up with the back of a knuckle to trace the edge of the climbing vines tattooed on his neck. There had been no hesitation in it, like Adam knew he had every right to touch or take of Rune as he liked.

Which maybe he did.

It had been in the rules, the first emails from Oliver, that he shared everything with Adam. They supported one another in whatever ways were needed. Adam needed more than Oliver, due to his lack of family support, and because Oliver was by far and away his closest friend. And from what Rune had seen, Oliver needed to be needed, so it worked out well.

The same reason why Oliver had fallen for David's offer of Rune was the same reason he clung so hard to Jackson and Adam as well.

Adam sat in front of the couch on the ottoman, scrolling through photos from his trip on his tablet. Oliver made constant commentary, but Rune wasn't interested, so he'd given Oliver permission to stop trying to sign everything too. Rune sat on the couch beside Oliver, with Oliver's hand wrapping his upper thigh, the fingers curled around. Head reclined, Rune rested, and plotted. But he kept catching Adam's gaze, and it kept giving him the chills.

Whatever Adam saw when he looked at Rune was going to influence his interactions with Oliver. They'd be discussing him, maybe planning ways to fuck him or use him, together, one at a time, or with friends. Rune didn't really want to know. He didn't want forewarning.

It was a given that Adam would be inside him soon. The knowledge of that had Rune scrambling for purchase, like he was sliding down a rocky slope. He used to solely be a top. He had done the fucking, called the shots, picked who he took. Now, he had relinquished all control.

The bitch of it was, he did trust Oliver. Completely.

He wished he didn't. He wished he had the excuse to use to fight back.

Because Oliver was a good guy. He didn't want to see the ugly shit Rune had in his face constantly, willingly. He didn't want Rune leading monsters on a chase just to save some strangers, if it meant he could get hurt or die.

And Rune didn't know what to do with that.

So he reclined and felt Adam's gaze like another set of fingers fondling him.

The image of that photo he'd taken earlier haunted Rune.

It showed how hard Oliver was going to fight to keep Rune safe, and how willing Rune was to do what he wanted anyway, no matter the casualties it created.

Maybe Adam was pissed at him. Maybe he was plotting ways to keep Rune caged and spare Oliver's feelings.

The complications around Rune were a web. Adam was the razor-sharp blade ready to slice through and send the ends tumbling down. Oliver was the force behind the blade, driving it on, invisible but more responsible for each slice than the weapon itself.

The next time Rune looked over at the others, Adam was focused on his tablet. Oliver was watching Rune.

Rune signed, *I'm leaving soon.*

Oliver said, over-enunciating and shaking his head, "No."

Rune rolled his eyes.

I'm your prisoner?

Sneering, then running his hand over his face, Oliver turned away.

They'd been over this earlier. Oliver's desire for Rune to be safe was not outweighed by Rune's need to keep his attackers from hurting others. He'd told Oliver he was willing to break their contract if he wasn't afforded some freedom to handle his personal matters his own way. Rune suspected Oliver didn't know how much Oliver had begun to mean to him, and how Rune was truly afraid of losing him as a Dom.

They were at odds, in a tug of war. Both of them stubborn, but Rune quite certain Oliver's feelings kept him more restricted.

I'll be fine, Rune promised. *No stunts.*

Don't go after them on your own, Oliver's fingers told him, his face steely and tense with anger.

Okay.

Promise.

Okay.

Adam glanced between them, trying to follow the signing. Oliver wasn't speaking his commands.

Adam said something Rune didn't catch. Oliver replied.

Pulling out his phone, Oliver typed something. Sighed. Showed it to Rune.

If you show up a bloody mess again, it'll be the last time.

Adam looked like he had something to say but was just barely able to bite his tongue.

Rune shrugged. *Okay.*

Again, Oliver and Adam exchanged words. Oliver typed something else.

Adam will be staying with us tonight. We start the scene at ten. Don't be late. If you are, there will be consequences you won't enjoy. We expect you showered, douched and ready to go. Understand?

Rune nodded, eager to put Oliver and Adam to the test.

"Do you remember Blaine?" Adam smirked. He picked at his vegetarian omelet, the twin mugs of coffee emitting long plumes of pale steam that snaked up through a band of bright sunlight slanting in through the café's window. Their table was tucked around a corner, out of sight of most other patrons. No one was in ear shot, except a teenage waiter that came and went at irksome speed.

"God, spare me," Oliver groaned. He risked scalded taste buds in order to get a sip of the caffeine-rich brew. The chocolate cherry blend had an overpowering smell, but he liked the arrogance of the bold scent. Sometimes it was refreshing to find something so obnoxious.

Other times, like with Blaine, not so much.

"It was hilarious. You have to admit," Adam chuckled. "A soap opera saga for the ages. I still think of the way he would fawn at you in Earth Science, doodling your name in a heart in the margins of his notebook."

"That didn't happen."

"Just because you block it out doesn't erase it from reality."

Oliver waved a slice of toast. "I was embarrassed for him. I'm still embarrassed for him." He ripped off a bite, chewed, tucked the food in his cheek and asked, "Why are we talking about this?"

"Humor me," Adam asked. "How did it start again? You snuck a look at him after swim practice?"

"No, he just thought I did. Screamed bloody murder to the whole locker room."

"You were out by then, right? Junior year?"

"No, not officially. But you were, and I was your bestie," Oliver smiled with a snide edge to the word. "Two plus two."

"So he just assumed. Had a moment of homophobic paranoia. Caused a scene. God, I wish I'd been there."

"I don't. Would've just made it worse," Oliver grumbled.

"Worse for who?"

Oliver gave him a look, shrugged, wondering where this was headed.

"But I wish I'd seen it!" Adam laughed. "They ganged up on you."

"No," Oliver argued. "It wasn't that dramatic. No one else wanted to get detention or cared enough to intervene. Blaine was just... unhinged." Adam waved him on. Oliver kept going, humoring him. "He came close, got up in my face, chest puffed out, flipping that stupid long hair back from his eyes, arms spread. 'You lookin' at me, faggot?! You lookin' at my junk?!'" Oliver mimicked, raising the pitch of his voice, adding a douchey, marble-mouthed accent but kept his volume low.

"And he faked a punch," Adam supplied.

"Yep. Pulled it way too soon. But I was pissed."

"You gave him a right hook, right in the gut."

"Collapsed. Whimpering. Calling for Mommy," Oliver recited, not nearly as thrilled by the memory as Adam.

"And they all scattered. No one had his back," Adam beamed, shaking his head. "How long before he started mooning over you? Slipping you notes in your locker? Trying to corner you in empty parking lots after practice?"

"It was like right away. Fucking stalker."

"I saw him."

"Wait... saw him recently?" His mind reeled, trying to advance the clock and picture Blaine in his mid-twenties.

"Yeah, down at Spark a week ago, dressed like a twink, drooling over some leather daddy."

"You are fucking shitting me."

Adam raised his eyebrows, took a bite of omelet.

"You led him on," Adam said. "The whole time. You gave him the barest hint of possibility, and then the utter refusal to engage even a little... it was brilliant. Masterful. He would have done anything for you. He'd have signed a lifetime contract, no stipulations."

"Probably."

"Hmm," Adam hummed, laughing to himself at the memory. He shook his head again. "So what happened?"

"To who? Blaine?"

"No, *you*, Olly." Adam set down his fork, leaned forward, lowering his voice. "What the fuck has happened to you? You destroyed that guy's life. He's probably still got a shrine to you that he jerks off to nightly. You saw it was killing him, for years, and didn't bat an eye. And it wasn't just Blaine. It was everyone who tried to get in your pants until Jackson. You cast spells over these guys with no effort at all, igniting obsessions. You were a legend. Still are to some. And I go on one trip, miss one introduction. One night. I hardly recognize you now."

"Is that why you took so many photos, then?" Oliver asked, drinking more coffee now that it had cooled a little.

"You do admit it!" Adam jabbed a finger.

Oliver rolled his eyes, sat back, spread his legs a little more. "Go fuck yourself, Buchanan."

Adam set his chin on a hand, studying him. "But... it's so bizarre."

"Yes, my life is hilarious."

"Is it purely the challenge? I can respect that, if it is. Or do you really get off that hard on his self-destructiveness?"

"Keep trying. Go on. It's fine." He checked his watch, then pulled out his phone. Adam snatched it away, set it out of reach. Oliver gave him a weary look.

Adam squinted, tilting his head like Oliver was a particularly baffling painting. "There is something there. Can't quite put my finger on it. I saw it when I walked in last night, with blood splattered everywhere, before he knew I was there, when you were rage-fucking him. The act itself was brutal, but Rune... he welcomed it. Trusted you. And this morning? He hated me for interrupting like that. Why? Jealousy? Possessiveness?"

Oliver gave him a fake smile, not rising to it. He'd had several years of practice at resisting Adam's banter and inquisitions.

"You really think he'll listen to you? That he won't show up in pieces again?"

Oliver slowly knocked his knuckles against the table.

"Okay. That's enough."

Angry now, the cool waters of his eyes set on fire, Adam seethed, "He could be out there, right now, getting his fucking brains blown out by some pants-wetting skinhead cum-stain and you could lose him!"

Cool, collected, Oliver said, "I'm always losing him. I was losing him before I even had him."

It crossed some bad line then. Oliver calmly witnessed Adam's terror seep over a sacred boundary. With wet, glassy eyes, he glared at Oliver, then pushed out of the booth and began to walk away, wiping a hand over his mouth.

"Adam."

He paused, kept his back turned.

"You don't have to save me from this. You're absolved. Officially. You don't owe it to me. Okay?"

Softly, a whisper. "Fuck you, I owe you everything."

And then he left, stalking over to the exit, blasting through the doors into the cruel light of day.

He was surrounded. Rune's whole body throbbed with the beat of his heart. The wind blew an arctic blast from the east, hard enough to nearly knock him off balance. Planting his feet wider, leaning into the gust, he focused his vision, keeping his target in sight. Nothing else mattered.

Lips moved. Expression contorted. Energy swirled with deadly force from all directions, but he was the eye of the storm. Nothing could stop him if he didn't want to be stopped.

Not even the voice whispering in the back of his mind, telling him it might be unrelated. That the crime against him and the crimes of the man on his knees in front of Rune might have nothing to do with each other.

They were still crimes. It was time for a little justice for once.

The circular, cross-shaped white pride symbol inked into the blond's neck stretched as his head was forced back by multiple hands yanking fistfuls of hair nearly hard enough to tear large bloody chunks from his scalp. Tendons popping, veins bulging, the pale-skinned, six-foot-whatever redneck dressed in a flannel and jeans sneered up at Rune with disgust, then hocked phlegm and spat it in Rune's direction.

Dodging the gob of saliva, Rune bounced on his feet and hit squarely, his fist whipping around as hard as he could.

He felt the snap. The crunch of bone against bone and the soft give of flesh before blood began to spurt from the blond's nostrils.

Max and Goat yanked harder at the golden tresses, keeping the homophobe still, forcing him upright with violent twists of the man's shoulders and a few kicks to the back.

Rune tuned it all out. Everything but the smashed ruin of the blond's nose, and the print-outs from the blond's social media account. His name was Kurt Radner. Each post was decorated with a clear photo of his face in the profile shot. Sometimes another guy was in the background, farther away, walking away, like the blond was following him. Kurt would hint in the post about what he'd done when he caught up with the other guy, without flat-out admitting it. Comment after comment on public posts, peppered with bigoted, hateful slurs, told teenage gay kids to go kill themselves and do the world a favor. Sometimes he just flat-out offered to do the job for them.

Rune yanked up the front of his shirt, flashing an old tattoo on his hip of an inverted rainbow triangle. He made sure the blond saw it. Then he cocked back his fist and let the blows rain down, long after his hand started to ache, letting the boiling of his blood carry him along and unleash a little hatred on the hateful.

The CCTV system was wired to the flatscreen in the bedroom. Adam lay reclined on the bed, arms folded behind his head which was propped up with pillows.

"You sure he's on his way?"

"Any minute now," Oliver replied.

"You're pacing again."

"Thank you, Captain Obvious."

"You're welcome. Here's something equally obvious: you can handle this, Olly. You can handle *him*. Whatever he brings you. I know you can. You know you can too, for the record."

Simultaneously keyed up and already exhausted by it all, Oliver shot him a weary look.

"He gets to you. He makes things more real than they usually are with your more boring, run-of-the-mill subs. I get it. And something tells me Rune gets it too. I think he keeps coming back here because he knows you can handle his shit more than any other Dom he's worked with before. Am I wrong?"

Oliver sighed and folded his arms.

"You know what I think?" Adam continued. "I think David facilitated this because he sensed Rune would get to you in precisely this way. That he'd wake you up and shake you up and force you to focus. Are you telling me you're not up for the job? When everyone else knows you can do it? When giving up would mean Rune's precious faith in you is all for nothing? If he steps over the line again and pisses you off, use that. Use that emotion, that energy to get his ass in line. You can care about him by holding on, but care about him like this too. It's what both of you want. And need."

Without knowing how to respond, Oliver just absorbed the words and watched the camera aimed on the apartment's front door, waiting and hoping.

The message he'd sent had been clear:

Let yourself in. Get undressed. Get cleaned up. Meet us in the bedroom. We'll be watching.

Rune had replied that he was on his way up five minutes ago.

Soon enough, it happened.

The front door inched open. Rune stuck his head in, looked around, then slowly came in, shutting the door behind him.

"You owe me twenty bucks," Adam sighed.

"What? Where? Is he okay? I don't—"

"His hand. The right one."

"Are you fucking kidding— Jesus wept." Oliver groaned, covering his face with a hand. Peering between his fingers, he saw the dark spots on Rune's knuckles and the way he kept the hand curled in front of him. "I need to take him to the hospital. Have them check for fractures. He needs his hands to speak!"

"Olly, breathe." Adam got off the bed and came around to him. Wrapping Oliver in his arms from behind, Adam held him by the shoulders, kissing Oliver behind the ear. Oliver overlaid a hand on Adam's, frowning, trying to calm down.

Rune toed off his sneakers, then crossed right to the kitchen. He took a bowl out of the cupboard and filled it with ice from the machine in the door of the fridge, the sound of cubes clunking in the bowl audible down the hall. Rune kept glancing around like he had something to hide, not like he was in pain. He let his hand slip into the ice and seemed to let out a deep breath, wincing only slightly.

"I'm gonna kill him," Oliver marveled.

"No, you're not." Adam took Oliver's hand, squeezing it. "He didn't mention it over text. Let's just see what he does. He knows himself and what he needs better than we do."

"He's been beating the hell out of someone! Look at his knuckles!" He kept his voice down, even though he knew how ridiculous that was. Ingrained instincts continued to be hard to break.

"I have. Maybe they had it coming. He seems committed to going through with the scene. There's a reason for that. Let's see if he has any other visible injuries, hmm?"

After a couple of minutes, seeing Oliver and Adam hadn't emerged to scold him, Rune took the bowl of ice with him to the bathroom connected to his room. As he moved, they switched to the feed in the hallway, then the bedroom, then the bathroom, pulling up both camera angles, side by side.

Favoring his right hand, but using it a little anyway, Rune shrugged off his hooded sweatshirt, then pulled his shirt over his head. Bare-chested, he opened his pants, pushing the jeans and underwear down to his ankles. They both came off, along with his socks, which he plucked off by the toes.

"I think he's okay. He hasn't flinched while using the hand."

"That's your official medical opinion? I should call Jackson."

"He's out with Jo. Leave him alone."

Oliver glanced over his shoulder at Adam, who was giving Rune's nude body a long once-over with plenty of interest. Adam noticed him looking, met his gaze and said, "I don't see anything."

"Yeah, right."

Adam did an exaggerated shrug, hands up-turned. "I'm here to fuck your boy toy. I'm not supposed to look? If looking makes you jealous, just wait until my cock is inside him."

"I'm not jealous," Oliver murmured, biting at his lip, studying the screen. He didn't see any new cuts or bruises. Rune wasn't looking for any injury in the mirror either.

"Should I go?"

"No."

"Why?"

"You know why. I need him in a submissive mindset. When I'm alone with him, the instinct isn't to dominate."

Adam breathed out a laugh.

"It's not funny."

"It's a little funny."

"His guard comes up with you. He feels like he needs to protect me from you for some godforsaken reason."

Adam laughed again, louder this time. He'd had a hand cupping Oliver's chest, feeling his pulse race. He caressed downward, grabbing a handful of Oliver's bulge instead.

Oliver knocked the hand away. "Not yet." He took the roaming hand, weaving their fingers together, leaning back into Adam to feel the heat of him against his back. "He needs to know we're in charge. That he needs to obey. That he can trust us."

"Present a united front. Mom and Dad, laying down the law."

"Something like that. I'll take the lead though."

"Of course."

Rune was in the shower, suds sliding down his wet, inked body. He rolled his head on his shoulders, the tension leaving his body.

"Doesn't seem to mind the voyeurism."

"Mmm."

After the shower, Rune started to use the douching bulb. He filled it with water, squirted it up his ass, and waited before letting it out again. Craning his neck to look in all corners of the room, he soon spied both hidden cameras, staring steadily into one, then the other.

When he'd finished and flushed, he washed his hands again, mostly using the left to soap up the right. After patting it dry, he wound some gauze around the knuckles, taping it in place, ripping off pieces with his teeth.

"He should keep icing it," Adam said.

Oliver glanced back at him and said nothing.

"Are you even capable of doing this?" Adam asked, an edge coming into his voice.

"Yes! Fuck," Oliver replied, knowing he sounded defensive but unable to do anything about it.

"Are you sure?"

He shot him a look of warning, then shook his head, muttering under his breath, "Hate when you get like this."

"I'm always like this," Adam answered calmly, not backing down. "It's why I'm here in the first place, right?"

Oliver didn't say anything to that, either.

Adam's prodding caused Oliver to think of all the times he'd helped Jackson work through his stress. The mental load of responsibility for his patients' lives, and the lives of his family weighed so heavily. It's why he came to Oliver to find ways to let go. If he could do that for Jackson, he sure as hell could do it for Rune, who was only responsible for himself and his own actions. Though he seemed to feel responsible for taking down every violent bigot he encountered, Oliver could show him how to let go of that too, at least for a night. If anyone was capable of doing that, it was him.

"We can change plans. Make it quick and dirty. Exhaust him and let him sleep."

"No. We stick with the plan. It's a good one."

He felt Adam looking at him, scrutinizing, measuring. "You still think you're losing him."

It was a knot in his chest, a rising panic that never quite bubbled over. Oliver avoided eye contact and watched eagerly as Rune headed out into the bedroom.

"I have him tonight."

Chapter 16
The Scene

Bracing himself for a lecture, Rune went into his bedroom. Oliver and Adam weren't there yet. Were they there at all? His skin tingled with the sense of being watched, something he'd learned to rely on over the past year. It helped him realize if someone was trying to talk to him or not. So yes, he did think they were there, somewhere.

Maybe they were too angry to face him.

A bench sat in the middle of the open space next to the bed. It was BDSM furniture like the kind he'd seen at Manse, though he'd never encountered any before in daily life. The bench was slightly raised on one end and was padded with leather.

Rune didn't want to fight. He didn't want to explain. He just wanted to feel connected to something, so he'd stop floating, get anchored. Unless he was touching or being touched, he wondered if all the world was a fantasy playing out in his head on mute. Nothing was real. He hated it.

There was a small side table against the wall by the door. He grabbed it and set it by the bench, then placed the bowl of ice on top.

He knelt at the bench and eased his throbbing fingers into the ice once more. The bandage was an effort to disguise the ugliness of the wounds rather than serve any other purpose. He didn't care if it got wet.

For a second, he was back in the lot. Max and Goat were holding Kurt Radner by the hair and the shoulders. Kurt had been bound. He'd been kneeling too. Lips moved, spittle flew, hate burned in blue eyes. Rune had caught a word here or there—like 'cocksucker'—even though he hadn't really been trying to lip-read.

Even though he'd been surrounded by riled men, it had been so still. The connection of impact the only thing grounding him, so he chased it, kept finding it.

He'd changed his shirt at the clubhouse, tossed the bloodstained one into his old closet bedroom.

Couldn't change his torn skin, though. He knew punishment was coming.

He was ready.

Leaning down over the bench, he relaxed into the pose, even though he was totally naked, ass up, his back to the door. It took some effort, especially since Adam was there, and Rune didn't know what to make of him yet. He'd sensed Adam would always be on Oliver's side first, above all, and it wasn't clear how that translated for Rune.

There were no footsteps to track, no warning of approach. The room was lit and not the hall, so no shadows moved over the wall. It was nothing but still air, and then—out of nowhere—a touch slid over the back of his thigh.

He flinched, gripped the bench with his left hand.

A tablet was set down and propped up on the same little table as the bowl of ice, the screen turned to face him.

A message popped up:

Are you ready?

He nodded, closed his left hand into a fist and rotated it up and down, keeping his wrist stationary.

Show me your safe sign.

He folded down all of his fingers except for his pinkie and thumb.

Rune glimpsed Oliver, turning his head to manage it, seeing only his chest, hips, and legs. Oliver gripped Rune's shoulder for a minute, hesitating.

He thought, this is when it'll happen. Oliver will call it off. Kick me out.

But, he didn't. He removed the wrapped hand from the bowl, feeling the joints, the bones of his fingers, the center of his hand and wrist. Rune waited. No sharp pains flared. Seemingly satisfied, Oliver set the hand back in the ice and let him go.

Oliver dried his hand on a towel, then caressed from the nape of Rune's neck, down his spine to the curve of his ass. Slowly, Rune let himself begin to believe he wasn't going to be rejected and abandoned for what he'd done. There was always the possibility, remote as it seemed, that Oliver just wanted to hurt him before sending him packing.

The caressing hand twisted, questing between Rune's legs and taking hold of his sac. Oliver nudged Rune's legs farther apart on the bench, pulled on his scrotum. A flare of want washed over him, heating him up from inside.

There was pressure, a tug. The tugging didn't stop. It was steady in a strange way, so he tried to move.

He let out a cry he couldn't hear as his movement yanked at his balls. He'd been shackled by then to the bench, with barely any slack. The realization made his face flush. He bit at his lip to keep quiet.

Something dangled in his field of vision.

A collar on a chain.

He was tempted then, to look up at Oliver's face. His guilt and desire to please kept him from doing it.

He pushed slightly up from the top of the bench as Oliver wrapped the leather around Rune's throat and connected the chain to a bolt on the bench. Rune wasn't going anywhere.

The proof that Oliver intended to keep him awhile evened Rune's breathing. He fought a smile.

There was no sign of Adam. The prickling at the base of Rune's neck remained, but he saw no evidence of the other Dom in the room. Trying to figure out if Adam's role would be a passive one, Rune was surprised by the touch of something cool to his crease. It didn't feel like any toy he'd seen before. It was pointed on the end and had a strange, uneven texture. It was pushed through his rim, the pointed end tapering to a thickness that tested him almost right away, especially without prep or lube. It was about three inches inside him, held steady there, his butt clenched up around it, when he started to feel something new.

He grunted, hid his face, felt his breathing quicken. He gripped the bench as the burning swelled, coating the inside of his ass, climbing up into his gut. Maybe they'd dipped the plug in hot sauce before stuffing it inside him. That's what it felt like. A gloved hand turned his face to the side again, so it was visible, and was firmly held there for study as the thing inside him began to push deeper.

Reflex kicked in, and he started to fight, but even the slightest movement pulled agonizingly at his sac, so he couldn't even writhe. Panic swelled, sweat breaking out over his whole body. He might have been grunting. He could have been screaming.

A message popped up on the screen.

It's ginger. It won't injure you. The pain is all in your head. Relax.

Adam. It was Adam reassuring him.

Rune forced himself to take a deep breath and blow it out. He closed his eyes, stopped fighting the bondage, but couldn't stop clenching on the ginger even when he wanted to. Oliver pushed it even deeper, and the root swelled thicker than ever. Then it narrowed rapidly, locking in place inside him.

A noise of terror escaped him, uncensored, unknown. He trembled, couldn't stop. He took a handful of the ice just to counter the pain of heat with the pain of cold. The hand on his head combed through his hair, soothing.

A gloved hand took hold of his softened cock, stroking it to hardness, and he didn't want it, but he didn't fight. All he wanted was that thing out of him. He pushed down on it with his inner muscles, but it did no good. Clenching only made the burning worse.

Now, it wasn't just hot sauce. It felt like a red-hot poker, like he was being burned alive from inside out.

He saw the blond skinhead on his knees, the smashed ruin of his nose, the blood-soaked teeth, smiling.

Maybe Rune deserved it. For scaring Oliver. For seeking out others in order to hurt them, to make them pay. For the arrogance of taking judgment into his own hands.

He sniffled, felt tears slipping from his eyes and didn't know if it was from being upset at what he'd done or from the burning pain. Oliver brushed the tears away, but pushed Rune's head down when he tried to turn it again. Oliver wasn't allowing that. He wanted to see.

Rune searched the tablet's screen, the room—anything—for a clock, a watch. There was nothing. No way to track it. It seemed to go on forever. Oliver kept stroking him, stirring lust even as the torment grew. Rune didn't adjust to the burn. It only compounded on itself.

He was still crying; knew he would have been ashamed of the sounds he was making if he could hear them.

The strange thing was, he was hard. Staying perfectly still, he liked and invited each slow tug at his dick from root to tip, even while wanting to claw at his own flesh to get that fucking thing out of his ass.

And then it moved. Was being withdrawn. But Oliver was already touching him in two places.

Control slipped away again, fast. Hands held him down in three places while the ginger root was withdrawn. It pulled free, leaving the burning behind. But then the root was rubbed up through his crack and he panicked, bucked, hurt himself and felt the pain climb down into his balls too.

There was a new message on the screen. How long had it been there?

Do you accept your punishment?

He stared at the words, let everything else fall away. He gave up struggling and just lay there, panting. His eyes traced the loop of the P, the curl of the U, the point of the I. When the ginger pushed back into him, began fucking him in a gentle rhythm, he didn't resist, but couldn't help his shuddering. He pulled against the binding on his scrotum just enough to distract himself with the pain there, which was fuller, broader and less sharp. He pulled his right hand out of the bowl of melting ice and flipped off both Doms.

The ginger began moving in longer strokes, riding him. Fingers rubbed in a circle around his rim, the flames climbing out to cover him there, too.

But that's when he realized, it wasn't even about the pain. He'd had worse. He'd lain broken and alone on asphalt, bloody from head to toe.

The real bitch of it was the shame. The helplessness. This was something he couldn't fight against, or undo, or decide to stop. There was the safe sign, but using it would only compound an already monstrous level of humiliation. Because he wasn't weak. He wouldn't give anyone the satisfaction of breaking him to that level again. Even Oliver.

He climbed back into his head, detaching, receding. It was a defense mechanism, but it worked. He lost track. The sharp edge of agony dulled.

Even when his head was taken between two hands, his mouth stuffed with a cock that slid over his tongue and into his throat, he didn't fully return. Gradually, he felt something else. Fingers. They were wet. Everywhere they touched, cooled.

Moaning, he wanted to push back onto them, and couldn't do that either. Recognizing Oliver's scent and feel, Rune finally came back. He started to suck, using his tongue, swallowing Oliver's taste. Just when he was really getting into it, loving the way Oliver pushed deep enough into Rune's throat to scare him, cutting off his air, testing his gag reflex, he pulled out. The hands that held his head moved, spreading his ass instead.

He waited, anticipating.

Something entered him, but it went deeper than a cock should have been able to. A desperate groan erupted in his chest. Goosebumps spread over his skin. Twelve inches of silicone-shaped phallus took him in slow, complete strokes and even if he wasn't bound, he wouldn't have dared to move. He stared at Oliver's bare hip, felt Oliver's fingers digging in to pull Rune's hole as open as he could, and wished for a gag because it felt fucking amazing and it was really embarrassing how much he loved it. He even loved the way the burn remained, spicing the pleasure.

Praying thanks for his limited senses, he knew he was too exhausted to fight the pleasure too. He willingly fell another rung on the pride ladder, urging Adam on with each stroke with his cries alone.

Oliver let go, moved to fill Rune's mouth again. Hungry for it, impatient, Rune chased Oliver's cock with his tongue, opening wide, humming with happiness as the crown pushed deep, lodging in his throat. Reflex kicked in, his body struggling with the obstruction. Fingers combed his hair back, caressed his jaw and neck. Pulling back, Oliver let him take a desperate breath then pushed back inside, choking him again. The whole time, Adam fucked Rune with the obscenely long toy. It was narrow but endless like a snake. It made his legs feel so weak, he was glad for the bench, certain he wouldn't have been able to hold himself up without it.

Taken at both ends, he lost himself in it. But Oliver came before long, unloading over Rune's tongue. Swallowing the salty, tangy come, Rune sucked him through the aftershocks.

Oliver pulled out, let Rune collapse down to the bench, panting.

The chain on the collar was released, then the one fastened to a leather cuff around his sac was freed, too. Fingers rubbed his rim as the toy withdrew completely. A warm body moved up behind him, skin on skin.

Frowning, pleading, he pushed back into the contact and onto the wet cock that breached him. He didn't care about anything but getting fucked by an actual person. He needed nothing else. The contact, the connection, the safety of it, the ways he'd been affected inside and out, it was the realest moment he'd had in a year.

There was a firm thrust, a hot, hard body at his back, and teeth bit down on his neck. He reached back, found a handful of hair and tugged on it, pulling the mouth against his skin, rocking back into the next thrust.

He cursed, begged, couldn't stay still. He bounced back onto the cock stuffing him, needing it. His erection strained, dripping. A hand caressed his balls, palmed his stomach as the cock thrust inside him. A palm rubbed up to his chest and fingers teased his stiffened nipple.

Delirious, Rune glanced up. Oliver stood there, stroking himself.

Feeling utterly undone, Rune turned his head, the collar pulling tight. Red hair fell in his eyes. It smelled like coconut and was soft as silk. He found Adam's mouth, opened for the tongue licking into him, forcing his jaws wide. Rune rotated his hips, grinding on Adam. Teeth nipped at his lip, and a harder thrust knocked the wind from him. Hands held him down while Adam straightened, pounding Rune's hole until he climaxed, then slowly rocked inside him.

Tingling from head to toe, dazed, boneless, aching everywhere—inside, out, hands, legs, knees, ass, stomach, balls—he let himself be moved. He was pulled to his feet, walked to the bed. Adam climbed on, his dark red hair tumbling into his blue eyes, his chest covered in thick red curls that stretched down his navel to gather at the root of his cock. Rune was pulled down with him, made to lay back on the soft fur on Adam's chest. Adam's hands hooked under Rune's knees, pulling them back and spread apart as far as they'd go, testing his flexibility. Rune's wet, throbbing, curled hand, chilled from the ice, rested on the bed. He tracked Oliver intensely, not even blinking, as he spread lube on his dark, heavy erection and climbed onto the bed.

The sight of him was so welcome, Rune felt his helpless smile and reached for Oliver with his good hand, needing to touch him. The hand curled behind Oliver's neck, the fingers twining in his dark hair. Oliver entered him with a complete thrust, bottoming out hard. Rune arched, his head fallen back against Adam's shoulder, his chest heaving. His ass was in torment—swollen from overuse, sensitive from the endless fucking and from the ginger. Sex had never felt so good or hurt so much.

Oliver's lube-slicked hand found Rune's cock and Rune pleaded with him, convulsing at the first skimming touch. Adam held him down, kept him spread, his lips pressed against the side of Rune's temple. Oliver stared deeply into Rune's eyes, pinning him down in more profound ways, and rode him gently. As his fist twisted on Rune's cock, they both held him trapped between them as he climaxed, shooting hot over Oliver's hand. Rune pleaded more fervently, but Oliver stayed a breath away, his lips barely skimming Rune's, stealing his air as he shivered.

When Rune was past it, Oliver finally kissed him. Rune wrapped himself around him, kissing back passionately enough that Oliver had to fight to take control again. Soon, he was panting against Rune's lips, rocking more slowly against him, holding him by the jaw to be kissed for a long time.

As he laid on Adam who caressed his legs, and was engulfed in Oliver who had him inside and out, Rune felt them suddenly grow still. Saw Oliver catch Adam's gaze, Oliver's hazel eyes wet and bloodshot.

Rune's hand had been pressed against Oliver's chest, all of his fingers extended except his ring and middle fingers.

Oliver cupped his hand against the sign for 'I love you', whispering unheard words against Rune's ear, a ghost of secrets. Then he kissed Rune, and it tasted salty. His thumb brushed Rune's lip. Oliver searched his eyes. Rune's hand held where it was, as it was.

Between them, Oliver's ring and middle fingers curled down too, his right hand pressed against Rune's chest the same way.

Letting out a sigh, Rune looped his right arm behind Oliver's neck and felt an anchor drop inside him, pinning him down like an unbreakable tether.

Chapter 17
Secrets

Oliver brought breakfast in bed. Adam had left a few hours ago, making Oliver promise to call soon. Even though he'd showered the night before, Rune went for a second one as soon as he was awake while Oliver prepared the food. Rune climbed back in bed, his hair dripping, once he'd finished.

Rune picked at a piece of toast while Oliver examined Rune's hand yet again before bandaging it for him. It didn't look swollen, and the wounds weren't deep. Rune insisted there was no sharp pain or stiffness, but Oliver still felt they should go for an x-ray, just in case.

Relax, Rune signed, smiling gently.

He waited while Oliver wrapped fresh gauze around, then reached for the large pad of paper and pen at the bedside. He wrote, then passed it over.

> *Tell me more about Adam. I've seen you touch. Kiss. Were you together once?*

Oliver looked at the looped letters and settled down on his stomach, propped on his elbows. Rune laid down beside him, caressing Oliver's back with his newly tended hand, pressing kisses to Oliver's arm and shoulder.

Oliver wrote, *No. It's complicated.*

Rune took the pen, added: *Tell me? Please?*

Oliver groaned, averted his eyes. Rune's fingers played at the back of his neck, tickling with their gentle movements over his skin.

The explanation was one he'd never had to make, except to Jackson, long ago and in pieces, gradually. Not all at once, not written down. But he'd already shared Rune with Adam. Rune deserved to have his questions answered.

He turned his head to look at Rune dead-on and said slowly, over enunciating, "It doesn't matter anymore."

Rune just kept watching him expectantly.

Sighing, Oliver picked up the pen.

121

We'd known each other forever. Since we were kids. It was never sexual. Sure, he was hot, but he was Adam. It just never occurred to me.

Rune plucked the pen from his hand.

So Adam started it?

Oliver nodded.

You seem uncomfortable.

Oliver took the pen back.

He's the one who took it there.

Rune raised an eyebrow, pulling a face that seemed to call out Oliver's defensiveness.

We were in college. Had just started training at Manse as Doms. Adam's parents had just been killed. He was looking for comfort.

Oliver remembered staying over at Adam's place all the time, keeping him company. They shared rides so Adam didn't have to be alone whether going to the university or to Manse. Oliver had his own room at Adam's new apartment. One night, Adam had slipped into Oliver's bed after he'd shut off the light, his textbook shut on the nightstand after studying for three hours straight. Adam had only been wearing underwear. Oliver had been in pajama pants.

Oliver had asked, "What are you doing?"

"Nothing," Adam said, sliding closer.

They'd been seeing each other naked frequently at Manse, which had added a strange twist to their previously normal friendship. That night, Adam had lingered to watch a submissive suck off Oliver rather than go to find one of his own.

He started to pay more attention during training. Watching me with subs. He's always been into watching.

That night, in bed, Adam had rolled toward Oliver, who lay on his back, and touched his chest, rolling his thumb over his nipple.

"I don't think we should do this," Oliver had warned. "It'll make things weird."

"Do what?" Adam asked, holding Oliver's gaze as he slid his hand down, under the sheet and inside Oliver's pants, going right for his dick. Feeling Adam's hand on it had been a shock to Oliver's system. It hadn't been hesitant or nervous at all, and from the first moment, Oliver knew he was screwed, fighting a losing battle. He hadn't been willing to do anything to hurt Adam's already sensitive feelings, but he also knew it was up to him to help Adam in whatever ways he could. There had been so much numbness and emotion. He'd found Adam locked in bathrooms, or smashing furniture by throwing it against walls. Adam always only seemed angry or dead inside. This though, was something new.

Adam's fingers curled around the shaft, picking it up, rubbing the head. Oliver's breath caught, a shiver working through him, the urge to knock the hand away really strong.

Adam kept fondling him and stared at him without looking away, which made it impossible for Oliver to engage in eye contact.

I was staying with him at the time. Keeping him company. He came into my room one night, after I'd been studying for hours. Got into bed with me. I knew it was a terrible idea. He was only doing it because he was upset and lonely.

As Adam fondled his best friend, the minutes dragged out, and Oliver remembered Adam's endless patience. Adam gathered up Oliver's sac, rolling his balls. Staring at the ceiling, biting his tongue, Oliver felt the first twitch of his dick against Adam's hand.

Adam pulled his hand out of Oliver's pants. He threw back the sheet, got up on his knees, took hold of Oliver's pajama pants with both hands and yanked them down to his ankles.

Oliver had told him, "Adam, I'm not your boyfriend."

Adam chuckled. "You think I'm an idiot?" He grabbed the lube from the drawer in the nightstand, squirted a handful on his palm, spread it around. He wrapped the hand around Oliver's dick and began tight, squelching tugs, lube dribbling between his fingers. "When's the last time you had a relationship?"

Never was the answer, but Oliver didn't trust his voice to speak. There was something dirty and wrong about letting Adam strip him and jerk him off that was making Oliver hard. In just a few squeezes, he was fully erect.

Smiling triumphantly, Adam played with it, pressing it down to make Oliver groan, knocking it back and forth, playing with the slit in a way that made Oliver's legs turn to jelly.

"You're alone. I'm alone. And I know what you like now."

Adam laid down over him, licking Oliver's bottom lip, angling to open him up wide, inhaling Oliver's heavy breaths.

It was just hand release and kissing, but it felt like a total mind fuck. You have to understand, I'd lost my virginity at the age of fourteen. I'd been having sex regularly for many years. It wasn't anything new, except it was. It was Adam.

Adam had played with him until he was right on the edge, his balls drawn up, ready to shoot, and then he stopped.

Adam climbed on top of him, straddling him, giving Oliver the deepest, dirtiest kiss Oliver had ever experienced, while masturbating. Maybe Oliver had just wanted it over, or maybe he'd just succumbed like Adam knew he would, but Oliver reached for Adam's dick. It had been like an out of body experience to jerk Adam off for the first time. Adam fucked his hand and came fast, shooting over Oliver's stomach. Then he'd leaned down and licked it all up with wide swipes of his tongue while slowly tugging Oliver to completion. Adam had opened his mouth to catch some of it, panting, and had rested his head against Oliver's chest briefly before getting up and leaving without another word.

You know what he's like. It kind of spiraled after that. The next week, during training, David bound and fucked me in the dungeon and I think it made Adam crazy to witness that. They were training us together, simultaneously, to work together and separately. They chained Adam to the wall, gagged, while David broke me. It was to show me what true helplessness felt like. It was consensual, but Adam hated it.

Rune wrote, *I can imagine. He loves you.*

Oliver had been lucky to get Adam out of there before he could deck David or one of his guards. They'd gone straight back to Adam's place. Oliver had been sore, exhausted. Adam gave him a few tall glasses of whiskey, massaged his shoulders as they watched a movie together on the couch.

Then the movie ended. Adam shut off the TV, knelt in front of Oliver, spread his legs, opened his pants, yanked them down and off. It was dark, and Oliver was drunk, but he still remembered the hungry look on Adam's face as he took his best friend's cock into his mouth for the first time. He'd taken his time, coaxing Oliver hard, sucking him down to the root. The slurping and moaning sounds from Adam had seemed way too loud to

Oliver, and way more obscene than the feel of the suction and silky rubbing of Adam's lips and the soft grip of his tongue on Oliver's cock. It sobered him up, fast.

Then Adam had started rubbing Oliver's swollen hole, which had caused things to turn a corner for him. He'd stopped watching, started to push up into each suck, his hand on the back of Adam's head to guide his pace. Which was when Adam fed two fingers through Oliver's rim, reaching for his gland and massaging it as he kept sucking.

Oliver had barely been able to breathe. It was the best blow job he'd ever gotten. He came down Adam's throat, then lay there, spread, letting Adam finger him while masturbating and licking at Oliver's balls.

Rune wrote one word, then underlined it. *What?*

Oliver gave him the cliff's notes version, not sure how to convey how confused it had made him feel, like he didn't know who he was anymore, or who Adam was, or who they were to each other.

But maybe Rune saw something in his face, because he responded:

I'm sorry. He shouldn't have done that. He just thought it was the best way to keep from losing you. He must have been so scared.

Oliver pushed the pad away, covering his head with his hands, breathing against the bedspread. The numbness was really strong. Rune kissed his neck and hugged him.

They laid there a while. Oliver marveled again at how easy it was to talk to someone who would never hear a word he said.

Eventually, Rune wrote: *Tell me the rest. I need to know this.*

Oliver accepted the pen from Rune and started writing.

It kept happening. It was a regular thing. He'd come to bed, or into the shower with me, or do it in the back of the car we'd hired. Blow jobs. He never asked me to suck him. And I never did. I don't know why I let him. I mean, they were incredible, but they were so fucking confusing, because otherwise we were still just friends. He still brought guys home. I still dated or hooked up. We used protection with others but not with each other. It got to the point where just looking at his lips could make me hard. And as soon as I was hard, he could tell. He sucked me in his studio, in the office while I was trying to study, in the kitchen, at his grandfather's estate when we visited for the holidays.

And one day, I just couldn't take it anymore. We were in bed. He stared at my cock from the moment he walked through the door, the only thing on his mind, I guess. I wasn't me to him anymore. I was just my dick. I was like a human fucking pacifier. And I was so, so angry at him for debasing me like that, for making me only good for that. That one thing.

He stopped writing, breathing harder, face flushed with shame. He felt Rune tighten his embrace, peppering kisses down his cheek.

He got in bed, started to shift down, leaning over me. I pushed him down, manhandled him onto his stomach, got on top of him, held him down. Fuck.

Rune took hold of Oliver's hand holding the pen, setting it back on the paper, demanding more.

I pushed until I was inside him, and then I needed to puke. So I pulled out, ran for the bathroom, locked the door.

I stayed in there for an hour, feeling like I was going to die. Like I was going to jump off the fucking balcony.

When I came out he was sitting there with his hands folded. He came over and hugged me. Told me he was sorry.

A couple of days later, he met Italo. They became a steady thing. It was the last time. We still kiss. Touch. That's it. It's hard to talk about.

Rune asked, taking the pen from him:

Do you think he'll ever do it again? Need you like that?

Of course, Oliver answered. *Sometimes I miss it.*

Maybe you should be together.

Oliver stared at him, rolled over. Shook his head vehemently. "No." Drew Rune into an embrace, pulling him against his chest, cupping a hand behind his head. "No."

Rune got on top of him. Oliver spread his legs, wrapping them behind him, offering his neck for Rune to kiss. His soft lips made a trail of them, down to Oliver's chest, down to his navel, down to his cock where Rune kissed the root, the shaft, the tip. Then he wrapped his lips around the head to suck a deeper kiss, licked the drip of pre-come away, opened and let Oliver slide back into his mouth.

When his fingers found Oliver's opening, teasing it, Oliver surrendered control. The need for power that fueled him and all of his balance slipped right through his fingers—a bolt of silk, yanked away. Giving over to need, he pressed down for more, thrust harder into Rune's sweet mouth, quivered and let out a deep moan as Rune's fingers entered him, searching for his gland.

Feeling frantic, Oliver rode it out, but Rune was still so calm, strong. He got up on his knees, sucking mostly on the tip, massaging Oliver's sweet spot to milk him like an expert. Oliver was happy to not have to filter any of his cries for modesty. He just kept caressing Rune's jaw, hooking a hand behind his ear, tugging at his black hair. When Oliver was about to come, Rune took every inch of him down his throat and Oliver growled, "Fuck..." as he shot, convulsing, giving Rune every last drip.

Rune was slow to release him, but Oliver wasn't done. He lunged sideways, opened a drawer, rolled onto his back again and passed Rune the lube.

Raising his eyebrows, Rune's surprised expression asked, *Are you sure?*

Oliver nodded, waved him on. Intuition hinted that maybe Oliver's trepidation concerning Rune would settle faster if there was a more even exchange of give and take between them. If Oliver demonstrated just how much he trusted Rune, hopefully Rune would keep trusting in him just as much. Oliver wanted to own Rune, but he didn't want to set any limits on the ways they could love each other, either.

Not wasting another second, Rune used the lube, lined up and entered Oliver like he'd just been waiting for permission since the first moment they'd met. A change came over him, his body strong, his rolling thrusts confident, his pleasure evident in the gasp of his mouth and the intoxicating moans coming from him.

Oliver wound his legs around him, pulling Rune's ass in tighter, holding him by the back of the head to be kissed whenever he had the breath to do it. It ached but in the best way, and he knew he had to be tight. It had been years since he'd last bottomed for anyone. The delirious roll of Rune's eyes and the frustration in his groans told Oliver as much too. Rune came quickly, panting, whimpering once while trying to bury his face against Oliver's neck.

Rune's arms wrapped around Oliver's back, and he held there, inside him, just breathing, for a long time.

Chapter 18
Y-E-S-M-A-S-T-E-R

Rune knew the tutor was due to arrive at ten. Oliver had told him he planned to split his day between ASL lessons and working, getting some trading done to get back into things after a month's hiatus. He delivered breakfast to Rune's bedroom on a tray after Rune didn't emerge on his own although Oliver knew him to be awake.

Rune had been busy when Oliver popped in. After signing his thanks, he went right back to typing on the laptop he was borrowing.

It wasn't long after that when Jackson arrived. Or, at least, that's what Rune assumed. He had no way to tell yet if someone was at the door like he had with his old closet room. But Oliver had been so impatient to have Jackson look at Rune's hand, he didn't think he'd delay the exam any longer than necessary.

Luckily, Rune was just finishing his report, and had sent it to the printer right before the door opened and the stern pair entered.

Jackson had a series of index cards in his hand. He held them up one at a time. They were written out in a surprisingly legible script in black Sharpie.

> *Do you have any pain in the hand?*

Rune shook his head. The card got shuffled to the back of the stack, the next revealed.

> *Did you have any pain last night? During the incident or immediately after?*

Again, Rune shook his head.

> *Any significant stiffness of movement?*

No, again. The next card read:

Are you being completely honest?

Thinking of the type of judgmental foresight that had gone into that question, Rune flipped him off with a subtle grin.

Do you realize the importance of protecting your hand from injury?

Rune promptly mimed jerking off.

Oliver was not amused. Jackson was unfazed. He came forward to where Rune sat on the bed, cross-legged. Taking hold of Rune's hand, he felt carefully around, watching Rune for any sign of pain. It was sore and his knuckles were just a little swollen now, but there were no other complaints. It hadn't been the first time he'd punched someone hard enough to break their nose, and it wouldn't be the last.

With his left hand, Rune pointed to the printer on a desk in the corner by the windows, where a page had spit out, the white sheet gleaming in a sunbeam. Oliver went to retrieve it. After he'd skimmed the first few lines, he said something to Jackson.

Jackson let go of Rune's hand and began to scribble out a new message on the back of a card with a Sharpie pulled from his pocket.

Please tell me if you experience any pain or it gets worse.

Rune held up the okay sign.

I'm doing online studies of ASL in my spare time. I'm hoping to pick it up quickly, but bear with me.

Rune smiled and fake-punched Jackson in the arm, which only got him a scowl and a waggling finger of warning. Hopefully they'd start to get his sense of humor soon, because it wasn't going anywhere.

Jackson walked over to Oliver and began reading over his shoulder.

As soon as he'd started to head to Oliver's place the night before, Rune had known he would need to explain what happened, but he was glad for the surprising reprieve that had lasted well into the following morning. Maybe there were some perks in not being able to verbally explain oneself.

The paper was a full report of what had gone down after Rune had left Oliver's place yesterday morning until he'd returned with a banged-up fist.

It started with a thanks for Oliver's patience and a promise that he wasn't trying to keep secrets or disobey any rules. The reliable presences in Rune's life had been few and far between enough for him to appreciate Oliver's support. Though they'd already discussed it, Rune had wanted to put it in writing that he intended to make Oliver, his Master, happy—no matter what that entailed. He did, however, intend to satisfy his drive to right the wrong done to him.

Oliver didn't get very far in his reading before he dropped the page, glaring over at Rune like he had a lot to say but not the skill to say it as immediately as he'd have liked. Then again, Rune knew sometimes it was better to have a minute or five to gather your thoughts before explaining why you were upset with someone or disagreed with their opinion.

Jackson grabbed the edge of the page, keeping it upright so he could keep reading. Oliver extended his wordless warning shaped only in the hard glisten of his eyes and the scary set of his lips, then kept reading too.

The morning had started for Rune with messages from Max and some of the other guys, letting him know about members of The White Lions getting arrested for throwing glass bottles at some kids. They told Rune—obliviously—how there had been witnesses describing a chase as the skinheads went after someone on a bike, and how the police had pieced the two incidents together after an anonymous tip messaged to them via Twitter.

Rune had expressed his (totally bullshit) surprise about the news to Max and the others—without letting on at all that the guy on the bike in said chase had been *him*—as well as his legitimate happiness that at least some of The White Lions were getting a taste of justice.

The arrests had riled the other Lions. Yesterday, a bunch of them were getting drunk and yelling things in the lot of their favorite bar, The Watering Hole, which was discreetly under watch by some of Rune's friends and an inside source at the bar itself.

It seemed only a matter of time before one or several broke off and went looking for fresh trouble.

When they did, The Born Soldiers planned to be ready to stop it.

But then nothing really happened, with the exception of one douchebag who kept boasting about hunting down the little fags and lesbos of the world—the new crop who thought their shit didn't stink—and laying the smack-down with some hard truths that the world would be better off without any of them in it.

The insider at the bar heard it all, relaying enough to get an ID. With the ID came proof. Evidence on public record, tying the guy to the skinheads. The same group that had gone after Rune.

So they suited up, leaving any identifying gear behind. Piling into a van led by a pair of bikes, they drove to the bar, and waited outside and down the road a bit, prepared to hang out as long as it took.

It had taken exactly two hours and ten minutes before the blond—a thirty-two-year-old janitor named Kurt Radner—had come out, staggering towards his blue 1994 Pontiac sedan with the bumper and fender missing and bald tires.

They had let Kurt drive a mile down the road, then had come up around him, cutting him off. By the time Rune had climbed out of the van, the others already had Kurt on his knees a few yards down a quiet, tree-lined side-road.

Rune wasn't privy to the run-down the others gave Kurt to explain why he was there, and that was just fine. Rune was there for one reason, and talking wasn't it.

Arms folded, Rune waited while Oliver and Jackson read.

The report ended with an admission that he understood Oliver would have a reaction to everything which would be slower coming than in a typical conversation. Rune was prepared to be patient while Oliver composed his thoughts, and promised to remain in the apartment until that time. He also promised that he was careful of both his hand and his identity. Everyone had been wearing masks, and had shown no identifying details, apart from Rune's rainbow tattoo. The last sentence told Oliver this wasn't going to be a regular thing, but it was something Rune needed to get out of his system.

Jackson finished reading first. He stalked over to Rune, a finger pensively to his lips as he fought back emotion and composed his thoughts. He was pissed, choking on words he knew Rune wouldn't hear.

Slowly shaping the words, Jackson got right in his face and said, "This isn't your job."

Rune considered not replying, but wound up pulling out his phone and typing:

> Protecting vulnerable people when I'm able is my job.

"You're not protecting. You're attacking!" Jackson replied. Or something like that. Rune wasn't the greatest lip reader of all time. It was the gist of his emotions, anyway. Closing his mouth, taking a deep breath, Jackson seemed to be trying to calm down. He pulled out his phone and typed:

> Next time, file a report with the police. Give them any evidence you have. Let them build a case and go after these guys. That's THEIR job.

Rune responded:

> *The police don't care about what happens to those kids like I do. We report what we can. But nothing the police can do will scare that fucker into laying off. We were careful. We just want them to know they can't get away with it anymore. That people are watching.*

Jackson rolled his eyes and gestured widely with his arms, then started typing some more.

> *You could just be making the skinheads madder. These aren't cool-headed, rational people. They lead with anger, hate & arrogance. You can't change that. Believe me. You need to protect yourself first!*

Rune signed okay. Holding up his hands in a gesture of surrender, he let Jackson win the argument.

Oliver was just standing there, staring at them. His face was unreadable. Something about the lack of response made Rune's pulse start to race and his stomach tie in knots. It would have been better if he'd been visibly angry like Jackson. The stone-faced stillness was so much worse.

A fresh shock of nausea helped Rune realize how much he did care what Oliver thought of him.

After climbing off the bed, Rune walked over to Oliver. Rune kept his head bowed, glancing up to try to maintain eye contact. More than anything, he wanted to reach out and get lost in Oliver's embrace again, where everything seemed safe and certain. The coldness of Oliver's glare put Rune off from trying. So instead he clasped his arms behind his back and dropped his gaze to the floor, using submissiveness as a peace offering.

The moment drew out.

Oliver hooked a finger under Rune's chin, forcing it up.

He signed three words: *Tutor. Soon. Stay.*

Rune finger-spelled: Y-E-S-M-A-S-T-E-R.

He'd barely finished the last letter before Oliver walked past him and left the room. Rune didn't see him again for hours.

"Hey Maggie. Remember that piece you did the beginning of June about the rise in racial tensions around the city, and the white power groups in particular? You don't still have your research on hand, do you?"

Oliver unlocked the car he used to use for scouting leads. It was an old Cadillac that blended in nicely with any surroundings, giving off none of the pompousness of Adam's bright blue Mustang, or even Oliver's black Jaguar. He drove the old Caddy once a month just to keep it from going entirely to shit, but other than that, he rarely used it anymore. Day trading didn't require as much stealth as journalism.

He loved that car too much to get rid of it, though. He'd spent hours upon hours scoping out stories, piecing together clues to form a tantalizing, shocking whole that would get served up for readers. He'd eaten breakfast, lunch and dinner inside it. He'd dozed off while stalking targets. He'd felt the rush of excavating truth in a world stuffed full of lies. The thrill had carried him through a couple of years until his priorities shifted. He never wrote off the possibility that he'd go back to it someday, so he kept the car.

It was coated in a fine layer of dust, but the key worked just fine and the engine turned over with a smooth purr like always.

"I know. I'm sorry for springing this on you, but it's important. One of the groups you investigated, The White Lions, have been really active lately. People have gotten hurt. If you're interested, I'll give you more details, just not today. Hit me up later. How's Steven, by the way? Pain in the ass as usual? If I wasn't such a fan of minding my own business, I'd try to talk you into moving on to someone new, who wouldn't shit all over your desire to make something of your life, but that's just me." He laughed. "Yeah, fuck you too. I know you missed me." He rifled through the glove compartment for a tablet of paper and pen. "Okay, shoot. Yeah, the main one. Yep. Weadley and what? Okay. Give me some back-ups too, just in case. Oh! Yeah, the bar on Dekalb I definitely need. Great. Thanks, Maggie. You're the best. Don't ever forget it. Yep. You too. Bye."

He hung up and had the GPS on his phone map the route, then cranked the volume so he'd hear every direction.

"Okay, you fuck-heads. Let's see what you're really up to, after one necessary detour."

Chapter 19
Needing to Be Needed

"Who the fuck is this guy? Hey! This is a private club!"

Oliver held up his hands, palms out, then signed as he spoke, "I'm here about Rune. I need to talk to Max. It's an emergency."

A bunch of the guys at the bar looked at each other blankly. One of them actually scratched his head. Another chugged his beer a little faster, muttering, "Shit."

A massive redhead big enough to make a linebacker piss his pants heaved himself off of a stool and said in the deepest baritone Oliver had ever heard, "Is the little guy okay?"

Oliver spotted Max walking forward, one of the others whispering in his ear as he walked. Waving, Oliver addressed the human mountain, "Yeah, Rune's fine for now. I'm trying to make sure it stays that way."

"Hey, Oliver," Max said, stepping up to him and extending a hand for Oliver to shake. Max's grip was dry and bone-crushingly strong. "What's the problem?"

Oliver glanced around, uncertain whether he should insist this stay a private conversation. "Can we talk somewhere less crowded?"

"Nope. No secrets here. Just tell me what's on your mind."

After a deep breath, Oliver widened his stance and stared Max down, not breaking eye contact once. "Do you know Rune's been going after The White Lions?"

"The hell do you mean, going after 'em? Yeah, we caught up with someone last night but—"

"Before last night. He led a bunch of 'em on a chase that got a few people arrested. But they got too close and Rune wound up with skin lacerations after someone started slashing at him with a knife. Then last night he showed up with bashed knuckles. It's become a pattern I need to stop."

"He don't know you're here, does he?" Max said softly, his eyes widening.

134

"No, but I wouldn't be here if I had a choice. I need you to be aware he's made this his mission. He wants to take these guys down, no matter the cost to himself. I need some support in changing his mind. He's already suffered permanent damage because of the Lions. I don't want him losing his life, too. Are we on the same page?"

Max frowned, cleared his throat and straightened up. "Yeah. I think we are." He shook his head, his gaze shifting sideways, focusing on something midair. "Always had a knack for sticking his head where it didn't belong. Never took no for an answer, that kid. Good heart, you know. Clear sense of the line carved out between the evil fucks of the world and the rest of us. But a little too reckless sometimes."

"What's this?" another Soldier asked, coming over, giving Oliver a long look before turning back to Max.

"Rune. He's been going after the Lions without any backup. Without telling us."

"What?! Why the hell would he be dumb enough to do something like that?"

"Cause he's pissed," Max said levelly. "Ain't no excuse. Oliver, I'm glad you told us. We'll have a talk with him. Set him straight. Assure him the guys can handle it together. Don't need to be a solo mission."

"Thank you. I'm not trying to deprive him of some vengeance, but I can't see him get hurt any more than he already is."

"Totally get it. I do. Don't sweat it, okay?"

"I already have your number, so I'll keep you posted if you do likewise, just where Rune is concerned. I'm not here to interfere in your business."

"You wanna see his room, while you're here? He ever tell you about it?"

"Sure. He hasn't told me much about this place. Just that he was staying here after he couldn't afford his apartment anymore. I'd love to see it."

"Follow me."

Max led him past the main room and bar, down a hall and around to a door. Max turned the knob, pushing the door open and switching the light on from the switch on the outside wall. "This is how we'd knock," he explained, flicking the switch a few times to cause a lamp to flash on and off. "A good amount of these boxes are his stuff. We cleared out a lot of the club's things to give him space, but he didn't really want a whole lot. Felt bad about sticking him in here, but it was all we had and he didn't ever complain."

Oliver gazed around the cramped quarters, the thin mattress on the roll-away cot, the dusty boxes and lack of daylight, imagining Rune living in such a place. No wonder he'd felt so hopeless there.

He also made a mental note about the light switch doorbell. He needed to set up something similar, and felt bad that he hadn't thought of it before.

There were a lot of boxes, which Rune had never asked to move to Oliver's place, like he was keeping one foot out the door. It gave Oliver a pang of unease and sadness, to know Rune didn't fully trust their relationship would last. Maybe that was the smart route, though. It hadn't been that long, really. But still...

"It's not what I expected," Oliver told Max.

"Yeah, it ain't much."

"Are you okay with keeping his things here a little longer?'

"Oh, yeah. Of course. It's his home now. We'd never keep him from it."

"Thank you." Oliver turned his back to it, not wanting to see it any longer. "I've got to get on the road, but I'll be in touch. Thanks for the help."

"No sweat. Take care of my boy, okay?"

"Absolutely."

Unease compelled Jackson to clean the kitchen. Rune sat at the counter on a stool, watching as Jackson hand-washed crystal tumblers and wiped down countertops. Whenever things were wrong, out-of-whack, disturbed, finding order was the only thing that calmed Jackson back down. He set pieces right. He diffused chaos. The work of it gave him instant peace. As long as he was moving, brainstorming, researching, studying, diagnosing, fixing, he was able to keep hold of hope that it would all turn out okay.

That's why Jackson understood why Rune did what he did—why he got on his bike and went after the monsters that hurt him. In different ways, they were both programmed with a deep-seated need to react to the unfairness of it all.

Before he was hit by that truck, Rune had a life. A whole life. A whole other identity. And some bastards with a hate hard-on decided he needed to die, just for being gay. Didn't know him. Didn't care. Just saw a person they could kill and get away with it, no problem.

Jackson knew the type. Anyone with a skin tone darker than cream did. Angry white assholes who thought they owned the world, just for being born in the skin-suit they wound up in. That they were God incarnate, able to cast judgment and choose who lived and died, who suffered, who begged for their life, just for being pale on the outside. Or having the 'right' religion, or sexual orientation, or political affiliation.

As a middle-class black kid who was seen by some of his white neighbors as nothing but a nigger, he knew what kind of darkness Rune had faced the day he'd been thrown over his bike, lying on the street with crucial parts of his skull broken beyond repair, just for wanting to go on a date with another man.

It was a lot to swallow. What could be done in the face of it? There was no un-making his injuries. He'd always be scarred. He might always be completely deaf. Of course he was furious. Of course he needed to react.

So he'd gone out there, hunting down evil, taking it on himself to clean up all of the shit he'd landed in.

Even if it killed him.

The balls of that. The sheer, glorious madness.

Maybe he'd gotten away with it so far in part because he was white. Or because he was crazy as hell.

Even if they somehow could trade places, trade bodies and lives, Jackson knew he didn't have it in him to go after men as fearlessly as Rune. Instinct only directed Jackson to work, to use his hands and his mind to make minor miracles out of order, medicine, and diligence.

Jackson felt it all settling across the span of his shoulders, heavy as a ton of rock. He set down the dishrag, planted his hands on the counter, and sighed.

When he looked up, Rune was still watching him like a hawk.

They stared at each other.

Without glancing away, Rune lifted his phone to show the screen and what was typed on it.

I'm glad he has you.

"Fuck."

Jackson felt it choking him and turned his back, blinking his eyes clear, running his hands over his mouth and leaning back against the counter.

He wished he was less observant, that he didn't see as much as he did.

Because it was painted right over that kid's face.

Rune was ready. He held on to nothing, no expectations. He took the good, the love, the moments of peace, but stayed ready. He was still lying on that road, even now, years later, waiting to bleed out. Waiting for his spirit to unknot and float away to somewhere better.

He was ready.

Rune walked around the counter, coming at Jackson slowly, stalking his pain.

"Fuck you, kid. For real," Jackson breathed, flipping him off half-heartedly, wiping his eyes dry, hating all of it. Rune got closer and Jackson glimpsed the bandage covering bashed knuckles, and the other covering thirteen stitches in his forearm from getting attacked with a knife, and the bright gleam in his dark eyes willing more, inviting it even.

He came into Jackson's personal space. Jackson shoved him off, pushing at his shoulder. Rune paused, came again.

Jackson shoved harder, seeing in memory the pain in Oliver's face from that morning, how this kid—this fucking kid—had the man Jackson loved as much as his wife in a cage. But the cage was in water and every step Rune took away from safety caused the water level to rise higher. Oliver was drowning. Doomed.

Because of this fucking kid.

And what the hell could Jackson do about it?

Nothing.

"FUCK!" Jackson screamed, his hands clawing at his head, curling forward.

Arms wrapped around him, drawing him into the embrace. Rune fit himself easily against Jackson, his smaller body tucking perfectly against Jackson's chest, his head resting against Jackson's shoulder. His fucking hands caressed Jackson's back soothingly.

Jackson held on too. He had to. It was a need from the core of his soul. He held on hard enough to bruise, breathing that kid's scent, pressing his lips to Rune's dark, soft hair. Keeping Rune's slim body flush against him like he could do it forever and keep him safe like that endlessly.

But there was no saving Rune, so there was no saving Oliver.

It was beyond him. Way beyond.

But he also felt how none of it kept him out. He was in it too.

The way Rune held on and comforted him said as much. They way Oliver had taken Jackson's hand before he'd left, and squeezed it like he needed the proof of Jackson's steadiness before he could take another step—that did as well.

Jackson wasn't stupid. He knew this was what Oliver had craved. What he'd chased as hard as Rune chased his attackers.

Needing to be needed.

And he was. Oh, how he was needed.

Rune pulled back just enough to look up into Jackson's eyes. He was so damned young. Wide-eyed. Clear-headed, like he'd never been confused in his life. Jackson cupped a hand against Rune's jaw, touched the soft curve of his lip, and just pleaded without words.

Not even for a specific thing. Just for all of it.

He prayed to Rune like he was some sort of God, too.

Rune smiled a little, infusing it with optimism Jackson didn't feel. He stretched up onto his toes and gently kissed Jackson's lips.

He laid a hand over Jackson's heart, caressing a little with his thumb, patting him.

And then Rune said, "Have a little faith, okay?"

Jackson stared at Rune's lips, at his thick eyelashes concealing his downturned gaze, and thought maybe he'd hallucinated the words he'd just heard.

Or maybe they were just another minor miracle.

He caressed Rune's jaw, his lips, took hold of his chin, turning it up and kissing him hard. Then he gathered Rune up in his arms, groaning. The soft tumble of his hair tickled the side of Jackson's neck and Jackson thought he'd hold on just a little longer. He held on the way he couldn't hold on to his dying patients, and everything else that kept getting away from him. Rune settled comfortably into the hug and let out a sigh.

When Rune finally pulled back, just a little, Jackson told him, "Oliver was right." He realized how much he needed what he'd found in Rune, in ways that didn't have a damn thing to do with anyone else. How he was the wildcard of life, incarnate, proving to Jackson over and over how he couldn't always have his precious order, and how that was okay too. How sometimes the reasons for pain and hardship were bigger than any one man, and how, in the end, when all debts were settled, the ride was well-worth the fear. "Kid, you're scary as hell," he said with a fearsome expression that got Rune to smile. He held up his hand, folded in a combination of the letters I, L, and Y. "But I love ya for it."

Chapter 20
Winging It

Oliver was paying for the tutor—same one he used himself sometimes, in addition to all of his other learning resources. The online tutorials. The friends of friends. Oliver was into diversifying. Rune respected him for it. Why get something from one source when you could get it from a dozen?

The tutor was helping Rune with the nuances of lip-reading to improve his ability to do it, and helping him catch up and expand his studies in ASL, enhancing his vocabulary. The piecemeal way Rune had initially learned how to communicate needed a little smoothing out. He'd learned a lot online, and had used MeetUp.com to connect with his neighbors in the local deaf community and do things in more of a one-on-one way. The human touch had helped a lot, but everyone had lives. They couldn't make teaching him their job.

The tutor, however, could.

Rune appreciated the guy—Mr. Hannover was his name. Older guy with an amazing, white, bushy beard and hands that flew through the air quicker than you'd believe. He was nice enough, and patient, and thorough. The lessons were helping for sure.

But sometimes Rune had other places to be. It was nothing personal. And he had no way to explain in a way that would satisfy.

When Jackson went to make a pit stop in the bathroom, Rune scrawled a message on a pad of paper, then left it on the floor just outside the bathroom.

Reschedule for me, yeah?

Then he took off, grabbing his bag, his jacket, and palming the keys to the bike. He slipped out the door and was gone.

The Watering Hole wasn't much to look at. The high, narrow windows were mostly obscured with neon signs advertising beer. The largest was the blue outline of a woman's torso in a bikini with Coors written across her stomach. Pickup trucks and some motorcycles filled the gravel lot. Everyone Oliver could see going in and out, or smoking by the door, was lily white and most were tattooed. They were subtle about it—a patch here, a tattoo there, and some bumper stickers slapped on grimy windows. But he'd been watching these kinds of guys longer than he'd known Rune. He recognized the pseudo-Nazi symbols, the skinhead trademarks and Klan references. There wasn't an overt swastika in sight, but there didn't need to be.

They didn't look dangerous or riled, but it was early.

The bar itself was located on a curve of the road. On the other side was nothing but a field run through with a snaky creek, decorated with an obnoxious billboard advertising a hunting store a few miles down the way. On the huge sign, a gigantic goose had taken flight and a man in orange squared his rifle in preparation for the shot to take it down.

"Charming," Oliver sighed, giving the board the side-eye before scanning the bar's lot again.

He'd been feigning car trouble, parking just down the road a little and milling around the opened hood. Now, he pretended to be on a call and walked closer to the bar, taking his time with his cell phone pressed to his ear.

There wasn't a plan, but Oliver wanted to go into the bar, maybe ask if they knew of a local towing company, maybe get a Bud Lite or some shit to get a feel for the crowd and eavesdrop.

The closer he got, the more an overgrown, ivy-covered tree blocked his direct view. He heard conversation carry over on the wind as a few men emerged from the bar, so he hung back in the shadows, listening.

And he heard the footstep behind him.

He tensed, adrenaline flooding his system, spinning on a heel to confront the person stalking him.

But before he'd completed the turn, he was knocked sideways, into the tangle of shrubbery, further into the shadows. Falling heavily onto his side, he braced his fall with his gloved hands, glad for the thickness of his woolen coat as branches tried to stab up at him.

A slim, dark figure wearing a balaclava jumped onto him, pinning him to the ground.

Oliver growled and took a swing, but had no leverage or a good angle, so the blow glanced off his attacker's chest. He looked for a weapon, a gleam of metal, anything. A hand reached for his face and he tried to bite, pushing back, but they managed to get a hand over his mouth, muffling his shout.

Using his larger frame, Oliver managed to shove them both sideways, rolling them so he was on top.

That's when he was kicked in the balls.

Groaning, cupping himself, he kept rolling through the ivy, lying on his back again and catching his breath. The dark figure leaned over him. They covered his mouth again with a gloved hand, punching his shoulder hard enough for ache to shockwave deep into the muscle. They reached for their mask.

He saw it right before the black fabric lifted away.

It was the eyes that did it.

"Oh, you massive pain in my ass," he grumbled against the palm covering his lips.

Rune glared angrily down at him, looking ready and eager to continue their wrestling match, punching Oliver's shoulder again, just as hard in the same spot, then raised a finger to his own lips. Then he jabbed the finger in the direction of the bar and promptly swatted Oliver again.

"Stop! Fuck," Oliver complained. He tried to grab at Rune's arms, not caring about the bar anymore, just wanting to get in a good hard smack of his own.

But somehow Rune was even angrier than Oliver was and won the battle for control of each other's arms, getting a hard grip on Oliver's wrists and straddling Oliver's chest to stop him from moving any longer.

"Do you have any idea the kind of damage I'm going to do to your ass later?" Oliver growled. "Epic. Devastating. Possibly legendary."

"Shh!"

"Did you just fucking shush me?"

Rune got right in his face, scowling like a demon. Oliver gave up a little more and stared up at the leaves swaying in the breeze, enjoying the ache climbing up into his gut, wondering if the kick had been intentional or not.

Detecting the end of Oliver's fight, he let go and started to sign.

Go home.

Oliver laughed.

"Shh!"

Go home.

You go home. Oliver replied with his hands, then said, "You fucking lunatic."

"Shh!"

"I swear to god."

Rune's fingers flew through the air. *Get in the car. Go home.*

Oliver signed in reply, *You come with me.*

He let it settle into his expression that he had no intention of moving an inch unless Rune was coming along. He didn't care that Rune had likely driven down on his bike. Fuck the bike. Oliver wanted to smash the damned thing with a sledgehammer, then chain his darling submissive in his bedroom for a while. One thing was for damn sure, Rune was not taking off again on some vigilante mission. Oliver intended to make sure of it.

Rune pointed to the car, hidden by foliage, his mouth screwed up with the disappointment of an aggravated father pushed to the end of his rope.

With the agility of a cat, he climbed off of Oliver and crouched expectantly.

Oliver got to his feet with a groan, brushing leaves, twigs and dirt from his black coat, straightening the collar and tugging at the sleeves. Rune swatted at him. Oliver pointed at him in warning.

He saw his phone lying in the dirt, picked it up and checked for cracks.

There was no immediate sign of Rune's bike.

Oliver started to walk back to the car. Hood pulled up, balaclava back in place, Rune shoved his hands in his pockets and stalked past Oliver, beating him to the car. He slipped into the passenger seat, slumped down, yanked the mask from his face.

Oliver closed the hood and got into the driver's seat.

Not bothering to sign, Oliver caught Rune's eye and ranted, "You little shit. I can't believe you shushed me. You're deaf for Christ's sake. And you can't hear me bitching at you right now anyway. Are you getting any of this at all?"

Rune waved his hands at the open road, looking frantic to be gone. His eyes were everywhere, behind them, in front, to the sides. He kept twisting in his seat.

With none of Rune's impatience, Oliver calmly shifted into reverse and started to do a three-point turn.

Once almost completely turned around, his saw Rune in his peripheral vision completely twisted backward in his seat. Ignoring him, Oliver kept his eyes on the road and began preparing all of the ways he'd rain some vengeance of his own down on his sub who was supposed to be with the paid tutor instead of tackling Oliver and kicking him in the balls.

Then Rune yelled, "The truck!" The force and volume of the cry startled Oliver to an embarrassing degree. Rune smacked Oliver's arm and pointed back at the bar.

With a heavy sigh, praying for patience so the urge to strangle Rune would pass, Oliver pulled to the side of the road again and looked.

A decades-old light blue Ford pickup had just pulled into the lot. Two men in nondescript redneck garb and baseball caps got out, then walked into the bar.

That truck hit me, Rune explained, his hands making shapes in the air.

"Are you sure?" Oliver both asked and signed.

Rune nodded enthusiastically, pointing. He grabbed for his phone, pulled up the camera and held it up so Oliver would get the idea.

"Stay in the fucking car. We'll drive past," Oliver explained, with words and hands.

He turned around again, and slowly drove by the gravel lot. Rune rolled his window down and snapped photo after photo of the truck, its plates, the whole shebang.

Satisfied, Oliver kept driving and planned to loop around a different way in order to head back to town. He went as fast as he could without speeding.

The robotic voice on Rune's phone asked, "Where are we going?"

"Police," Oliver answered, holding his right hand in a C shape over his chest where a police badge would be found, then returned his hands to the wheel.

"I can handle it," the phone insisted in monotone.

"No." He used one hand as in command, bringing his first two fingers and thumb swiftly together, closing the argument.

The rest of the drive was silent. Fifteen minutes later, they had pulled up to the police station. Oliver cut the engine and turned toward Rune.

"You need to file a police report about the attack. Give them the photos." He pointed to the phone.

Rune pressed play on his phone, which dictated his message. "The cops will do nothing. It's hearsay. No evidence. They'll let them go and they'll keep attacking people. I need to handle this on my own. I need to stop them. If I file a report, the Lions will know I'm gunning for them. They'll know I'm coming."

"No." Again, Oliver brought his fingers together, infusing the gesture with his anger.

Rune huffed and moved to start typing again.

"No," Oliver repeated, slicing through the air, smacking Rune's arm to get his attention. He said it slowly, exaggerating the words so they'd be understood, waiting until Rune's gaze was on his mouth. "Report or we're done." He gestured between them, then cut through the air.

He saw the pain in Rune's expression, the hurt, the frustration. It was grasping, fevered, driven. But Oliver was resigned and held his place. He would not be moved. Not anymore. Because he knew what was right, and the best ways to protect Rune from the consequences of his ferocious crusade against his attackers. He also knew he loved Rune too much to stand by and watch him sacrifice himself for the cause.

There was a pause. Stillness. Tension. Rune gazed up at the station, licked his lips, bowed his head and slowly nodded. In the silence of the car, he wadded up the balaclava in his lap, gathering the fabric in a hand and slid the phone back into his pocket.

Oliver sighed, relieved.

Rune opened the door, got out, slammed it shut and started to jog away, in the opposite direction of the station.

Oliver realized he had his answer.

Chapter 21
Choices Made

For a while, Oliver couldn't move. He sat in the parking spot outside the police station, hands on the wheel.

He could just let Rune go. Arrange to have his things returned. Avoid further confrontation. Oliver could move on with his life. He still had Jackson.

He could do it.

But he kept looking in the direction Rune had walked. He was long gone now, but his ghost remained, taunting.

"He's gonna fucking get himself killed. He doesn't even..." Oliver punched the steering wheel with a closed fist, as hard as he could. He growled, then yelled. Then screamed as loud as he could, until his chest ached. It was the futility of it all that hurt the most. Gasping, head fallen back, he finished, "He doesn't even care."

What the hell was Oliver supposed to do?

Let Rune kill himself? Not give a fuck?

He'd given the ultimatum. Rune had chosen. He chose more pain and revenge over Oliver. It was done.

"Fuck. Fuck!"

He blew out a breath through his nose, closed his eyes, tried to calm down.

"Let him go. Let it be. He'll come back."

But he wouldn't. Rune was stubborn as hell. He'd probably blame Oliver for the pain he felt, then use it on some suicide mission to take out a bunch of drunken, backwoods morons, or die trying.

Oliver had tried to out-stubborn people before. He'd always been successful. His will was iron-strong.

It wouldn't work this time. Not with Rune.

Oliver could see it all taking shape—how Rune might not even care about getting his stuff back. How he might be stalking the neo-Nazis right now, no waiting, just get it done and go down, guns blazing.

It made Oliver feel shaky and nauseous.

He was losing. Losing everything.

Not only would he be back to square one, with that empty pit in his chest eating him alive, but he'd miss Rune forever. He wouldn't get past it. The guilt would consume him.

This was his fault.

His balls still ached. Same with his shoulder. He was sick, the urge to vomit stronger by the moment as he imagined Rune tied up and dragging behind a beat-up blue Ford truck, the road acting as a meat grinder on the man Oliver loved.

Oliver fumbled for his phone. It almost slipped out of his shaking hands.

He dialed and it was picked up after three rings.

"Hello?" said a confused, gravelly voice.

"It's Oliver. I don't know what to do. I think he's going after those shitheads. Or he's gonna kill himself trying. I don't know how to find him, or stop him, or—"

"Come by the clubhouse," Max cut in. "I'll send some guys out looking for 'im. He'll come by sooner or later, trust me."

"I, um, I have a license plate number for the truck."

"The truck? *The* truck? Are you shitting me?"

"No, but Rune has it too."

"All right. Give it to me."

The first thing Oliver did when he got to the back to the bar was have a drink. He figured he'd be there a while and needed something strong to kick him in the ass.

"We're looking for him," Max assured Oliver. "Got eyes on The Watering Hole. Got guys doing a sweep of places Rune likes to ride, but his bike is still hidden over where he left it. He won't get to it without us seeing."

"Thanks. That's good. I've got people at home looking for him there too," Oliver admitted. Jackson was holding down the fort for the time being. Adam was driving around town looking for any sign of Rune traveling on foot on the miles-long route to the clubhouse.

"Well, sit. Relax. Ya look like hell. Ya need something to eat?" Max asked.

Clutching his stomach, which was still in revolt, his sense of impending doom not lessened one bit, Oliver shook his head and did another shot of scotch.

"He won't do anything suicidal. Trust me. He's emotional, sure, but he ain't dumb. Am I wrong?" Max challenged.

"No, you're not," Oliver allowed.

"What happened, anyway?"

Oliver groaned, rubbed his eyes. He sat on a nearby stool and leaned on the bar. "After we saw the truck, I told him if he didn't file a police report, we were done. I can't keep watching him act like a fucking vigilante with a death wish."

"Oh," Max said heavily, leaning against the bar top beside Oliver. "Huh. Well, I can see why he'd run off. Never been a fan of the law, 'specially since they dropped the ball with finding these guys and haven't been able to keep the hate crime attacks under control either. Thinks he can do it all himself. Hates asking for help. All of that. Same reason he wound up living out of the storage closet for so damned long. Stupid kid."

He gave Oliver a heavy-handed pat on the shoulder. "He'll turn up. I know it."

Now and then, Jackson texted Oliver for updates or to say there'd been no sign of Rune. It was the same case with Adam, who offered to come wait with Oliver, but Oliver waved him off. He wasn't in the mood for company or talk. He also wasn't in a rush for Adam to see how miserable Oliver felt, with his heart bleeding on his sleeve. There was no excuse for it. He'd fallen too hard, too fast. It was his own fault.

A few hours passed with no change. A football game played on the TV screens around the clubhouse, which was less than half empty.

When Oliver's phone rang, he checked the caller ID, and answered for maybe the only person he was ready to talk to.

"Hey," Oliver said. "Has he caught you up?"

"Sure has," Josefina told him. "How are you?"

"How do you think?"

"Hmm. So, what's the issue here?"

Oliver sighed, knowing how much Josefina knew about him both from personal experience and from what she'd heard for years from Jackson. She likely knew Oliver had been actively avoiding talking to Jackson and Adam, that he was sulking and acting totally unlike himself.

"How do I let him go?"

A yell went up from the few guys glued to the screens. No one was paying Oliver any attention, though Max was hanging out somewhere nearby. Oliver had lost track of him after a while.

"Let him go?" Josefina echoed with incredulity. "Of course you're not letting him go. You? *You* are going to let him go? It's just as likely Jackson would ever let *you* go."

"Then what the hell do I do?" Oliver asked, getting upset, wanting to hit or drink something again out of sheer frustration.

"Just wait. Wait, sweetie. Once he sees you, he'll understand. Trust me."

Oh, how he wanted her to be right, but he couldn't go there, or hope that much.

"Now is not the time for pride, Olly."

"Mm. Thanks, Jo."

"Hang in there."

He hung up, felt a little better.

And waited.

Rune built a wall in his mind. He fought to keep Oliver on the other side of it.

Oliver had made him choose, and there was no choice. Rune knew he was being a rotten little shit, but he just couldn't let it go. He couldn't let the bad guys win. Not when people were actively being hurt. Not when they'd taken his whole life away with no consequences.

That's what he focused on.

Even when his chest got tight and his vision blurred. Even when he felt a magnetic pull drawing him toward Oliver's apartment, where he suspected Jackson still waited for his return.

Rune had started on this road a while ago. For most of his life he'd been selfish, shallow. But he got it now, how important it was to get your head out of your ass and try to improve the state of the world rather than sitting by to watch it burn. They were all responsible for knowing when to stand up and say enough was enough to the hateful and the damned. Before, he'd been failing on all counts. Karma caught up with him. Taught him one hell of a lesson. Now, Rune knew he had a chance to do something important. If he let it pass him by, he'd feel personally responsible for anything else the drivers of that blue truck did from here on out. He had to keep his head down, ignore Oliver's distractions, and see it out to the end. He had to do what he knew in the core of his being was the right thing.

He was capable of letting Oliver go. He would. He'd just do it. He'd stay active, go for the people he knew he could find now. And figure out the rest later.

If there was a later.

It was for the best.

That's what he told himself every time he remembered coming upon Oliver just as he was about to walk up to the lair of a bunch of corrupt shitheads to do god-knows-what like some big suit-wearing hero. Over Rune's dead body would he let Oliver waltz right into the firing line of these guys. They'd taken enough. They wouldn't get any more. Not if Rune had a say about it.

He was doing the right thing. He was protecting everyone who needed protecting—other kids who were as oblivious as Rune had been, Oliver, Jackson, Adam, and any current or future targets of the hate of The White Lions. This was his fight. No one else's. No one would miss him if he fucked it up, not in any way that mattered. Maybe on some level Oliver would, but Oliver had also been the one to make the ultimatum. He'd made the call, not Rune. Oliver would get over it in time if there were consequences. He'd still have Jackson and Adam.

Unlike Rune, Oliver had people who would miss him. Who counted on him. He wasn't disposable in the same way.

There was a pain in Rune's chest every time he thought of himself as disposable, but he ignored that too, pushed it behind the wall to be ignored along with everything associated with Oliver.

Rune kept walking, burning off the frazzled energy and self-doubt that kept grabbing at him.

He didn't even know where he was headed, he just walked.

And when he got tired, he got an Uber and was ready with his directions pre-typed into his phone.

He got in the car, let the phone dictate his instructions to the driver, who looked confused but drove on anyway.

Fifteen minutes later, Rune was pulling up to the clubhouse of The Born Soldiers.

After getting out of the car, Rune sat down on the curb, letting the growing chill of the waning day sink into his bones.

He wasn't ready to go inside yet, or explain anything to anybody. He just wanted to be left alone with his impossible situation. It was going to keep hurting until he solved it, eating away at the inside of his chest like a monster he'd swallowed. But he was going to have to get through the bar before reaching the sanctuary of his room. He waited for courage to show itself before trying.

A hand shoved his shoulder.

Jason stood there, cigarette in hand, gesturing widely with a confused expression.

Rune shrugged.

Jason jabbed a finger at the club, his eyebrows raised, his mouth set in a tight line. He looked ready to drag Rune's ass inside if need be.

Rune flipped him off.

Jason mumbled something, stuck the cig in his mouth and started to come at Rune, who dodged away, scrambled to his feet and raised his hands in surrender.

Then he flipped Jason off again, this time with both hands, and headed toward the front entrance of the club, whether he was ready or not.

He punched the door to open it, letting it swing violently away from him as he stalked through the doorway.

Eyes on the ground, posture hunched, trying to exude a powerful don't-fuck-with-me vibe, he stalked three steps forward.

And stopped short.

He saw perfectly shined shoes. Tailored pants. A crisp white shirt with the sleeves rolled up to the elbows. And Oliver's expression, a wreck.

It was all there—right there on the surface—in his shining-wet, wide, bloodshot eyes, the twist of his lips, the furrow of his brow, the hopelessness in the set of his shoulders, his hands held palms out as if he was just waiting for a tidal wave to carry him away, like he needed it to take him.

Seeing him like that felt like a punch to the chest.

Stunned, Rune fought to breathe, his gaze darting around to the others in the bar who watched them, and those that didn't. He saw Max a few feet away, looking displeased.

As much as it hurt to do it, Rune looked back up at Oliver, and knew.

He was so screwed.

Royally.

There was no conscious decision. There was no choice.

He just dropped it all. The pretense. The belief in how things were going to go. The things he had told himself he needed. The plans.

It rolled off of his back and vanished like smoke.

Oliver moved his flattened right hand in a circle over the center of his chest—the sign for please.

Rune felt a hand squeezing his heart, crushing his lungs. He cleared his throat, brushed his thumb over his bottom lip as he hid behind the curled hand.

A force moved him, silent and unbeatable. It pushed him the few steps forward until he was being folded into Oliver's embrace. Rune's mouth pressed against the warm, smooth skin of Oliver's neck. Wrapping an arm around, he held on, closed his eyes. A hand clasped the back of his head and he sighed.

He knew what it meant; that in a way, he was losing.

But next to what he was gaining?

Well, there was no comparison.

Chapter 22
Getting It

They took care of it that night. Within the hour. Oliver drove Rune and Max over to the police station. A few of the other guys who'd been there after the crash and during Rune's recovery, or who'd seen the guys with the blue truck around town causing other sorts of trouble, came on their bikes to help support Rune's case and make their own statements.

It was paperwork. It was fielding questions from people who struggled to communicate with him clearly. It was letting Oliver take charge and seeing the deep, crushing relief in his eyes the whole goddamned time. To Rune, just seeing that awful gratitude in Oliver's face felt like he'd actually been the one to find Rune after the crash when he lay there on asphalt in pieces and now Oliver could finally see the ambulance coming down the road. Like there was hope he'd survive, against all odds.

And that hurt too, but Rune knew he had it coming.

Once the forms were handed over, Oliver pulled him into a hug, pressing a hand to Rune's chest, his index and pinky fingers and thumb extended. His voice was a tremble against the side of Rune's neck, his lips kissing there softly.

Rune pointed to himself, closed his fist and moved it in a circle over his heart to say he was sorry. Then he folded his hand in a combination of the letters I-L-Y, just like Oliver. Stepping back, he let Oliver see his hand, shaped the same way, hoping love would be enough.

They didn't go straight home, even though both of them were exhausted. There was no discussion about it. Oliver just took Rune out of the city, into an expensive suburban neighborhood about twenty minutes away. The homes were surrounded by low stone walls and iron gates. Lush landscaping covered rolling lawns of an unnaturally vibrant chemical-green color. The houses themselves looked like mini castles, with towers and spires and grand entryways.

Rune didn't have the faintest idea why the hell they were out there... until they pulled slowly into a driveway where two young girls in braids were playing on the lawn with bubble wands. Tiny gossamer bubbles filled the air. The setting sun's rosy purple light added even more magic to the moment. Somehow, they'd broken out of time and entered a safe, wondrous place with no fear, no need for police or vengeance.

Jackson sat in a white rocking chair on the front porch, a ceramic mug in hand. He raised a hand to them and began to walk over. A moment later, a beautiful woman in a light-as-air floral dress stepped through the doorway, her hair wrapped up in a cranberry-colored scarf on top of her head. Josefina.

Rune glanced over at Oliver in the driver's seat, saw his sad smile and an echo of longing or pride. Rune felt how they were closed into the stuffy air of the car, sealed inside, while the idyllic scene played out before their eyes, close enough to see, but not to touch. They were apart from it, just enough to know exactly what they were missing out on.

There was no place for Oliver in that scene. Sure, he was a cherished guest. A friend. But nothing here included him or ever would.

No wonder he'd been so lonely.

Rune felt it too, how it was too perfect—a nice story instead of real life. He couldn't relate either, as much as he did care for Jackson.

This, for Jackson, was his world. It came first, and always would.

Oliver was first to get out of the car. Jackson embraced him in a close hug, clapped him on the back. They whispered into each other's ears in a way that was just a step or two beyond friendly. Jackson clasped the back of Oliver's head, kissed him soundly on the forehead, then cupped his cheek before stepping back and letting Josefina come in to give a hug of her own.

Jackson went to the passenger side of the car and opened the door, waved Rune out.

There was lingering fear and pain in Jackson's expression as he caught and held Rune's gaze. Taking Rune's jaw in hand to keep him focused, Jackson mouthed carefully, "He needs you."

It was a warning, a plea.

Blinking as his eyes began to sting and water, Rune nodded, lowered his gaze.

Jackson drew him close, enfolding him in arms that felt warm, safe, and steady. Jackson kissed the side of Rune's head and lingered with his lips pressed there.

The two girls wandered over with their wands, curiously watching the newcomers. Rune tried to smile and gave a shy wave.

Oliver was still chatting with Josefina, so Jackson made some introductions, saying, "This is Rune," while finger-spelling his name. He pointed to the slightly taller girl who gave her father a shy glance before finger-spelling J-A-D-A. The smaller twirled herself in a dizzy circle, giggling before pausing long enough to name herself as K-A-Y-L-A.

Rune gave Jackson a proud smile and a slight nod.

Josefina came up to Rune. Her sad smile was a strange mix of both Oliver's and Jackson's. He wondered how much she knew. He saw on her lips: *thank God.* And she gave him a hug.

Oliver translated for Josefina when she said, "We were so scared we'd lost you. I'm so glad we have you back."

Rune wasn't sure what to say, so he just nodded a little in acknowledgment and kept his hands in his pockets.

A few moments later, they got back into the car and left.

Rune typed into his phone and waited for the first red light before pressing play.

"I get it now, with you and Jackson."

Oliver nodded, kept his eyes on the road. There was a haunted look about him that wasn't going away, but Rune told himself it was just tiredness.

Soon, they finally were parked in the garage at Oliver's building. It felt good, like coming home. It wasn't lost on Rune how important it was to feel like he belonged somewhere, and he did.

Oliver waited in his seat, the engine off, until he had Rune's gaze. *Adam is here*, he signed. *He was worried. He helped look for you.*

Rune nodded.

I'm going to bed. To sleep. He wants to talk to you before he leaves.

Are you okay? Rune asked, letting his worry show.

Oliver's gaze slid away. He turned his head, licked his lip.

Rune smacked him.

Oliver barely frowned in reaction, then shrugged and answered, *I'm tired. Let's talk tomorrow.*

Rune grabbed Oliver's arm, held him there after Oliver moved to open the door and get out.

Oliver sighed heavily.

Then, he asked, *Are you staying?*

Technically, the question could have meant anything, but Oliver's face said it all, especially how he diligently avoided eye contact, like it hurt too much to look at Rune. Rune had never seen so much pain in him. The whole day came crashing down on Oliver's shoulders then—how he had been driven by fear for Rune to try to handle the neo-Nazis for him, how he'd given the desperate ultimatum to either report or end things, the way he'd nervously waited at the club for Rune to come back, the patience and need he'd shown as he supervised the reporting process at the station, then the last-ditch cry for help that had been hidden behind the drive to Jackson's home to show Rune everything Oliver could never have.

There was too much bare honesty and pain in it to disrespect Oliver by instinctively reassuring him that of course Rune was staying. Instead, Rune took time to actually think about his answer first. Oliver deserved at least that much.

The moment drew out, an echo of that moment hours earlier, outside the police station. He remembered the feeling of Oliver's hand signing *I love you* pressed against his chest. He again heard the last thunderous crash he ever would and felt pavement scraping his skin away while pathetic men laughed.

Rune put his face in his hands and groaned with force, hearing only silence. His fingers scraped over his head, grabbed tightly at his hair as he stayed like that, folded in half.

Then he sat up, looked Oliver dead in the eye.

He raised his right fist, then bent it at the wrist slightly up and down as if his hand was nodding.

Oliver smiled a little and nodded toward the elevator, looking ready to fall asleep right there.

Rune reached out to hold Oliver's hand in the elevator. He kept it in his grasp on the way to the door, and as they walked inside.

Adam stood waiting right inside the entryway, hands on his hips, wide-eyed and tense.

He and Oliver spoke a few words to each other. Oliver let go of Rune to go and kiss Adam on the lips, then headed to the bedroom without a backward glance. Rune lingered just inside the apartment's entrance, hands in his pockets again.

Adam turned and walked, waving Rune over to the couch on the far end of the large room, by the windows. The stars had begun to come out, the sky clear with a small sliver of a crescent moon, showcasing the tiny pin-pricks of light.

Rune took a seat on the couch. Adam sat on the ottoman directly in front of him, so close their knees touched. Adam took a deep breath, his eyes focusing on something not in the room for just a moment. He pulled himself to sit up straighter. Then, his hands began to move.

It's okay to be angry, but don't let it destroy your life. Don't let the anger win. People will always get hurt. You can't fix the world. You can only control yourself.

Confused, Rune signed only: *how?*

Adam held up a pad of paper that had been sitting behind his back. On it was written:

Elet taught me a few sentences via Skype while I was waiting. I'm not fluent yet.

Rune chuckled a little at the "yet".

He leaned forward, hands folded in front of his mouth as he thought about what Adam had said.

Taking the pad, he wrote:

There's a lot of anger. How do I deal with it if I can't use it to do some good?

Adam shifted the paper to his lap and replied:

Purge it in safe ways, with your Doms. I know what it's like to feel helpless because others have robbed you of crucial parts of your life. You can't let it turn you into a monster too.

It was the first time he really realized that Adam, of all of them, knew how he felt. Really knew. Because his parents had been killed by the foolish actions of others, also in a traffic accident. It had destroyed his world too. But Adam had pulled himself back up. He was finding a new way forward.

Adam's looped handwriting scrawled:

You can still be the good guy. You can keep fighting. There are ways to help others. Safer ways.

For a while, Rune just held the tablet and hung his head, staring at it. Adam's fingers combed through Rune's hair, tickling over his scalp in ways that sent pleasant shivers down his neck and through his back.

He closed his eyes, enjoyed the soothing feeling.

Time slipped by.

He picked up the pen, wrote:

I've been angry for a long time, before the accident. That just amplified it. I was just constantly let down by important people— my parents, teachers, cops. CPS workers. No one ever fixed what needed fixing. I couldn't rely on them, so I just relied on me. Even with my crew, they never knew the whole story. I felt safer that way, being independent. But now Oliver, Jackson, and you are showing me I can rely on people again. I really need that. But I have to ask, does it still ever drive you crazy?

Adam gazed down at the white paper, watching the blue ink dry. His hand moved to cover the letters of the question. His other hand caressed back along Rune's jaw. Bowing his head, he laid it on Rune's shoulder. Rune moved his arm to wrap Adam's back, feeling the strength of it through his thin t-shirt. He felt Adam's breath hitch and held on tighter to him. Rune turned his head toward Adam's heat and breath, felt dampness on his skin, then lips on his mouth. He opened for the kiss, pressed in with hunger and need. Adam licked into him, held him there to use his mouth and Rune poured his fear and uncertainty into Adam, who gladly drank it all down.

When they broke, his lips tingling, his head spinning, Rune felt better.

Adam got to his feet.

Rune brought his right hand up to his mouth, flattened, the fingers touching his lips, then moved it away and a bit down. Immediately after, he finger-spelled S-I-R.

Adam gathered him once more to his body, with Rune's forehead resting against Adam's hip.

Once Rune was able to let go, Adam walked away and slipped out of the apartment, leaving Rune lighter, and less scared of the choice he'd made.

Chapter 23
The Watering Hole

A text message came in around ten o'clock that night, while Rune lay awake in bed beside Oliver who was heavily asleep. Rune had been scrolling through the local police station scanner's twitter feed when the phone vibrated with the arrival of the new message.

It was from Max.

> *Cops are headed to The Watering Hole looking for the Lions. Got a call out that way for disturbing the peace and heard they're doing a follow-up on your report.*

Right away, Rune replied:

> *Swing by and pick me up?*

After a short pause, a new text popped up:

> *Kid, just stay away from it.*

Knowing he should, but also that he couldn't, Rune insisted:

> *I just want to see if they take anyone away, or if the truck is there.*

Three dots blinked on Rune's screen, indicating a new message being typed. It read:

> *We can tell you that much.*

Rune glanced at Oliver's sleeping form, knew he'd be out for hours with how tired he was, and sent his last text:

Come on, Max. Please? I won't get involved. I swear.

There was a solid minute before Max's verdict came through.

Fine. Be ready.

Eagerly, Rune sprang out of bed, pulled clothes on and scribbled a note for Oliver:

Couldn't sleep. Went on a walk to clear my head. Be back soon. I have my phone if you need me.

Four cars with flashing red and blue lights had swarmed the bar's parking lot. In the flood illumination from the headlights, countless patrons were gathered in small clusters around the officers. More police vehicles approached from farther away, their lights growing larger and brighter the closer they got.

Max and Rune stayed across and down the road a bit, out of the light, watching. Max wore his club leather jacket. Rune was in his hoodie again.

He couldn't tear his eyes away, praying the cops would start to load people up in the backs of the vehicles to be taken downtown for questioning and hopefully charges.

There had been no text from Oliver, who Rune would have bet was still deeply asleep.

As the additional police arrived, it only added to the confusion.

Rune kept glancing at the dark tangle of brush near the large tree on the opposite side of the road where he'd wrestled Oliver to the ground earlier that day. After they'd gotten into Oliver's car, Rune had gone through his pockets to make sure he'd not dropped anything, but he still felt a little paranoid about it. Temptation lured him over to scout out the area again, just in case. Especially now that the Lions would be on alert that someone was after them.

The additional cop cars added to the overall illumination of the area, some of it creeping their way.

Rune swatted Max's arm, pointed to the road, thinking they should at least back up a little more.

Max nodded but at first made no move to go.

Then, from the swarm of people in front of the bar, someone broke off, smoking a cigarette. It was a huge bald man, the red glow of his cig sparking up as he inhaled and began to stroll right toward them.

Rune tapped Max's arm again. But Max was looking in another direction, the far end of the lot.

The bald guy started to jog, coming right for them.

Rune got on Max's bike, made a frantic cry to Max who finally saw their pursuer—now mere feet away—and got on as well.

A hand reached for them, skimming the back of Rune's hoodie.

They peeled out of the dirt on the hard shoulder and sped down the road, leaving the light and the Lions behind.

When Rune got back to the apartment, Oliver was right as he'd left him, the note untouched. Scooping it up and taking it into the kitchen, Rune set the edge of the note on fire, dropped it in the sink to burn up and out. Then he went through his pockets again, trying to remember.

He always kept a small notepad in his left pocket with a pen. When a page was full, he tore it off and threw it out. But if he wasn't near a trash can, he didn't litter—he'd stick the crumpled page in his pocket to be thrown out later.

He had three crumpled pages in there at the end of the day, but had that been all of them? He scoured his memory, trying to count the times he'd torn pages away. He even smoothed out the pages he still had, reading them over, trying to tell himself there wasn't one missing.

But he'd stopped for coffee on the way to The Watering Hole, looking for Oliver, wanting the energy boost to fuel him. He told himself the page he'd scrawled his order on, along with some leftover conversation from that morning with Jackson, had been tossed in the trash at the coffee shop.

He couldn't be sure.

If the Lions found it, surely they'd make nothing of it.

It was nothing.

Rune was so successful at reassuring himself that it took four more hours until he finally calmed down enough to fall asleep from pure exhaustion.

Luckily, Oliver let him sleep in. When Rune finally rolled out of bed, it was just shy of noon.

Before waking his phone or unplugging it from the charger, Rune headed to the bathroom for a shower. Part of him dreaded facing the day and what might have happened while he slept.

He used the toilet, brushed his teeth, then climbed into the billowing steam of the shower, planning to shave once he was done.

Hands planted on the tile, he let the hot water blast down on his back, his thoughts in a whirl.

The first sign he wasn't alone was a touch to his back, making him jump, sliding up to the nape of his neck to grasp hold. The hand used the hold to bend him sharply over at the waist, and kept him firmly in the position. Rune got the briefest glimpse over his shoulder. Dark-eyed, Oliver glared down at him, his lips sealed tight. Guilt swelled in Rune's gut. Bowing his head, he could only yield to Oliver, who kicked Rune's feet apart into a wider stance.

Insistent pressure against his hole told Rune what was coming—no prep, but a good hard force-fucking he completely deserved for many reasons. He'd scared Oliver in so many ways the day before. He'd even intentionally kicked him in the balls. Even though he welcomed Oliver's need to dominate and take him, Rune tensed with worry and nerves. He didn't resist, but found he couldn't unclench his ass. It took an especially hard thrust from Oliver to breach him. Pain flared. He knew Oliver was likely hurting from the friction burn as well, not that Rune could hear or see his reactions, or thought Oliver would have cared enough to let it stop him. Rune's hands slipped against the tile wall. Gasping through the ache, he tried to loosen up, denying every instinct that kicked in to fight back. His body wouldn't cooperate, wouldn't relax. The pain continued to be intense. He knew it colored his cries, which he couldn't hold back or measure. Everything Oliver did to him was reflected raw and unfiltered in Rune's every whimper and shuddered grunt.

Burrowing deeply into Rune's ass, Oliver kept a tight grip on Rune's hip and his neck. Oliver forced him to take every inch. When Rune writhed, Oliver stayed with him, kept thrusting. Once Oliver's cock was fully sheathed, it got hard for Rune to breathe through the pressure of penetration. There was plenty of humiliation for him in that moment. Rune knew all of his failures and selfishness had gotten him there, bearing his punishment.

Remembering kicking Oliver, knocking him down, punching him, Rune let the throbbing low in his body sink into him. He gave over to it, panting. Secretly, mentally, he urged Oliver on, wanting him to do his worst, welcoming everything Oliver could dish out if it would help him feel more in control again.

The surrender of that helped center Rune a bit. His trembling eased. His heavy breathing began to steady.

Oliver took tight hold of Rune's hips with both hands, then began to fuck him, going harder, and harder. Rune growled through it, ricocheting off of each thrust as Oliver's hips beat a steady rhythm against Rune's parted cheeks. The continuous dry friction burned deep inside and at his rim. It was all he could do to stay on his feet, and keep his knees from buckling.

Rune felt Oliver climax, holding inside him with a tremble as he unloaded. Abruptly, he pulled out.

He shut off the water, reaching around Rune to do it, then resumed his bruising hold on the back of Rune's neck to guide him out of the shower, dripping in more ways than one.

Rune left soaking footprints as he was manhandled from the room and out to the bed. Oliver pushed him down onto it on his back, grabbed at Rune's legs to bend them sharply back, forcing him to fold in half as Oliver swiftly cuffed Rune's ankles, locked them snugly together. Then, Oliver slipped a collar around Rune's neck, buckling it shut. There was a metal ring in front which Oliver connected by a short chain to the ankle cuffs, pulling it as tight as he could before locking it in place. It kept his legs folded back with his knees in his armpits, his sore hole exposed for further torment. His sphincter throbbed already from the force-fucking. As his anxiety spiked, Rune's breathing remained out of control.

He flashed back to that night with Elet, years ago, and being chained, being made to take a cock of monstrous size, his yells echoing from the walls as he felt like he was coming apart, as if Elet was wearing him like a particularly delicate glove, like his body would never recover, as if he had no power at all except the power to submit to his Master's lust.

Water continued to fall off him, soaking the sheets. He shivered with a chill.

He barely had a chance to get his bearings before seeing Oliver with a massive silicone phallus in his hand, and a bottle of lube. He fisted the slick over the long, thick cock, then moved up to Rune with it.

An embarrassingly nervous, shouted plea for mercy was felt rather than heard.

The cool, firm end of the toy touched Rune's sensitive opening. Oliver's fingers parted him with gentle but determined coaxing, stretching his rim to hug around it, feeding it into him. Once the head was past Rune's rim, Oliver palmed Rune's right cheek to steady him. Ruthless but slow pressure worked to penetrate Rune with the shaft, stuffing it through his clenched outer ring of muscle. Rune's aching ass swallowed the toy, pulling it in like it was starved for it. It sank farther than Oliver's cock had gone. Head thrown back, Rune gasped for air, quivering, holding onto his thighs, breaking into a sweat.

When he thought the phallus couldn't possibly penetrate him any deeper, it kept going. Rune kept crying out, his mouth working as he struggled to bear it.

Finally, stuffed impossibly far into his ass, the toy stilled. Oliver held it, watching him. Rune lay there, afraid to move, impaled and chained, made utterly vulnerable and helpless. Though Elet possessed the largest cock to ever fuck him, the phallus Oliver had just forced into Rune was longer, if not thicker. It had to be the size of a small arm.

Rune reminded himself again of how much he'd scared Oliver lately, in so many ways. He understood Oliver's impulse to pin Rune down, to chain him and overpower him and physically conquer him. Because in that moment, spread, bound and fucked, Rune had no escape. He had given himself over completely to his Master. Though he had his safe sign, it was Rune's only out. Oliver had no reason to listen to Rune's pleas or whimpers. He was fully empowered to keep Rune in that bed, chained and violated, as long as he wanted. It was just another way their tug-of-war for control continued, and now Oliver was certainly winning.

More than a little scared of the insane phallus stuffed inside him, and what might happen to him next, Rune felt his heart race. He tried to get his breathing slowed down and regulated, but then Oliver took hold of him by the balls, and pulled, and squeezed.

Instantly, Rune's stomach and thighs clenched tightly, cramping, and he coughed, whined, moaned. Reflexively, he bucked, but Oliver had him in two places, so he couldn't go far.

Oliver kept applying pressure to Rune's testicles. It was steady, careful, awful. He didn't let up or let go. Still, it was much nicer than a kick. Rune had enjoyed kicking Oliver in the nuts quite a lot, actually, though he had no plans to admit as much; not that he needed to, clearly.

When the hand squeezing him released, the cock began to slowly withdraw. The sensation was startling, but welcome, giving Rune some relief from the maddening pressure. It didn't last long. Oliver pushed to reclaim him right away. On the in-stroke, back into him, Oliver started to lightly slap Rune's sac where it hung, over and over. Rune groaned in protest and clenched up, tried to curl forward. It didn't help or work, so he pulled his legs back, drawing them together. He tried everything to fight it, uselessly, the pain of each light smack a shockwave that made him feel panicked and desperate. He pleaded wordlessly, too far gone to care what he might have sounded like. Oliver ignored it, and Rune's guilt became more and more satisfied with his torment. He stopped fighting or protesting and just surrendered to it. The big fucking arm kept riding his ass and Oliver kept batting away at Rune's sac, though his ass was still clenched in protest and it made the penetrations ache that much more.

The thrusts grew longer, more complete as Rune's body adjusted. It quickly made Rune dizzy, unable to stop panting for air, his body tugged and pushed with each thrust. The slapping stopped and Oliver roughly massaged Rune's balls instead. Rune kept waiting for a squeeze, a slap, and they came, but not at predictable intervals. There was no anticipating anything.

More control slipped from him. He'd never felt so helpless in his life. He forgot everything but enduring each moment.

It went on and on. He feared Oliver planned to keep this up all day long, working out weeks of worry in one session. A new level of exhaustion and nervousness began to take over, the throbbing in his rectum the loudest thing he'd ever experienced. The shaft was grinding on his gland, and the push and pull of the deep fucking continued to mortify him.

The toy stilled. Rune breathed his thanks, but realized Oliver wasn't taking it out. He'd buried it again to the root, left it there.

Oliver climbed on the bed, by Rune's head.

Before Rune could anticipate it, Oliver wrenched open Rune's mouth and fed him Oliver's cock, which pushed fast into his throat. The angle helped Rune be able to take it. Reflex kicked in, so he fought it at first, gagging on it. At the same time, a wet hand started to tug Rune's erection and he hated the rush of pleasure. Fought against it harder than he'd fought the pain.

Convulsing, unable to breathe, Rune kept choking on the cock in his throat, which was riding him gently, shallowly, but too deep. The hand jacked him faster, bombarding him with a building need to come, his balls full and heavy. Oliver rubbed down over them, likely causing a rising sharpness in Rune's cries, but Oliver stayed fairly gentle with them.

As blackness crowded in at the edges to Rune's vision, Oliver finally gave Rune some air, letting him gasp, then plunged in again. He caressed Rune's throat, tracing the edge of his stretched, wet lips, and clasped his jaw.

The hand jacked Rune harder and orgasm slammed into him without warning, his vision completely blacking out. Semen flooded Oliver's fingers which squeezed the thick fluid over his shaft, his fingers constricting around the head as he shook drops free of it.

Rune moaned around Oliver's cock. When he let go, Oliver went back to fucking Rune with the toy, watching him writhe and quake as he was taken from both ends at once, proving to him that it was always possible to be made even more powerless. All it took was some incentive and imagination.

Oliver's come filled Rune's mouth. Rune worked to swallow it, but Oliver pushed back into Rune's throat and kept shooting down it. His hand caressed Rune's neck as he struggled, feeling Rune's throat continue to swallow around him.

When Oliver pulled out, Rune gasped for air like a drowning man.

Oliver gave him a moment to recover, but kept fucking him at a steady pace, then caressed Rune's stomach as he began to hammer the cock into his ass at a bruising speed.

Yelling, cursing, fighting the chains, but not dreaming of using his safe sign, Rune took it. He had to. Because finally, he really, truly, understood. It didn't even matter whether he had any control. Where he'd been, what he'd done, what he planned—it was inconsequential. Nothing in the whole world came close to what Rune felt when Oliver was driven to consume him. That was Oliver's gift. His blessing. The salvation he offered.

The fear and the rage had no room in Rune when he was Oliver's.

Chapter 24
Punish the Wicked

Oliver's mouth watered as he pulled the phallus out of Rune again, taking his time to ease the head past Rune's impressively swollen rim.

Rune was dazed, delirious, softly muttering an endless, "Fuck you... fuck you..." Oliver was pretty sure Rune had no idea he was doing it.

When Oliver leaned forward and took a wide, slow lick over Rune's rim, the next "fuck you" broke apart in the sweetest, most beautiful way, the tone of Rune's voice climbing up and up. Oliver licked him again, and again, loving how still and relaxed Rune became at the gentle petting of Oliver's tongue.

Oliver plunged two fingers roughly through the puckered, hot opening to rub around inside, savoring the tenderness of the passage and the way Rune gasped harshly and flinched in reaction.

Rune sobbed a little, but didn't clench.

Oliver found his gland, massaging it lightly, and Rune's breathing choked off, his tension coming right back as he combated the stimulation, then convulsed, a broken sound leaving him.

Licking around where his fingers were nestled, Oliver felt a hand grab hold of his cock in warning, squeezing it, and he laughed.

He kept going, applying his tender torture, until the hand shifted to grab his balls instead.

"Okay, okay."

He withdrew his fingers, kissed Rune's puffy, pink rim, plunged his pointed tongue through it once, then sat up and unlocked the chain.

Rune rolled to his side, boneless, panting, his eyes closed. He didn't react or respond as Oliver removed the collar and the cuffs.

When his eyes opened a crack, gazing up at him, Oliver told him, "You're not the only one who can punish the wicked." He leaned in and kissed the tumble of Rune's black hair.

Rune's eyes closed again. His breathing evened out. Oliver lay down behind him, spooning up close.

An arm looped around Rune's chest. Rune wove their fingers together, and fell right asleep.

It was a couple of days before Rune heard from Max. Finally, the message came through. He wasn't even really surprised to get it.

The Lions were staking out the clubhouse. They were on to them. Had it been Max's jacket? The bike plate? Something they'd found in the brush by the bar? There was no way of knowing for sure.

But the chance was there they suspected Rune as the guy who'd been hounding them, who'd beaten up Kurt Radner and who'd called the cops.

It meant Rune had to stay away for a while. Keep his distance.

It meant The Born Soldiers had to lay off the Lions right when they were so close to nailing them to the wall.

But close wasn't good enough.

They knew it. So did Rune.

It had always been a possibility that when Rune and The Born Soldiers had sent an anonymous message of warning that night with Kurt Radner, it would have repercussions. They'd gone for Kurt because of his homophobia, specifically. They'd made a point of letting him know it was why they'd singled him out. Oliver always suspected it would go wrong on them somehow.

It did.

Five days later, the report came over the news, tossed out during the morning segment on a local station between the performance of a mid-level tween pop singer and a segment on how to cook a delicious vegetarian lasagna.

Rune lunged for the remote, just to keep it out of Oliver's reach, his eyes glued to the screen. Oliver listened while studying Rune, who stared, unblinking at the closed captioning.

"...A seventeen-year-old male was found dead this morning out on route thirteen near Reading. Reports from local police indicate he was tied to a tree and shot several times by assailants. His name and identifying details are being withheld at this time as suspects are pursued. Stay tuned right here to channel six for more on this developing story..."

Rune's expression was strained, his hands shaking as they clutched the remote. Reading was where the White Lions were based. Route thirteen was where Rune's crash had happened, over a year ago. The tone of the story sounded too much like them for Oliver to dismiss it outright.

Trying to figure out what to do, how to reassure Rune, Oliver was almost caught off guard as Rune turned on a heel and began to sprint to the door and exit.

Oliver caught him, barely managing to step in his path just in time. Clutching Rune's upper arms, Oliver held him there, trying to meet Rune's frantic gaze which was glued to the doorknob. For a long moment, he fought Oliver's hold, then stilled.

Instead, he reached for the phone tucked in the back pocket of his jeans.

Oliver slipped it from his hands and held it high up over his head as Rune tried to jump for it. When he couldn't reach it, Rune punched Oliver's shoulder, then tried to climb him like a monkey on a tree.

"Stop!" Oliver yelled, uselessly. "Fucking stop!"

He peeled Rune off of him and held up a finger. "Wait. Wait!"

He woke up the phone with a tap and called up Max's number. Peering over Oliver's shoulder, Rune calmed down just a hair.

Oliver placed the call.

A very confused Max answered, "Hello?"

"It's Oliver. I have his phone. He's here, just upset. Too upset."

"Oh," Max said with relief. "Makes sense. Figured he'd be calling, just… you know. A video call."

"So you heard?"

"Yeah, I heard. Poor kid."

"It was them?"

"Sure was. News isn't saying so, but the kid was gay. Got a source downtown that gave me a few extra details. Story is, the Lions set the kid up on an online date, waited for him to show, just like Rune. Got him way out in the middle of nowhere, on route thirteen where there's fuck-all in every direction, then did some target practice. The sick fucks."

"My god," Oliver groaned. Rune was right in his face, inches away, inhaling his air and following the movements of his lips like his life depended on it. "It's the same thing. Same trick as with Rune."

"Yeah. Bet it's the same guys, too. Just seems stupid, you know? Rune just gave his statement. The cops're on their scent. Why take the chance?"

"Because they can. Because they don't care about anything other than hurting the people smaller than them to make themselves feel big."

Oliver felt sick to his stomach. That could have been Rune. Was Rune.

"What… what can we do here, Max?"

"Just let it be. Let the cops handle it."

"You really think I'm gonna be able to keep Rune away from this?"

"You've gotta try. They're still coming around here all the time. Keeping watch over us. Like they want us to make a move. We can't give 'em the satisfaction. He's gotta stay way the hell away from here until we say otherwise."

"Okay. Thanks Max."

"Hey."

"Yeah."

"Don't tell 'im more than you need to, ya hear?"

"Got it."

Oliver hung up, walked a few steps, crouched, jumped as high as he could and stuck the phone on top of a decorative beam running across the ceiling of the kitchen.

Rune growled, yelled and came charging at him, knocking Oliver back into the wall.

Setting his teeth, Oliver willed himself to do what needed to be done.

Rune started hitting him. Oliver grabbed hold of Rune's wrists, twisted one around behind Rune's back, pushing it up, forcing him to bend over and struggled to bring the other arm back too.

Rune broke free of the hold, too slippery to pin. He spun, sweeping Oliver's feet out from under him and sent him falling sideways. Landing heavily, Oliver cursed and twisted onto his stomach, ignoring the ache in his shoulder and hip from the collision with the floor.

While he was down, Rune started to go for Oliver's pockets, digging for his phone instead. Rather than trying to stop him, Oliver lunged forward for the side table nearby, located on the far end of the couch nearest the kitchen. He got the drawer open and palmed what he was looking for inside while Rune started trying to unlock Oliver's phone.

Springing up into a crouch, Oliver took a deep breath and went for Rune. The phone went flying across the floor. Rune sailed into the wall, face-first, though he managed to brace himself with his hands.

Oliver snapped on the first handcuff. Rune stared at it with incredulity while Oliver yanked the cuffed arm behind Rune's back and snapped on the other one too.

Rune yelled, fought, kicked.

"I'm sorry," Oliver said circling the front of his chest with a closed fist, nuzzling the back of Rune's neck, trying to show Rune he was calm, composed. "I know I'm breaking the rule, but it's for your own sake here, okay?"

Rune threw his head back and bashed Oliver in the nose.

"Fuck!"

Stars exploded in front of his eyes, his hand flying to his nose to check for blood.

Rune spun, plowed into Oliver, who skittered backward but stayed on his feet. Rune squared up for another charge and Oliver dodged out of the way, then stuck out a foot to trip Rune as he went past, even though Oliver felt like a total asshole for doing it.

Rune crashed to the floor with a bang. He writhed, groaning after landing on his shoulder rather than his face. While he was down, Oliver grabbed hold of him by the cuffs and dragged him over to the larger cabinet in the living room where more supplies were kept. Rune yelled in pain as his shoulders strained in the wrong direction, but he wasn't going far. After a few feet, Oliver was close enough. He found the leg cuffs he needed and got them on before Rune had the ability kick him more than three times for his trouble.

For the finishing touch, Oliver connected the ankle cuffs to the wrist cuffs, hogtying Rune where he lay.

"You fucking suck, Oliver!" Rune screamed, his voice cracking.

Oliver laughed breathlessly. "You know, that's the first time you've said my name, you little shit."

He dabbed at the blood trickling from his nostrils, examined the broken skin on his knuckles from one of the kicks, then crouched to check for injuries on Rune, who was still fighting the cuffs in a rage.

Oliver gave the side of Rune's face a slap. Then did it again. And again.

Finally, Rune stopped bucking and glared up at him.

"Calm down," Oliver commanded, doing a soft, soothing, sweeping gesture from the center, downward and out with both hands and projecting all of the power and control of a Dom.

Rune gave one more primal, blood-curdling yell, then shut up and fell still. He lay there, panting, stomach down, facedown, arms and legs connected behind him.

Oliver retrieved his phone, unlocked it, then started dictation on it. He crouched by Rune's head and held the screen up for Rune to read.

> *The police are handling this. You are not going over there. Max says to stay away. Lions are watching the Soldiers. You're not going over there, so calm down. Are you hurt?*

Rune hocked up some phlegm and spit it at him.

Then he seemed to notice the blood on Oliver's face and hands and dropped his eyes.

Oliver felt around Rune's body, especially the side he'd fallen on and his shoulders, but there was no reaction that spoke of a break or anything serious.

Oliver cleared his screen and started again.

I'm sorry about the cuffs, but I need you under control. If you can stay calm for a little while, I'll unfasten your right cuff so you can type or write.

Oliver left him there for a moment and went to the kitchen to get an icepack. Then he sat with it, leaning up against the couch by where Rune lay, pressing the ice to his nose.

When Rune had laid still for a solid five minutes without any yelling or squirming, Oliver unfastened one cuff, as promised. Rune reached immediately for the pen and pad Oliver had set out for him.

This is really your plan?

Oliver nodded, muttering, "for now, anyway."

They killed him, Olly.

"I know, kid," Oliver said with regret.

Rune's hand hovered over the paper, then scrawled, *I don't know what to do.*

Oliver crawled over to him, pressing kisses to Rune's cheek and forehead. Oliver held onto him, weaving his fingers through Rune's dark hair. He tried to push all of his love through the connection and into Rune.

He took the pen, wrote beside Rune's words:

There's nothing. I just need to keep you safe. It's all that matters now.

Chapter 25
The Price of Freedom

Rune knew what was up. Oliver meant to stick around night and day, watching over him to make sure he didn't slip away to go after the Lions. Rune knew he meant business, especially after everything with the ultimatum and the cops, but also just from Oliver's expression alone. It was like he kept imagining it was Rune who'd been shot to death on that tree.

It made Rune feel bad for worrying Oliver so much, but Rune also couldn't ignore instinct, especially the one as strong as the gnawing pit in his gut demanding some kind of justice for that poor fucking guy who'd been killed.

Because Rune knew on a spiritual level that it was in his power to rain hell down upon those bigots. His rage and fury was intense enough to manifest miracles.

The next day was spent trying to figure out how to skirt both lines. He had to keep Oliver sated and he also needed to get his ass in gear and do something productive. Something smart but effective.

After Oliver returned his phone to him, Rune covertly texted Max, Goat, Jason and as many other Born Soldiers as he could to pull all of the info they had on what was going down. Rune knew they had inside info on what the cops were doing, thanks to a friend in the force, but also because they monitored the calls going out from the local station more reliably than Rune was able to by checking the online feed whenever Oliver wasn't actually looking over his shoulder.

And it was a weird fucking day because Oliver kept Rune chained to various objects at all times, if possible. For a while he was on the bed, chained to the footboard, and was given a bell to ring if he needed to take a leak. Then he was locked in the bathroom until he was finished. Then he was chained to a pipe in the kitchen while they ate together. Later in the day, he was shackled to a mysterious bolt in the floor in the living room that looked like it had gotten some good wear.

Even the cuffs weren't enough to pacify Oliver, though. He stopped trying to get work done and mainly just hung out near Rune to physically watch him as well, just in case.

The stress was getting to Oliver. Rune saw it. He looked exhausted.

So Rune played nice, didn't complain or protest, smiled at Oliver as much as he could without drawing suspicion, and waited for him to doze off.

In his comings and goings from the bathroom, Rune had secured a few paperclips and pins to use to pick the lock on the cuffs, which were not some fancy extra-secure kind but just the normal variety. No sweat.

Just as the sun was going down, with the Discovery Channel playing a documentary on giant squids, Oliver's eyes drifted shut as he reclined on the couch next to Rune. His mouth fell open, his body went lax.

Rune waited a few more minutes, then got to work.

After five minutes passed, he'd scrawled a note of apology and explanation, ended it with a sincere "I love you" and took off.

It was a decision he would soon, painfully, come to regret.

Rune's bike was waiting for him in the garage, though the last time he'd used it was before he and Oliver had fought. Max had been the one to drop it off for him.

Climbing on, Rune took a last spare minute to check his text messages, sent one of his own, then sped off with one goal in mind.

Oliver startled awake, jumping up, arms flying into the air, gasping aloud.

He scanned the room.

"Fuck! Oh, you little shit!"

Rune was gone. The cuffs were still there, now unlocked by a damned paperclip. On the seat where Rune's ass should have been was a note. Oliver grabbed it up, crumpling it in his haste.

> Going to the clubhouse. I'll check in. Just need to help out somehow. I'll be fine. I'll check in when I get there. I love you.

"Yeah, my ass are you going to the clubhouse, you filthy liar."

Oliver palmed his phone, sprang to his feet and placed a call. Keys in hand, he made right for the door and elevator.

"Yeah?" Max growled.

"Looking for Rune again, that little shit."

"He's on his way here. Texted me about ten minutes ago. Come on by if you want 'im."

"You really think he's coming there instead of going after the Lions? I mean, come on, Max."

"After that whole search party we put together looking for 'im? Yeah, I believe him. I do. He knows we'd skin his hide if he pulled major shit. He's dumb, but he's not *that* dumb."

"All right. I'm trusting you here, probably with his life. I'm on my way. Keep an eye out for him for me?"

"Will do."

There was no plan, just intention. He wouldn't know for sure if the Born Soldiers had been holding back on him, information-wise, to keep him out of trouble until they were face-to-face. He needed reassurance they were keeping an eye on the Lions in whatever ways they could. And he didn't know how to reassure Oliver he wouldn't actually go after the murderers alone without a demonstration of being true to his word.

Sure, he was tempted to go straight for the Lions, but all of Oliver's passionate devotion held Rune back just enough. It was time to start playing it straight, and using help when he could easily get it.

Now, all he needed was to get inside the clubhouse. Get to his crew. It was a simple goal. Even if the Lions were watching, Rune needed to be with his people.

The closer Rune got to his destination, the more he laid on the accelerator, flying faster down the road. The freedom of movement, the righteousness of his cause, it lit him up inside. It gave him hope, purpose. His problems didn't matter. He wasn't moping around feeling sorry for himself. He was doing shit. He was alive.

He wasn't going rogue this time, trying to do everything on his own. He'd gotten Oliver's message and was going to do the smart thing this time by playing it safe, working with the others and not alone. Already, he imagined Oliver's relief that Rune had actually come through, that he'd learned. Maybe it would be enough to earn Rune some more leeway and freedom, in showing Oliver how he really could trust Rune to stick to his word.

He broke into a smile, feeling it all the way down to his toes and the ends of his fingers.

In moments, the building loomed up before him, the most beautiful sight he could have wished for. His life's most familiar landscape welcomed him home, where he'd always have a place, and people. It wasn't much to speak of—just some scrubby brush and tangled trees crowding in around ramshackle buildings on one side and opening up to a barren field on the other—but to him it was his world. It was his family when he'd had none, his

174

sanctuary when he'd been broken, and his peace when all he'd known was chaos. Oliver was lucky enough to have Adam and Jackson to run to when things got tough. Rune had his crew. A couple of overexcited bigots had no chance of keeping him away.

With something like tunnel vision, he locked onto his target and went for it. Nothing else mattered or crossed his radar.

Not even the pick-up truck that spun out into the road from a parking lot at a gas station across the way, coming right at him.

Rune slowed as he got closer to the entrance, preparing to pull into the lot and coast right up to the doors, and it was good he did. In a sickening echo of his accident, a beat-up pickup truck—the same one as before—cut him off. It had crossed into his lane, swinging out to make a big target of its side to splash Rune's guts across. Part of his mind played it out like it had happened—showing him how it felt to go flying over the handlebars again only to hit metal instead of pavement. Trying to snap out of it, to keep a firm grip on reality, no matter how much cold fear tried to claw at him, he was just able to get it under control. By some small miracle, he managed to corrected the course of his bike, wobbling to a stop without falling off.

He was jittery though, his head spinning and heart pounding. He instinctively reached out with what senses were still intact, becoming more aware of the bike's bulk between his legs and the scene playing out around him. His mouth was too dry and the smell of the air was strangely sweet.

Steps away, two men jumped out of the truck. Furious energy came off of them in waves as they locked eyes with him and charged over.

Their arms swung up at the same time, the bright sun flashing off of the metal of their guns, aimed right at him. He resisted the urge to stare down the dark, hollow barrels, keeping his eyes instead on the two men doing the aiming.

And just like before, way back at the beginning, it was so damned quiet.

Perfectly so.

If they were yelling, he didn't hear it. He couldn't even see who they were in order to give a description later, though they were almost in grabbing range, thanks to the bandanas tied over their faces, and the sunglasses hiding their eyes.

He raised his hands, exuded calm.

The guy to Rune's left grabbed at Rune's arm and hauled him off his bike, then shoved him down to his knees on the asphalt. The rocks dug into his kneecaps, anchoring him to the same earth that shattered the bones in his inner ear, and a breeze blew the scent of freshly cut grass to him. His heart thumped away in his chest as the same guy who'd pulled him from the bike stuck a gun to the center of his forehead. He caught the smell of oiled metal, felt the cool weight of the barrel against his skin. And, somewhere far out of his reach, the two men standing over him screamed warnings he couldn't hear or lip-read.

He knew was fucked. The truth of it settled on him gently, like a tender apology.

This, he thought. *This is how I die.*

Deafness was a horrifying obstacle in emergency situations. Especially when those situations were full of people who couldn't sign.

Oliver imagined a theater where someone yelled, "Fire!" People jumped from their seats, screaming, bolting without warning to those around them in a stampede for the exits, and Rune got lost in the confusion, looking for insight that never came.

He imagined Rune walking across the road while checking a cell phone, and stepping in front of a speeding car, its horn blaring in useless warning.

He imagined a hike through the wilderness, and Rune stepping in the wrong place as a rattlesnake shook its tail.

So many scenes flashed through his head, the helplessness compounding upon itself until Oliver felt strangled by the force of it.

And it all happened in the awful seconds before he jumped out of his car. It hadn't even come to a complete stop, his foot jammed on the brake but his speed causing the car to hitch and strain, the wheels squealing. He was in the middle of the road with nothing nearby so he didn't bother steering, just flung the door open, threw himself out from behind the wheel and almost fell into the street on hands and knees as he screamed and screamed in wordless protest.

All of the awful imagined scenes melted before the terrible force of reality, set right there, neatly before his eyes, like the universe wanted him to see this. Like this had been their true destination all along.

Rune, on his knees in the road, his eyes calmly scanning masked faces.

Rune, helpless before a hateful stranger pointing a gun to the middle of his forehead.

Rune, with his hands raised in surrender.

Rune, beyond Oliver's cries, unable to even realize Oliver was there, because Rune wasn't turning, wasn't looking, not even to say one last, silent goodbye.

Mentally clawing at the sight, Oliver prayed it couldn't end like that, making silent vows to do better, to try harder, sacrificing anything he could, if only...

But it was. There was no denying it, or stopping it.

He was too far away. He had no weapon, and neither did Rune. And there was no stopping the men who wanted to tear Rune down, who were fueled by blind ignorance and hatred alone. It was too late, too little, and no matter how much Oliver loved Rune, it wasn't going to save him. The fact that Oliver had known that all along only made the hurt more brutal.

But Oliver couldn't just stand there, doing nothing.

Just wanting to look into Rune's eyes one last time, knowing it was useless, Oliver screamed again. The bellowed protest exploded in Oliver's throat, ripping apart.

The man with the gun to Rune's head—he could hear just fine.

So, he turned to look.

The barrel of the gun swung away from Rune, as if moving in slow motion, pointing Oliver's way instead.

Watching it happen, Oliver stopped running just before he heard the shot, just before his knees gave out, his body blown backward. Long before the pain—and realization of his fate—had a chance to kick in.

The shrieking was all inside Rune's head, but it filled the world. It split through the deadly color and primal wrath. It grabbed hold of things and tore them to pieces.

He'd seen the flash from the gun, the recoil, felt the air shift.

He'd followed the gun's site to its target, even as he denied it was happening, his thoughts an endless howling *no, no, no.*

Oliver.

His Oliver.

Falling to the road. Twisting to one side as he was knocked back and went down, collapsing, then colliding with asphalt. Crimson bloomed on the front of his white shirt, growing, spreading. His eyes were wide with disbelief as he looked right at Rune, seeing him in ways no one else could, even at the end.

In Rune, something snapped. He let go, let it take over.

There was no logic. No thought. He just moved.

Rune flew to his feet, launching himself at the shooter, who was still turned away, watching Oliver bleed, and Rune was determined to rip him to bloody pieces with bare hands.

He zeroed in on his target. The rest of the silent world fell away.

His momentum allowed him to easily tackle the masked shooter to the road before the other one had time to react. Rune grabbed hold of the gun they'd shot Oliver with, flipped it so it was butt-down, barrel-up and brought it down again, and again, and again. He kept going, unable to stop, his rage at so much unfairness fueling him as he pistol whipped the guy's head. He heard nothing, and no one stopped him. Soon, the sight of nothing but a wet mess of red filled his vision and the feeling of crunching kept vibrating up his arm.

Then, movement caught his eye.

The other masked man from the truck collapsed where he stood like a rag doll, part of his head obliterated in a cloud of red mist and large disgusting chunks that splattered in all directions.

The sight of that allowed Rune to stop and get control of himself again, just a little.

He dropped the gun with shaking hands. Looked around.

Several paces back, Max held a rifle, and slowly lowered it to the road where the bloodied but still living White Lion lay beneath Rune.

Max waved Rune away.

Goat was there too, holding up a cell phone, the lens of which was pointed at the scene. Nearby, closer to the clubhouse's entrance, other Born Soldiers flooded out, most of them also using their phones to record what was going on.

Even as Rune acknowledged the sights, he let them go without giving them time to really register.

In a daze, he struggled to his feet, his legs not wanting to hold him up, and pushed himself toward Oliver. Getting to Oliver was all that mattered. Staggering, Rune crossed the few steps between them and fell to the pavement one last time, scraping his knees, and gently pulling Oliver into his lap.

Rune touched his face, his chest, saw him breathing as it rose and fell. Oliver's eyes stared straight ahead, confused, unseeing, shocked. He didn't react to Rune's presence at all.

Rune bent to kiss Oliver's forehead, put pressure on the gushing wound, and prayed.

Just prayed.

Jackson watched the video playing on the borrowed phone, his numbness too strong to fight.

Tinny voices shouted through the small speaker. On the screen, about a hundred feet away and in the middle of a road blocked by a light blue pick-up truck, a figure knelt with their hands raised and the barrel of a gun pressed to the middle of their forehead. Two men loomed over him, as jittery as he was calm.

Someone a fair distance from the mic said, "Yer the faggot who's been playing us, ain'tcha? Went after Kurt. Been coming around where you don't belong. That ends today. Right now. Gonna punch some fresh holes in you the way we did that other cocksucker, huh? Go on an' cry. Go on an' piss yerself, you fuckin' trash."

From off-screen, farther away, Oliver's voice cut in—a guttural, formless protest of pure desperation.

The gun previously aimed for a direct headshot swung around to a new target.

A shot rang out.

Or, the first one, anyway.

Wordless, primal howling filled the air as Rune sprang and took out the shooter. Rune's arm swung down, raining blows on the assailant, creating meaty thwacks.

A second shot blasted through the noise. This one was fuller, louder.

The camera's view shook a little as the masked man who'd been left standing had his head blown apart in a spray of red, and took his last fall.

Bile rose in Jackson's throat. He lowered the screen, covered his mouth.

"Jesus..."

"That ain't even the best angle on it," the Born Soldier named Mark who stood at Jackson's side explained. "Cops took Goat's phone. Steady hands on him, what can I say. He was closer, too. Ran out there at the first glimpse of Rune's bike. Max was coming up on 'em with the rifle but couldn't get a clear shot without circling around. Refused to shoot if there was a chance of hitting Rune. Then Oliver came through with his distraction. Damned effective. Bless 'im."

With a thick, heavy hand, Mark patted Jackson on the back.

"He's tough. He'll be just fine."

Jackson nodded, feeling sick and cold, and passed the phone back. "Thanks."

Police milled about everywhere, taking statements from the leather-clad Born Soldiers who filled the hospital's hallway. Seated in a nearby waiting area, Rune bent over a tablet, busily providing a written statement of everything he remembered. Jackson was impatient to get to him and give him a hug. There was nothing more he wanted in the world, apart from seeing Oliver.

He wasn't going to feel steady and his thoughts wouldn't settle until he did that.

Jackson's phone vibrated in his pocket. He stepped aside, drifting slightly farther from the crowd to answer.

He muttered, hollowly, "Hey, hon."

"What's going on?" Josefina demanded, her voice sounding as rattled as he felt. Panic lent an edge to her questions. "Is Olly gonna be okay?"

"I think so." Jackson let out a frazzled sigh. "He's in surgery now. The bullet passed completely through his left shoulder and they don't think it hit anything vital."

"Oh, thank God," she said heavily. "Do you know what happened?"

"I'm, uh, still figuring that out. Sounds like the same guys responsible for the original attack on Rune have been on a spree, trying to take out gay people. They shot and killed that poor person just the other night, and now this. The Born Soldiers are testifying that the White Lions have been doing stake-outs of their club, not even to start something with them but more like they were looking for someone. Like this was premeditated. Now I guess we know they were looking for Rune. Maybe they figured out he was the one gunning for them. I mean, he's got all of those tattoos. Even when he's covered up, you can still see some, usually.

"Anyway, they intercepted Rune as he was pulling up to the clubhouse, pulled him off his bike, moved to shoot him execution style right before Olly distracted them. They shot him instead. Then Rune and one of the Soldiers—Max—took both the guys down. One's DOA. The other has severe head trauma."

Josefina, horrified, whispered her husband's name.

"I know."

"And Rune? How is he? I can't imagine…"

"I don't know yet. Haven't gotten close. He's still with the police. He looks okay, but… tense. Angry."

"Can you blame him?"

"No. I just… I almost lost him tonight, Jo."

"But you didn't. And now the world has one less psychopath in it to terrorize people."

Softly, dazed, Jackson wondered, "Why do people do this to each other? I just don't understand."

"That's because you're a good man, Jackson Whitney. And I love you for it."

"Love you too, baby. I'll keep you posted, okay?"

"You'd better."

Five minutes later, Jackson caught Rune's eye from across the hall. Rune's dark, intense gaze locked on him with laser precision, and Jackson couldn't look away. Not when Rune got up, oblivious to the spoken questions from a nearby officer, or when he walked past the mass of police and crossed the hall to approach Jackson, weaving through the Soldiers, or when Rune took hold of a fistful of Jackson's shirt and kept voicing the depth of his horror through his eyes alone.

Jackson gently took hold of Rune's head with both hands, framing his face, letting his own pain and fear rise to the surface, past the composed doctor's mask he usually wore. Rune seemed to invite it, demand it. The weaker Jackson let himself feel, the stronger Rune seemed to become. It didn't matter that Jackson was taller, bigger, more muscular, and older. Rune's spirit was indomitable. He took control, his energy charging until it almost sparked from his skin.

Jackson knew Rune wasn't done fighting. Maybe he never would be.

Maybe that was okay.

Everything was right there, in the air between them—Rune's vow to protect them all, to never back down. He would always fight for those he loved with his last breath, follow his heart, and stay with Oliver until the stars crashed down from the heavens.

Rune was not afraid, like Jackson.

No, not a bit.

He was furious.

Jackson gathered him up in his arms and breathed like he could inhale some of Rune's power for himself. Rune pressed a kiss to Jackson's neck, rubbed his back. It was the first thing to help calm Jackson down since he'd gotten the text about Oliver being shot.

When they broke apart, Rune had his phone in hand instantly, typing. The phone's voice read, "No one will ever hurt him again. I swear it."

Doubt crept into Jackson's heart. Rune saw it there.

He typed again. "The Lions aren't a problem anymore. Not after this. Not for a while, anyway. Now, my job is being there for Olly."

But was it the truth? Thinking of his three- and five-year-old daughters, and the way their most solemn vows were always expressed, Jackson stuck out his pinky expectantly. Rune frowned in confusion. Jackson took hold of Rune's hand, hooked his pinky with his own.

Rune smiled, understanding. He nodded. Crossed his heart with an X drawn over the spot.

Then he stretched up on his toes and kissed Jackson's cheek. When he pulled away wearing a warm, affectionate hint of a grin, it sparked hope in Jackson's heart, melting some of the lingering chill. It made him want to pull Rune close again, and not let go for a long time.

With a raised eyebrow, Rune finger-spelled C-O-F-F-E-E?

Despite the late hour, Jackson knew there'd be no sleeping that night.

He replied in kind: H-E-L-L-Y-E-S.

Rune gently bumped Jackson's shoulder, took his hand and led him toward the direction of the cafeteria.

Chapter 26
Taking Care

Standing in the kitchen of Oliver's apartment, Rune's blank and unfocused gaze pointed to a spot in mid-air about a foot from the tip of his nose. The fingers of his left hand drummed a steady, rolling rhythm on the countertop. His dark hair was disheveled. Barefoot and bare-chested, he wore only a pair of pajama pants.

Fighting the nonsensical urge to call out and alert Rune to his presence, Jackson eased into the room, wriggling his key from the lock. He made a mental note to take on the job of calling about getting some electrical work done to set up a visual doorbell. It was just one of those tasks that had fallen by the wayside and Jackson needed to correct it.

Setting his keys down on the table by the door, Jackson continued to fail to catch Rune's notice. The bags under his eyes and his sagging posture spoke of an exhaustion of the sort Jackson had never seen on the feisty submissive. For once, he actually looked older than Oliver, which Jackson knew he was.

It had been a few endless days at the hospital with Rune trying to stay awake twenty-four seven to watch over Oliver's recovery. Jackson had been the one to physically drive him back to the apartment for some mandatory sleep in an actual bed, but hours later and looking at him again, Jackson wasn't sure Rune had slept at all.

Dawn was breaking over the city. An amber haze shifted the darkness to light and spilled through the huge windows at the far end of the living space. Jackson had to go into the office soon, but planned to bring Oliver some supplies from home first, like some fresh clothes, pajamas, and toiletries.

Jackson was about to wave his arms to try catching Rune's eye when he saw Rune's gaze shift without any indication of surprise to Jackson's lower legs, tracking them as he walked around and into the kitchen, behind the island where Rune stood. Then he unfocused again, his head slightly bowed.

Jackson wasn't sure what in particular haunted Rune, or if it was all just catching up with him. All Jackson knew was he couldn't force Rune to talk if he didn't want to.

Putting himself in Rune's shoes, Jackson could imagine a spectrum of hate, helplessness, elation, and terror taking a toll on his mental state. He'd had a loaded gun pressed to his head, sure to succumb to a murderer's wrath if no one had stepped in to stop it. And instead of getting hurt, Rune had seen his lover shot in his place. There was misplaced guilt there Jackson yearned to soothe away.

Stepping up behind Rune, Jackson set a hand gently on Rune's right shoulder and caressed the warm, firm muscle. Burying his nose in the top of Rune's tumble of hair, Jackson inhaled the musky, natural scent of him.

Jackson wondered how he could possibly help Rune.

There was no question of Rune's devotion to Oliver, but Jackson could so easily see Rune getting swept away in a new obsession of righting the latest wrongs done. Avenging Oliver or undoing what was done—it was impossible.

The White Lion who wasn't dead on arrival had been pronounced brain dead that morning, and nothing Rune could ever do would remove the bullet wound from Oliver's shoulder.

Rune couldn't use it as a cause for vengeance like he'd done before. Not in the same way.

He needed to find a way to work through it. To let it go.

But how?

Rune pressed himself back against Jackson, his head falling to the side to allow Jackson's lips to skim over his temple, a severe frown furrowing his brow.

He took hold of Jackson's left hand, guided it around in front of him, pushed it down inside his pajama pants. Jackson found him, held on and started to gently tug him hard. Turning his face away, Rune tried to hide his expression, but couldn't mask the heaviness of his breaths or the quivering coming from the low center of his body, radiating outward in all directions. He gripped the edge of the counter, bent slightly over in front of Jackson.

Taking the hint, Jackson spit on the fingers of his right hand. When Rune slid his pants down in back to bare his ass, Jackson reached downward, pressed two fingers into him, heard Rune grunt. Jackson saw Rune's clenched jaw and his renewed grip on the granite. Jackson pried at him a little more, going slow but forcing Rune to yield quite a lot.

Rune's control of his breathing slipped with a heavy exhale and gasp, but his eyes were closed. He just braced himself and stayed open, giving over to it. He'd become fully erect, pre-come slicking his shaft as Jackson played with it, pressing it down with a hand to encourage Rune to bend over more sharply. Letting the elastic of Rune's pants hug just below his sac, Jackson reached to open a drawer and fish out what he needed.

When he withdrew his fingers from Rune's body, Jackson felt how tangible Rune's displeasure was, and his impatience for more. As Jackson pulled out his cock and rolled on a condom and lube, Rune gave a tormented, yearning look back over his shoulder before facing front again and willing Jackson silently to get on with it already.

Jackson lined up, held Rune by the junction of his shoulder and neck, and himself by the root, and pressed to enter. Rune's mouth fell open with a small cry as he pushed back onto Jackson, his pleasure at the pain audible in the soft breaking of his moan when the head breached him and locked their bodies together. His back curved in a graceful line, his ass pushed out to receive more, his arms trembling, Rune let Jackson force his way to full penetration despite the inner resistance of his body. And when Jackson was seated, he didn't wait but kept taking Rune harder on each thrust, letting him try to withstand it. Soon, Jackson pounded him, sliding more easily, enjoying the little clenches of Rune bearing down on him and gripping him from inside. Rune's right hand let go of the counter to find his straining erection, jacking it as he got fucked.

Rune's orgasm hit first. He gasped, shuddering, and Jackson came right after with a satisfied moan, folding himself over Rune's back and winding him in an embrace as he slowed down.

The frown was gone, Jackson saw, though not the weariness, or the sadness.

Jackson turned Rune around to face him.

"It's gonna be okay, kid," Jackson promised, kissing his jaw. "We're in this together. All of us."

Overheated and breathing easier, Rune undulated in Jackson's arms. Jackson reached down to caress over the hip marked with the rainbow triangle tattoo.

Rune reached for his phone, set on the counter beside them and typed:

I'll shower and come with.

Jackson shifted the screen so he could type instead, and replied:

No, you'll sleep. You need rest. That's an order. He asked me to pass it along. I promised him I'd take care of you.

Rune gazed down at the message, then closed his eyes and kept rocking ever so gently against Jackson's cock still buried in him. Jackson took Rune's chin in hand and kissed him for a while.

After he pulled out, Jackson led Rune by the hand to the shower, set the water to run hot, and took Rune's face in both hands. He enunciated slowly, "Stay in bed. Stay."

Then kissed the soft bow of Rune's lips.

Rune watched him with wonder and gentle submission.

Rune touched his chin with the fingertips of his flattened right hand, drawing the hand away and down.

Jackson kissed him once more and Rune wove their fingers together. Jackson turned to go before temptation got the best of him again, but Rune didn't let go until he was forced to, their arms stretching out between them, then slipping out of reach.

Everything had flipped, and it left Oliver with whiplash. Days slipped by in a fog of poking, prodding, arguing with nurses, and living with the constant annoyance of being stuck in bed because of the undeniable reality of his exhaustion.

He hadn't even felt the shot when he heard it. He'd been too busy dealing with the onslaught of utter terror of waiting to see Rune die right in from of him. In the moment, it had been unavoidable. In fact, part of Oliver had subconsciously convinced himself that it had happened, like part of his mind splintered off into a hellish parallel reality where Rune was dead and refused to leave.

Back on that road in front of the clubhouse of The Born Soldiers, Oliver hadn't any time to think about himself when Rune's grisly murder was taking place a few strides away.

When Oliver's legs buckled and his body stopped cooperating, Oliver's only thought had been for Rune. That he had to get to Rune. He had to do something. Stop them. Help.

When one of the Soldiers knelt by Oliver, a cell phone pressed to his ear, the stocky, leather-clad guy looking Oliver over and relaying things into the phone, all that mattered to Oliver was trying to stand up again, and trying to keep calling Rune's name.

Even when Rune had appeared at Oliver's side, the dread didn't lessen, because delirium took over along with a thick helping of pain and shock.

Paramedics eventually arrived and sedated Oliver because he wouldn't fucking lie still.

He remained so agitated when he came to again, the decision was made to keep him sedated well after the surgery was complete.

Needless to say, he had no memory of the lead-up to the surgery or the immediate aftermath. He stopped being able to track time and lost several hours at a stretch to sleep that he couldn't shake off no matter how furious he was.

Now, Oliver knew days had slipped by. He didn't know how many. What he did know was that Rune was always there when Oliver woke up, holding his hand. The only exception was when it was nighttime, and then Oliver tended to slip into panic attacks until a nurse came to reassure him Rune was alive. They regularly helped him call Rune to ease his mind.

It freaked Oliver out how dependent, mentally, he was on Rune's presence, especially given the look of Rune. He was pale, with bags under his eyes and a drawn expression. Oliver could see that Rune was physically drained, but it was the listlessness that worried him the most. The sight of him like that, with so much fear and intensity reflected in his eyes and tense posture, didn't really help Oliver calm down.

So, he'd ordered Jackson to order Rune to get some damn sleep at home, in a real bed.

A big chunk of hours had passed since then, in which Oliver's vitals had been tested regularly. His heart-rate had been monitored, and his unshakable sleep was constantly disturbed.

But Rune was back. He held Oliver's hand with both of his own, and Oliver hadn't even opened his eyes yet, but he felt the welcome touch. It helped calm Oliver and reassure him like nothing else could.

Something in Rune had changed. Something in Oliver had also changed.

Even though he understood now that Rune hadn't been shot, Oliver still carried the echo of devastation in his heart. It made just having Rune there, nearby, touching him, the greatest joy Oliver had known.

From Rune—the steadiness of his haunted eyes, the persistence of his ass remaining in the chair right by Oliver's bed no matter what the hospital staff said about it—Oliver understood a lot.

He understood that Rune wasn't going to take off after some thugs anymore, like he'd been doing. Oliver had him now. No question about it. But Oliver's weird delusional fear was equally matched by the guilt he saw in Rune's expression. As time slipped by, Rune's guilt began to outpace it.

And Oliver didn't know what to do about that.

He didn't care he'd been shot trying to save Rune. Not if it helped distract those fuckers long enough to spare Rune's life.

The physical pain was an annoyance he had no time for. He paid it no mind.

There was a big problem now, though. Oliver's arm was unusable, and his best means of communicating with Rune was via sign language or typing, both of which required use of his arm. They were using the voice-to-text feature in the meantime, but with mixed results. And it hurt Oliver to feel a space between them. The communication barrier had never been so maddening.

Oliver lay in that hospital bed, knowing he was going home soon, trying to let go of his certainty of what would have been, holding on to Rune and settling into a fevered sort of gratitude.

Peering at Rune's handsome face through barely-opened eyes, Oliver drank in his seriousness and the alert, furious air swirling around him. With his fair skin scrawled with ink, his dark hair hiding soulful eyes, his slim body hinting at none of the history he'd endured, he was quite a picture. Even without Adam's artist's eye, Oliver knew as much.

"God, I really do love you, you know," he mumbled.

Rune sat forward, trying to track Oliver's lips. Rune frowned a little in confusion, letting go with just one hand to pull up the voice-to-text app. He held the phone out by Oliver's lips to capture his words with the purest kind of desperation. Oliver's heart ached to see it, like the sweetness of Rune might kill him since the bullet had failed.

Sitting right on the edge of his chair, Rune kept holding out the phone, hoping Oliver would say it again, his eyes so focused on Oliver's mouth, his lip bitten with worry.

Oliver's vision blurred and he rolled his eyes at himself before lowering his gaze.

The phone fell to the bed and Rune's hand caressed Oliver's cheek. Rune's fingers brushed away a pair of tears and he kissed Oliver's lips over and over, as light as the brush of butterfly wings.

"I love you so much," Oliver told him.

Rune pulled back just to peek at the phone's screen, but Oliver never dared look away.

Rune's bloodshot eyes filled with shine and he moved even closer to press a kiss to the side of Oliver's neck, laying his head there and breathing him in. Oliver heard Rune's breath hitch. Letting go reluctantly of Rune's hand, Oliver instead brushed his fingers through Rune's soft, black hair and gave him the tenderness he so deeply deserved.

Oliver had always seen himself as a man who could have it all. Any lover. More money than he could spend. The lifestyle of his dreams. Power. Envy.

But, God, he'd give it all in a heartbeat just to stay there a little longer with Rune.

And he savored the new reality he'd landed in, where he had no power at all; where blind, arrogant confidence had been traded for faith and trust; and where he didn't really need anything, other than the beautiful man oh-so-carefully measuring each of Oliver's breaths and taking far too much blame for the cruel twists of fate.

Chapter 27
Mother Hen

Oliver discovered Adam's response to the news of the shooting was delayed by a good fifteen hours. Of course, by the time Oliver had his wits about him again and had calmed down enough to think about anything but Rune, Adam's presence in his room had become a constant.

"Excuse me. Excuse me!" Adam exclaimed, intercepting a nurse who'd wandered up to check Oliver's chart. Arms folded, bitch-face on, Adam sternly said, "I'm going to need to know the soonest Mr. Hughes can be discharged. He's already been here far too long. I need to speak with someone about this."

"Hey Mom," Oliver interjected tiredly, "un-twist your panties and relax. Leave the poor nurses alone."

Adam had been channeling his inner mother hen for days, clucking and pecking at anyone who got too close to Oliver or who displeased him in any way.

For a second, Adam remained torn between continuing his tirade and responding to Oliver's jab instead. Then he held up a finger to the nurse and turned his attention to Oliver, who saw the nurse roll her eyes and walk away.

"You're practically being held hostage, Olly."

"They said today or tomorrow morning," Oliver explained. A combination of severe blood loss, unsteady blood pressure levels, and Oliver's lack of cooperation in his care due to the shock and upset of it all had kept him under watch longer than usual.

"I need to get you out of here. I hate seeing you like this." Adam's blue eyes shone down at him with all of the determination of someone prepared to hijack a wheelchair, load Oliver into it himself, and wheel him out of the building, permission be damned.

"Well, I'm sorry to inconvenience you. Take a break. Go get something to eat. Go for a walk."

"I can't leave you," Adam said with offense at the mere suggestion.

"Honey. Sweetie. Babe. I'm fine."

Adam quirked his mouth to the side and raised an eyebrow, then sighed and came to sit perched on the side of Oliver's bed. He took Oliver's hand and held it in his lap.

Rune snoozed in a chair in the corner of the room, peacefully undisturbed and finally getting some more rest.

"I'll never forgive myself," Adam murmured.

"Would you give yourself a break, please? I'm fine."

"But you weren't fine. You were fucking shot, Olly, and I was..." he blew out a breath. Shook his head full of brick-red hair.

"Where were you, exactly, by the way?"

Adam groaned, his gaze failing to stick on Oliver's for long.

"That bad, huh? What's his name?"

"Vincent."

"Mmm-hmm. And?"

Adam's attention twitched toward the door as he glimpsed a white-coated person breeze past.

"Focus, babe," Oliver urged, patting Adam's hand. "And?"

"And he's recently divorced. Three kids. Ended it with the wife when he fell in lust with the male nanny and realized he wasn't completely straight after all. Never let on with the nanny though, just suffered blue-balls in private over it. I ran into him at that gay bar on forty-fourth street. He stuck out like a big, straight, nervous apple in a basket of oranges."

"So you pounced?"

"Oh, come on, you say that like it's a bad thing."

Oliver laughed, then groaned in pain and tried to stop.

"And fifteen hours later..." Oliver encouraged.

"Well, it took a little while to convince Vincent to come home with me and to get a hold of Andrew."

Oliver grinned. "Oh, that old trick. Sic the human sex doll on the hard-up gay-curious guy. Andrew is kind of delicious. Has one of the prettiest cocks I've ever seen, and does such magical things with his tongue."

"Mmm," Adam smirked, as if drifting into fond memories.

"So you got poor confused Vincent alone with you and set temptation itself at his feet to beg, lips parted, wet and waiting? Went a few rounds in a few different Kama Sutra positions?"

"Something like that. I wasn't there for you when you needed me... It's inexcusable, Olly. I'm horrified. I—"

"Stop it. You're allowed to have fun. You're not tied to your phone. I know that."

"But I could have checked. It won't happen again."

"Well, I don't plan on getting shot again, so I think you're off the hook."

Adam frowned at Oliver's bandaged shoulder, then leaned down to kiss his forehead.

"No one gets to take you from me. Ever," Adam swore.

"Aww, I love you too, Mom."

"Stop that."

Oliver chuckled.

The session didn't take long to come to fruition. Rune's need for it sat right there in his expression for anyone to see. As soon as Oliver began to suggest it, Rune latched on to the idea and wouldn't let go until they'd scheduled it and made it official.

One of the new developments in post-hospital life was Rune had taken to staring at Oliver's sling. He glared at it like it was the enemy now, rather than the White Lions. Oliver didn't know for sure about the details of what ran through Rune's head those days, because as soon as Oliver initiated a conversation about what had happened, Rune just kept signing his apologies and took all blame on himself, sparing none at all for Oliver, or even the rednecks from that light blue Ford truck.

So, Oliver slowly, one-handedly, typed up everything he needed to say, explaining how, in fact, it wasn't Rune's fault at all and he was doing harm to himself by assuming any blame. It had been Oliver's choice to be there. No one had forced the shooter—Dale Murtaw—to fire, unprovoked. And Oliver also spoke at length about how terrified he'd been to lose Rune. That getting shot was a price he'd pay any day, anywhere, anytime, to save him.

Oliver had sat with Rune in bed, watching him read the letter. Making sure he did.

If anything, Rune's need for the session increased after that.

They arrived at Adam's apartment early in the morning. Rune had awakened well before dawn. Oliver woke to find him sitting up in bed, clear-eyed, lost in thought.

The three of them settled in Adam's living room. Adam sat across from Rune to better communicate with him and read his expressions. Next to Rune, Oliver settled into the role of observer only after Adam provided him with a pillow to rest his arm on, a fresh cup of coffee to sip, a blanket to keep him warm, and several other ridiculous displays of unspoken devotion that Oliver found quite sweet.

As Rune typed on a tablet, it read the words aloud; the larger screen allowed for more speedy typing than his phone.

Adam's replies were typed as well, sent directly to Rune's screen, though he spoke aloud as he typed them for Oliver's benefit. It was a little stilted, but it worked well enough.

Adam started, "I need brutal honesty. Tell me exactly what's bothering you, even if it's ugly. We both support you. We're here to help. You won't scare us off."

Rune's gaze settled on screen, his furrowed brow doing all of the speaking for him as his fingers lay still.

"Get it out. Let it go," Adam added. "This has to come first. We agreed."

Finally, Rune began to type and type. The computer's voice relayed as he went, a few sentences at a time. "He can't fucking talk to me. We can't talk. He can't sign. Can't type as quickly. We're trying with lip reading, but it makes me so angry. All of it makes me angry.

"I was so fucking stupid. Selfish. Dangerous. I should have known Olly would follow. I should have seen the Lions coming, or known to beware of them staking out the place at least. I'm mad they got me again. That they had me on my knees out there and I didn't even fucking know what they were saying. I just knew I was about to die.

"I'm mad at how scared Olly was. He's never scared of anything. Pissed off maybe, but you saw him. For days he was out of his mind with terror that I'd nearly been shot in the head right in front of him. I did that too. I did that to him.

"For so long, I just wanted someone to give a shit about me for real. I'd survived that first crash, pieced myself back together through sheer spite and anger, and for what? For who? To sit in a storage closet feeling bad for myself?

"I'm not sorry I did everything I could to stop those guys. I don't regret any of it, even when it made Olly worry. Because it made my life mean something again. Showed me I could still make a difference.

"In the end, I got what I really wanted. I know he loves me." He hesitated, and refused to let Oliver catch his eye. Rune was tearing up, refusing to let them fall, his hands shaking and his face flushed red. He looked ready to throw the tablet across the room. "But I love him even more and I didn't really see how much until he was lying there, bleeding out in my arms. Until he was raging at the nurses busy trying to save his life because he thought I was still in danger. Until he kept waking up looking so fucking scared until he felt me holding his hand, and saw me sitting with him, and how then the fear melted away for a while. And I can't..."

Oliver caught Adam's eye. Adam was leaned forward in his seat, phone in hand, soaking it all in, his fingers likely itching for a camera or a canvas. He held up a hand to Oliver, pleading silently for patience.

Rune continued, "I can't take how much it hurts. This hurts more than anything they've ever done to me. I never had anything I couldn't walk away from before. I don't know how to stop being so angry. I don't know how to stop it from hurting so much. There's no one for me to go after anymore. Olly's healing. I'm the problem that needs fixing."

"Don't touch him," Adam quietly warned Oliver as he moved to reach out. "Let it be."

Then, typing, Adam asked, "What we previously discussed—you still feel that will help?"

Rune nodded, his gaze locked with Adam. There was something so focused about it, it signaled to Oliver that Rune was trying to keep him out of this, even before he typed another word.

"He should stay out here," Rune's tablet dictated.

"No, we already agreed. He's your Dom. He gets to watch. He won't interfere. Right, Olly?"

Oliver nodded when they both looked his way.

It had to be that way. He needed to be present. They were both angry, not just Rune. Adam was still tearing himself apart about the same damned things he thought he should have done differently for Oliver's benefit. No, in the scene, Oliver had to be the control. The calm.

Adam asked, "Olly, your conditions still hold?"

"Yes," Oliver told him, nodding.

For the first time since they sat down, Oliver found Rune looking at him. He was tensed, ready, alert, the tablet forgotten.

Oliver tilted his head toward the shadowy hallway.

Rune sprang to his feet, setting the tablet on the couch. He stood with his feet spread, head down, arms clasped behind his back, more eagerly submissive than they could have hoped. The sight of it released a knot in Oliver's chest, helping him breathe easier. It showed him there really was control to be found. That things didn't have to be chaotic anymore. That they could do this. It could work.

Adam stepped up to Oliver, helping him stand, then pressed a kiss to the corner of his mouth. "You trust me with him?"

"I do," Oliver admitted.

"Tell me why."

Oliver almost smiled. "He's part of me now, and you'd never dream of hurting me, would you?"

Adam caressed Oliver's cheek, "I'd sooner die."

Adam turned to Rune and moved to fit a collar around his neck, buckling the clasp shut and testing its fit. Then he wrapped a strong hand around the nape of Rune's collared neck, grabbing tight hold, and led him forward, to the shadows.

Chapter 28
Kicking Ass

If Adam and Rune had their way, they would have gone right to the gym, but that's why Oliver made the conditions he did. His goal was for this to help all of them, and hurt none of them.

As stipulated, Adam detoured on the way to the gym, into a guest bedroom. There, a bench waited, ready, with supplies already set nearby. As Rune glimpsed them, Oliver heard his breathing quicken. Coming up short, he was jolted forward by Adam, who pushed him toward the bench, then down to kneel on it. Adam's grip forced Rune to bend sharply forward. The ring on the front of his collar was secured to a clasp on the bench, keeping him in place.

No other bonds were attached. Rune's hands wrapped the sides of the bench, his eyes watchful, his body alert.

Adam removed each of Rune's boots, then his socks.

Rune's pants were opened. Along with his underwear, they were slid down and removed, with Rune lifting his knees slightly to allow them to come free.

Adam left Rune's t-shirt on, for now. Oliver knew sometimes it played mental games on a sub to be partially clothed in situations like this, with only the areas of interest exposed. In fact, Oliver was tempted to ask Adam to put Rune's boots back on, just for fun.

He held his tongue just because he knew how impatient they were to get going, but next time, perhaps.

Oliver hung back, leaning against the wall, wanting the others to mainly forget his presence. He knew he got in the way. It had everything and nothing to do with his injury. Adam and Rune needed this from each other. Oliver couldn't give it to them. But, he could give them each other.

The first glimpse of the force of Adam's need showed itself as soon as he moved up behind Rune. He squirted plenty of lube on his hand, the pressed two fingers through Rune's opening, twisting them around. While doing this, he knelt with one knee between Rune's legs, straddling Rune's left leg and leaning over him so his chest was flush to Rune's back. Adam wore one of his trademark outfits—button-down shirt barely buttoned with snug jeans splattered with paint and cowboy boots.

Oliver heard Rune grunt as he watched Adam's arm flex, the muscles working as he pumped his hand. From the wet squelches and breathy sounds of protest from his usually silent submissive, Oliver knew Adam was being fairly rough on him.

Before it had a chance to ease or fall into a rhythm, Adam pulled out and grabbed a huge, clear, tapered plug. Oliver had seen Adam use it before, trying to fit it inside the snug asshole of a whimpering, blushing sub, but had never seen him succeed. He didn't think he would this time either. Not with how tense Rune had been lately.

Rune kept trying to glance over his shoulder and must have noticed what Adam had in hand. He started to growl when the narrow tip first grazed his pucker. His back and arms flexed, gripping the bench. His toes curled and feet flexed. Adam glanced down to watch Rune take the first inch or so, adding more pressure as he went, then leaned down again to breathe over the back of Rune's neck and shoulders, the ends of his blazing red hair tickling the skin at Rune's exposed neckline.

"It's really true Elet had him?" Adam asked, just before pressing the plug harder and drawing a small cry of protest from Rune.

"Sure is," Oliver replied.

"Must have been something to see. Wish I'd been there. Would you let it happen again?"

"Mmm, if Rune asked, maybe."

"Liar," Adam chuckled. "I know you too well for that, Olly."

He twisted the plug deeper, like a massive screw on which he worked to impale Rune's body. Rune cried out, writhing on the bench. He had a couple more inches inside him now, but the dramatic width of the plug at this point prohibited any further movement.

Adam started to fuck him with it, shallowly, gently, trying to coax it deeper. Or maybe just trying to push Rune's fight instinct to start to kick in.

It went on like that for a while. Oliver savored the soft squelches, Rune's gasping struggle, Adam's silent determination to conquer and tame.

"I can feel it," Adam wondered aloud. "How he doesn't want me to keep trying to feed this into him, but he's not fighting me as hard as he could."

"Maybe he's saving it for when he can do more damage."

"Maybe."

Adam reached around Rune's hips with his free hand, causing more growling, more squirming and tensing all along Rune's body.

"He's not hard," Adam reported. "He's taking this as a punishment, only. Let's see what I can do about that."

Gradually, unhurriedly, he removed the toy. Oliver watched Rune's ass expel its wet cone shape. He heard Rune's grateful panting for breath. He lay nearly boneless on the bench.

Adam stood, setting the plug aside for something else.

It only took him a moment to fasten the harness around his pelvis. Once it was secured, he stepped up behind Rune, spread his cheeks with both hands, lined up and breached him with a hard thrust.

Rune gave a softer cry, but tipped his ass up to receive and stopped trying to catch glimpses, his head faced strictly forward now in a resigned sort of way. He seemed to push back onto the dildo as Adam kept hold of him, drawing Rune's hips back onto the lube-slick cock.

A lilting whimper broke free from Rune as Adam bottomed out, making Rune take the whole shaft at once. Caressing Rune's neck, kneading his ass, fingering his rim, Adam began to ride him with long, complete strokes. Rune's skin glistened with a light sheen of sweat, his breathing steady but heavy. Oliver walked soundlessly around the carpeted room to see the expression on his lover's face.

Rune was frowning, but not with anger. Sadness, grief, regret, pain, and surrender were all there, though.

Adam shifted his angle, and Rune shuddered visibly. His knuckles grew white as he gripped the bench. He bent his head slightly to hide his face and let out a gruff cry, writhing with torment with each push, convulsing a little against the movements inside him.

Adam reached around again, fondling Rune. Oliver heard the wet squelch of a squeeze.

"Mmm, better," Adam grinned. He tugged Rune counter to the rolling thrusts of his hips, the cock sliding easily now. He kept triggering Rune's gland as they listened to his cries grow in urgency and pitch.

He let go well before Rune had a chance to come.

There was a frustrated snarl from their captive.

Adam pulled out, removed the harness. He unfastened Rune's collar. Rune stayed where he was placed, face-down, expression hidden from sight. He shifted his knees together as if to hide his arousal. His breathing slowed.

Only once, but deliberately, Adam stepped up behind Rune and reached out. His fingers went right for Rune's tender entrance, rubbing slowly at it as if to remind him of his vulnerability and place as a submissive. It was meant to underscore he'd been taken, used, and would be again soon. Oliver heard Rune holding his breath, saw his tension return.

"Crouch in front of him," Adam commanded. "Make him look at you."

For another moment, Oliver watched Adam literally and figuratively pushing Rune's buttons, seeing Rune's discomfort climb. Then, he obeyed.

He crouched just in front of the bench, and wasn't surprised when he needed to reach out and lift Rune's chin before he'd meet Oliver's gaze.

There was a soft squelch as Adam's extended arm flexed, though anything he did to Rune was hidden from sight. A muscle twitched in Rune's jaw. His breath rushed out his nostrils. With his free hand, Adam reached for Rune's shoulder, using a firm grip on it to draw him upright, then to his feet. Adam kept hold of him by the shoulder. His right hand stayed buried with an uncertain amount of fingers stuffed through Rune's hole. Rune's hands twitched restlessly at his sides. He nearly moved to cover his erection, which bobbed obscenely in front of him.

Something like embarrassment colored his dark eyes. He let his gaze fall to the floor, away from Oliver.

"Show him, Olly. Show him what he's so damned angry about."

"Are you sure you want me to do that?" Oliver asked.

"I am."

Oliver reached for the buttons of his shirt and undid them, yanking the fabric to the side and pulling the bandage away from his wound.

Rune's gaze went right to it with intense scrutiny. He didn't look away, didn't blink.

Just like that, the touching became unacceptable.

Rune threw an elbow back into Adam's stomach, causing a grunt as the air was knocked from him. He twisted out of Adam's grasp and out of reach, glancing between the wound and the redheaded Dom.

Adam held a hand out, gesturing to the doorway, inviting Rune to go through it. Rune's frown returned. He reached behind his head, grabbed his shirt and pulled it over his head. Letting it fall, he stalked toward the door and left.

Adam quickly washed up, undressed. Oliver paced nervously, far out of the way. Rune waited on the mats Adam had placed on the floor in the middle of the room.

As soon as Adam advanced on him, Rune had his fists up, his stance guarded, his feet light as he bounced a little, his chin lowered.

"God, you're gonna kick my ass, aren't you?" Adam wondered.

"Yes, he is," Oliver agreed.

Adam was a little taller, and broader. He was bigger all around. But Rune? Rune had strength that had nothing to do with his size.

Once it started, it all kept happening, fast and without pause. Oliver stayed back but was willing to play referee if needed.

Rune let out a furious yell and charged at Adam, who dodged aside and swept Rune's leg. Rune fell to the mat on his side. Adam dropped on him, trying to pin him there by twisting his arm behind his back and using his legs to tangle Rune's. Adam panted against Rune's neck, who strained and fought the hold. With his free arm, Rune rolled them, and was able to get out from under Adam. He pounced, getting on top of Adam, bringing Adam's arms up above his head and holding them there. Rune used his body weight, sitting on Adam's hips to keep him down. Smiling, Rune leaned down and blew Adam a kiss. The lull lasted a beautiful moment before Adam's strength won out. He broke the hold, bucked Rune off of him and threw them both sideways. They rolled on the mat, grappling, trying to get a hold on each other. Rune's arm went around Adam's throat, his thigh twining around Adam's torso and lower leg wrapping his hips. Adam pried Rune's arm from his neck and spun to face him.

It wasn't precise or skilled. Neither of them were professionally trained. They were just naked and very pissed off. For a minute or two, they wrestled each other, throwing elbows, or pinching, or slapping out of frustration or anger. When they did get a hold on the other, it seemed to drain their energy fast just to fight it off or fight to keep it going.

Soon, they were both panting and sweating freely.

But Rune was grinning like a madman and Adam kept breaking into soft laughter at the ridiculousness of it all.

Rune pinned Adam with his legs and gave Adam's ass a few hard slaps. This made Adam angry enough to slip away. He twisted around and bit Rune's nipple, drawing an offended gasp from Rune, who reached for Adam's nipple in retaliation and twisted it sharply until he let go.

Adam slapped the side of Rune's face. Rune slapped him back. Oliver rolled his eyes.

The wrestlers both growled and charged again, landing in a tangle of limbs.

They both looked fatigued but, as hoped, Adam's endurance held out. He pinned Rune face-down on the mat, forced his legs apart, and waited just a moment for Oliver to pass him an opened condom and help him roll it on. Then, without any other warning, Adam lined up and entered Rune with a heavy sigh. Adam kept Rune's arm pinned behind his back as he buried his cock to the root, and held there for a long moment to let Rune know he was beaten.

Rune panted, skin flushed and body glistening, but the fight drained from him. Oliver saw it leave his eyes first. Adam kept him pinned as he started to pound Rune's ass, fucking him hard, with all of the leftover anger of Adam's own frustrations, borne of feeling like he lost control of someone else he loved. Rune gave over to it and didn't fight Adam one bit. Sensing it, Adam let go of Rune's arm and just focused on giving it to him as roughly as he needed to, driving the air from Rune's lungs with the beating of his hips on Rune's cheeks.

Adam's pace slowed, his breathing heavy, his energy fading. Rune reached for a handful of Adam's red hair from over his shoulder, pulling Adam's mouth against his neck. Moaning, Adam shivered and slowed even more, still shallowly rocking in and out of him. Rune rocked down against the mat, as if rubbing off on it.

Adam pulled out and basically lay there, collapsed, on top of Rune, who carded gently through Adam's hair. Rune glanced back over a shoulder with a smile.

"Yeah, I feel better, too," Adam agreed, breathlessly.

He shifted to catch Rune's lips, kissing him briefly. He hummed with pleasure, then collapsed again. Oliver saw Rune's amused grin, his peacefully closed eyes, and knew it had worked. They'd got it out of their systems, for now at least. Taking Rune on the bench first had prevented him from getting hurt during the forced sex after the match, and it had also helped break Rune's frantic energy by having him submit to Adam that way before the fight. Otherwise, Oliver would have bet Rune to be the victor, no question.

Adam rolled off of Rune, helped him stand. He stepped back, then, and gestured to Oliver.

Head bowed, Rune walked up to Oliver while rubbing his arms, looking a little shy. He was still hard, flushed, his skin beaded with sweat from head to toe, his dark hair stuck in black curls to his forehead, his ink stark in the bright morning light.

"Hey beautiful," Oliver murmured, drawing a loose hand over his face in a sweeping motion.

Rune looked up at him, so open, shining with utter devotion and love, his body heavy with tiredness.

He eased into Oliver's space, self-conscious of himself, and pressed a reverent kiss to Oliver's shirt, just over the bandage on his wound, then his neck, then his lips. His hand folded with his middle and ring fingers in, the other fingers out, and pressed it to Oliver's chest. Oliver did the same, holding him there. "Love you too, kid," he sighed.

Chapter 29
Cherished

Rune showered. It took him a full three minutes. Then he sprinted from the bathroom, slipping a little on the tile with his bare, wet feet, and dove into bed beside Oliver, who smiled over at him.

Biting his lip, Rune pushed the sheet aside, needing much more access to Oliver's naked body. The bench he'd been chained to was just a few feet away. Morning light spilled in through the parted curtains of Adam's guest room. Oh-so-careful of his movements and Oliver's shoulder, Rune moved to straddle him, dripping water everywhere, slippery as a fish. He found and fondled Oliver's cock, shocked at the starkness of Oliver's hunger and focus. Beneath him Oliver seemed open, clear, peaceful, like nothing else in the whole world existed but the two of them, nothing else mattered other than their love, trust, and respect.

Rune steadied Oliver and sank down onto him with a happy sigh. Bending forward over him, a human shield, Rune rode him slowly, wanting to draw it out. When Oliver took hold of Rune's erection, playing it through a wet fist, Rune caught Oliver's mouth and licked into it. Melting into the three points of contact and the mind-blowing pleasure found in each, Rune gave over to him.

He shivered and gasped as he raced toward climax, fast. Rather than drawing it out more, Oliver sped up, jacking Rune to force him over the edge. He brushed his parted lips over Rune's as he gasped and came, spilling in a hot flood over Oliver's fingers, rocking down against him as his skin pebbled in goosebumps from head to toe.

Tingling, head spinning, awash in bliss, Rune's world narrowed even further, to touching Oliver with light caresses of his fingers, and light kisses here, there, and everywhere he could reach. He kissed Oliver's eyelids and the tip of his nose, then circled down below his ear, the edge of his jaw, finishing up at the center of his forehead. All the while, Rune clenched and rolled his hips, giving Oliver all of the pleasure he deserved. The slight quiver of Oliver's lips, the high color in his cheeks, the urgency of his thrusts and grasping of his hand all urged Rune on.

When Oliver came inside him, Rune hummed with satisfaction and caught all of Oliver's panting breaths, feeling the racing of his heart with the press of his palm against Oliver's chest.

Behind the bed, there was a window. In the glass's reflection, Rune saw Adam lingering in the doorway, sketchbook in hand, drawing furiously as he glanced between the bed and the page.

Smiling, Rune helped Oliver pull out, then settled down next to him, laying inside the circle of his arm, and savored the rare, true joy of being home, at long last. He loved and was loved. He protected and was protected. He cherished and was cherished in return.

"How is Max?" Oliver signed and asked.

Rune's ever-watchful gaze followed the movements of Oliver's hands as he sipped his mug of coffee. Max had been providing regular updates on their monitoring of the Lions. There had been no activity in the handful of months since the day Oliver had been shot. Everything was quiet. Maybe it wouldn't last—it never did—but for now, there was nothing to be concerned about.

Rune typed into his phone, which dictated, "He's good. They've been keeping an eye out with the scanner and regular patrols of the area. Nothing major to report. It's quiet. How are you?"

Oliver flexed his left arm, stretching it, and signed, "Good. The exercises aren't fun but they help."

He was out of the sling, but still was working the kinks out of his range of movement and stiffness.

"When's Jackson getting back from the convention?"

"Friday," Oliver replied, making a circle of his thumb and index fingers, his other fingers straightened as he rotated it to face him and circled the upright hand twice.

"I miss him," Rune's phone read.

"Me too," Oliver smiled. Then he paused, thoughtful, before asking, "Are you interested in surgery, for your hearing? We could look into it. I'd be happy to cover the costs."

It was something Rune thought of, now and then, a puzzle he toyed with at the back of his mind, especially now that he had less pressing concerns to divert his attention.

So, he had an answer prepared.

"Right now, I don't need it. I'm happy."

Oliver came over and kissed him. "I'm happy too. If you change your mind, tell me."

Rune nodded.

"I've never asked," Oliver started, "but your parents—do they know about your accident?"

Rune held Oliver's gaze, letting him see some of the cloudiness he felt in response to the question before typing his answer. "No. I never told them. They honestly wouldn't care the way parents should. They've always been too wrapped up in their own problems, with little room for mine. We all have our own lives. It's better this way. I feel more stable standing on my own or leaning on you, than trying to go back there."

Oliver drew him in for a hug and another kiss, then signed and said, "Okay. I'm sorry you've had to handle so much on your own. If you ever need to vent about any of that, I'm here."

Rune held the fingers of his right hand to his lips and moved the hand forward, then down slightly.

"I'm headed to the office if you need me," he gestured to the hallway. "The tutor is coming at eleven?"

Rune nodded and pointed to his laptop, where he'd been doing some studying of video tutorials to get a jump on things. Now that he didn't have to worry about the Lions, he realized how important it was to broaden his ASL vocabulary, not only for himself but in order to better communicate with those he loved, and to help others. There was a small but vibrant local deaf community, which he was discovering and yearning to be a bigger part of. They were another group of people he wanted to be able to watch out for, and speak up for.

Oliver walked over to him and kissed his forehead. "I'm so proud of you," he enunciated, letting Rune study his lips.

"Me too," Rune replied aloud, letting the words go, filling them with everything in his heart. With his hands, he said, *You, Jackson, Adam, Max— you're my family. You're what I fight for now.*

With a bittersweet expression, Oliver pulled him close and held him. Rune kissed Oliver's healed wound, as he kept finding himself doing, like a little prayer of thanks.

Oliver let go, turned to head to his desk, located just down the hall and in the first room on the right. He hesitated to say and sign, "Saturday, Manse?"

Rune smiled, and nodded, wiggling his eyebrows and winking once to show he was ready. In fact, he was looking forward to it.

Rune stood beside his motorcycle as Oliver pulled up in his black Jaguar with Jackson riding shotgun. Rune grabbed the door for the backseat and slid in with a farewell wave to Max who stood smoking a cig nearby.

Rune had been spending some of his free time at the clubhouse, working on ways the Soldiers could do community outreach, offering ways to help like providing moving services for women and kids who were looking to escape abusive or dangerous situations, or participating in the local big brother program to help mentor kids, or hosting charity drives for people in their community going through medical emergencies. It took a lot of secretarial coordination and a flexible schedule, so Rune's typing and organizational skills, his drive to help others, and his lack of a paying job all made him perfect for the role.

Jackson held up the screen of his phone:

How was work?

Rune gave him a thumbs up, then buckled his seatbelt and settled in. He pulled out his phone and typed a reply, which was read aloud. "I told Olly I'd find a paying job if he gets sick of me mooching off of him."

Rune caught one glimpse of Oliver's severely offended expression and grinned, flapping a hand at him as Oliver started to rant and complain, not bothering to try lip-reading any of it. Rune just pointed to his ear and shrugged.

Oliver twisted in his seat, gave Rune's cheek a little slap and pointed at him in warning. Rune just blew him a kiss.

Jackson's phone now displayed the message:

I don't think he's a fan of that idea.

Rune's phone spoke his reply, "Really? I couldn't tell. It's not like he's controlling or a worry wart or anything. Even my mom wasn't this protective of me."

Oliver scowled at him once more. Rune patted his arm and gestured for him to go ahead and drive.

Jackson texted Rune as they drove out to Manse, filling him in on the conference he'd returned from, and news from Josefina and the kids, who were doing well in school but were dealing with a bit of bullying. Rune offered right away to handle it for them, but Jackson assured him it was under control, then made sure Rune understood that wasn't an invitation to investigate the bullies on his own. He made Rune promise not to do anything crazy but offered to let him talk with the kids and offer advice if he wanted, which Rune was more than happy to do.

Rune knew he was done with focusing on his own problems. Now, he devoted himself only to helping in every way possible, as much as possible. The more he gave, the better he felt. Because Oliver, Jackson, and Adam had all shown him how letting go of fear and selfishness, holding on to his faith in those in his newfound family, and following his heart were the ways forward.

Good to have you back, Rune typed to Jackson. *You're staying over tonight, right? If so, I call dibs on your ass.*

Jackson glanced back over his shoulder, raising an eyebrow. He messaged:

Yeah, we'll see. I think it's my turn.

Maybe you'll have to fight me for it, Rune replied with a chuckle.

Oliver and Jackson exchanged a look, then Jackson sent:

That can be arranged.

Rune laughed again, looking forward to everything the night might bring.

Manse was packed, or at least it seemed to be from what Oliver could see as they were escorted by a member of the staff to a secluded room on the basement level of the mansion. They left the drunk, dizzy, and horny patrons behind, along with the noise and the crowds.

In the room stationed with guards, they found David, Shea, and Elet waiting for them. Staff approached with trays of champagne and finger food.

Welcome, David signed, waving horizontally toward himself with an opened hand.

"You've been learning?" Oliver asked, opening for David's embrace as Shea hugged Rune and Elet kissed Jackson's cheek.

"Starting to. You?"

"Yeah, I'm getting there."

The initial greetings continued and David urged them all to make themselves comfortable. It was a low protocol kind of night, but Rune seemed to be enjoying a more submissive role. When Oliver sat on a couch, Rune sat at his feet, resting against his leg. Jackson sat on the couch on Rune's other side, idly brushing the soft, dark hair at the nape of Rune's neck.

Oliver felt David and Elet watching them, measuring them.

A large, well-placed mirror on the opposite wall, probably installed for voyeuristic pleasure, helpfully allowed Rune to see Oliver as he spoke and signed, "I need to express my thanks to all of you for how you brought me and Rune together. I don't know how I could ever pay you back for helping me find him, but I'll always be grateful."

Rune nuzzled Oliver's thigh with his cheek, wrapped a hand around his lower leg.

"We're just glad it's working out," David said, with Elet translating for him. "I worried about you both. Not you, though, Jackson. You're fine."

They all chuckled. But when Oliver frowned at the enthusiasm of Jackson's amusement, it just made him laugh harder. He leaned in and kissed Oliver's cheek.

"Yeah, we're all a mess, but Jackson's always fine, as usual," Oliver said with pouty sarcasm.

"Hey, you said it," Jackson teased.

Oliver whispered, "I'll get you for that later," then saw from the corner of his eye that Elet was still translating everything and Rune was chuckling.

"How's your shoulder doing?" Shea asked.

Oliver saw a cloud pass over Rune's joy, felt the strength of his grip increase, so Oliver stroked Rune's hair to try to soothe him.

"Fine. It's fine. We were all glad to get out of that safely."

"And Rune, how are you?" David asked, with Elet echoing his words with his hands.

Rune signed his answer.

Suddenly choked up, Oliver bowed his head to compose himself. The room was so quiet, echoing the world in which Rune lived, every day, every moment.

When no one translated, Shea asked, "What did he say?"

Elet spoke up, telling them with emotion in his voice, "He said, all of my dreams have come true."

Oliver caught Rune's eye in the mirror's reflection and told him, "Me too."

"I think that deserves a toast," David declared softly. He made sure they each had a glass, except for Elet, who was too busy shaping David's words, then they raised them together. "To love, life, and happy endings."

Their glasses clicked, and they drank deeply. Oliver knew it wasn't really the end, but that every moment they had together from here on out would be a gift, an adventure. He wondered how he'd gotten so lucky to have so much.

If you enjoyed this story, you can sign up for a free membership at ForbiddenFiction and discuss it with other readers and the author at the *Hush* Story Page.

We do our best to proof all our work, but if you spot a text error we missed, please let us know via our website Contact Form.

Author Notes

I'm pretty sure Jay over at Joyfully Jay was the first one to ask if I'd considered writing a story about Rune, Oliver, and Jackson. I credit her for that initial spark of wonderful inspiration, because that was the moment I first seriously considered really doing it. As soon as she planted the idea in my brain, I knew I absolutely had to write Rune's story.

The first thing that grabbed me was that I loved the intensity of his challenges in doing things we all take for granted, like small talk or ordering a burger. But he struggled with the big stuff too, like figuring out what the hell the point of it all is anyway. I could relate to the sense of being bizarrely adrift and alone while simultaneously surrounded by lots of people, and wanted to investigate that further. But I also saw Rune as a force of nature—untamable, wild, and with an almost singular focus once some key pieces began to line up for him. From the start, I saw him—to be blunt—as someone with no more fucks left to give. He was going to do whatever he was going to do, and there was almost nothing anyone could do to stop him. Fueled by a righteous cause and with nothing tying him down, he was able to throw himself into the fire with no thought given to getting burned.

But that's where Oliver and Jackson came in. They're the necessary balance, a pair of mostly-sane bystanders who arrange their lives around rules and responsibilities. They actually, unfortunately for Rune, give a shit about what happens to him in the end. Rune appreciates that about them enough that he doesn't discredit them entirely. They're what he bounces himself off of, symbolizing everything he thought he'd never get to have. While Rune is out there, risking his life and telling himself it's okay because he's disposable anyway, there are these men suddenly in his life, showing him all of the ways he's wrong.

The interesting thing about this book, like some of my others (*Loving the Master*, *Song of the Lonesome Cowboy*, and *Caged Jaye*, to name a few) is that it takes place before another book I've already written. Some things had already been set in stone before the first word on page one was ever written. More, I had never planned to write any of those follow-up books, so it's not like I intentionally wove things into the story to easily pick up later. It was a case of dealing with the threads which naturally appeared in the original stories, and figuring out ways to weave them into a new pattern that still made sense and honored the first. Little details about the three guys were already sprinkled through *Bare*. I couldn't change any of those. Just like I had to work with the complex triad Dominant/submissive relationship between them. Most of all, we already knew how things turn out. We know the guys wind up together. With that as a given, I wound the clock back a few years and explored just how they came together in the first place. And honestly, I had no idea until Rune showed me the way.

Here's a confession: I loved driving Oliver crazy in this book. He's the perfect sort of guy to torment, because he's so good at convincing everyone he's unflappable, going after the money, the quick and easy buzz, the good sex, bouncing around to chase whatever feels nice in the moment. But we discover the truth fairly quickly, that Oliver's heart is a tender one, and the rest is just an act borne of self-preservation. His undying loyalty to his best friend, Adam, proves as much (another confession, the Oliver/Adam banter gives me life). I knew as things progressed, I could let Rune be as bat-shit crazy as he wanted to be, and Oliver would fight just as hard (while completely freaking out) to cage him again, for his own good, of course.

And then there's Jackson. The true grown-up who's not afraid to be weak. The stable, level-headed presence with too many ties anchoring him solidly to earth, who appreciates the crazy adventure both Oliver and Rune bring. He's there to help pick them up, to remind them who they are, who they can be, and he shows them how clearly he sees them despite it all. No matter what lies Oliver and Rune try to tell themselves, Jackson is always there to reflect truth back if they need to see it, and I love him for that.

It was profoundly important to me in tackling this story to pay proper respect to the deaf community. Like Jackson, I wanted to reflect back with this book how relatable the simple, daily struggles are when one part of your body suddenly stops working properly. I needed to show how strong these people have to be in order to navigate a rather unforgiving cultural landscape. There's a lot of ugly noise in this world, but when it gets stripped away, beautiful things can be revealed. The language of gesture is something I find gloriously intentional and emotive. Things like lip-reading require a focus and skill that's hard to comprehend. All of the ways the hard-of-hearing communicate require a sort of real human cooperation of which I truly stand in awe. I sincerely hope all of this is reflected in the book. My heartfelt gratitude goes out to Hope Vincent for all of her input in helping me do right by Rune and my deaf or hard-of-hearing readers. It was the key to the whole thing for me, so Hope, you're my hero.

This book was a real whirlwind for me from start to finish, but I learned a heck of a lot along the way. These guys made me laugh, cry, and stole my heart. I thank you, my lovely readers, for taking the ride with me.

Lynn Kelling
January 9, 2018

About the Author

Lynn Kelling began writing in order to tell stories that aren't afraid of the dark, don't hold anything back and always strive to be memorable, forging lasting attachments between character and reader. Her inspiration comes from taking a closer look at behaviors and ideas lurking at the fringes of life—basically anything that people may hesitate to speak of in mixed company, but everyone wonders about anyway. Her work is driven by the taboo in order to expose the humanity within it. Lynn is an artist, designer and lover of any form of creative self-expression that comes from a place of honesty and emotion, whether it's body art or opera. She is an award-winning author who has written over seventy-five works of erotic fiction of varying lengths, and always has several novels in progress.

Other Works by Lynn Kelling

Deliver Us series:
Deliver Us (Book 1)
From Temptation (Book 2)
Forgive Us (Book 3)
Twin Ties series:
My Brother's Lover (Book 1)
Dual Affairs (Book 2)
Double Heat (Book 3)
Arctic Absolution Series:
Arctic Absolution(Book 1)
Caged Jaye (Book 2)
Arctic Restitution(Book 3)
Other Works:
Whatever the Cost
Song of the Lonesome Cowboy
Bare
Becoming Kerry
Cursed Blessings (short story)

The Manse Series

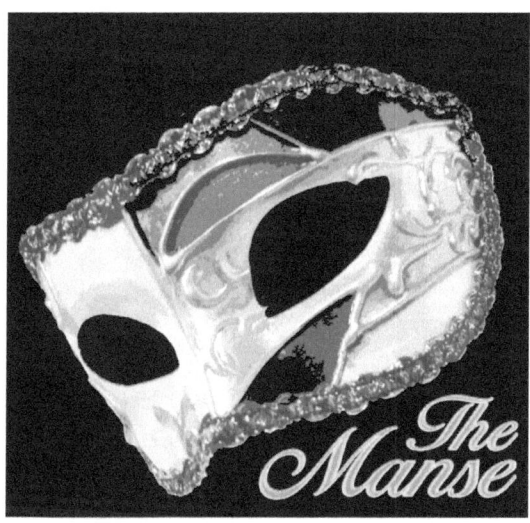

Erotic stories in the world of author, <u>Lynn Kelling</u>. These are a part of The Society of Masters shared world.

The Manse series focuses on the lives of men who play at Manse, a private club in rural Pennsylvania, catering to gay men. Billionaire David Davenport runs the club as he sees fit, and he's used to getting his way. So when he decides he wants to fill the place with gorgeous men in masks for a night, that's exactly what happens.

Loving the Master
Learning from the Maste
Bound by Lies
Hush

About the Publisher

ForbiddenFiction.com is a publisher devoted to writing that breaks the boundaries of original erotic fiction. Our stories combine intense sexuality with quality writing. Stories at Forbidden Fiction.com not only arouse readers through sensations, but also engage them emotionally and mentally through storytelling as well-crafted as the sex is hot.

ForbiddenFiction.com is also designed to be a social reading environment. You'll have fun even if just reading the latest post each day, yet you will have the chance for so much more. Readers and authors can be part of ongoing discussions of specific works and individual authors as well as more general topics.

Sign up for a FREE Membership today at <u>ForbiddenFiction.com</u>

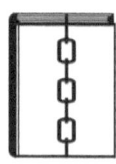